Breath of Knowledge

The Generations of Noah Series:

Blood of Adam – the story of Japheth and Denah

Bones of Rebellion – the story of Ham and Naomi

Breath of Knowledge – the story of Shem and Eran

Breath of Knowledge

Rachel S. Neal

A Novel

Generations of Noah

Book III

withallmyheART

Published in the United States

Cover design by Rachel S. Neal
Cover model photo from Dreamstime.com

ISBN: 978-1494378103

Printed in the United States of America

This book is primarily a work of fiction. Names, characters, dialogue, and incidents are the product of the author's imagination and are not to be construed as real. Any resemblance to actual events, locales or persons, living or dead, is coincidental.

Scripture quotations are from the Holy Bible, paraphrased by the author.

To Nathaniel and Leah,

With more love than I can express,

and

In Memory of

Bob and Eva Longnecker,

The heart and hands of Jesus.

Cast of Primary Biblical Characters

Noah –Builder of the ark

Jael* - Noah's wife

Shem – Noah's second son

Eran* – Shem's wife

Japheth – Noah's firstborn son

Denah* – Japheth's wife

Ham – Noah's youngest son

Naomi* – Ham's wife

Eber – Shem's great-grandson

King Amraphel – Ham's grandson, also known as Nimrod

Abraham (Abram) – Shem's eighth generation descendant

Sarah (Sarai) – Abraham's wife

Lot – Abraham's nephew

Additional Characters*

Fatimaa – Servant in the palace of Amraphel

Tolo – Caravan guide

Okpara –'King' of Zoar

Khepri – Okpara's daughter

Malina – Slave in Okpara's home

Rez-Nahor – Guard in Okpara's home

(*names provided by the author.)

...and they exchanged the truth about God for a lie, worshipping and serving created things rather than the Creator...

-Romans 1:25-

It is the Spirit within a man, the breath of the Almighty that gives him understanding.

-Job 38:2-

Historical Timeline *

4004 BC: Creation

2348 BC: Flood

2242 BC: Languages are confused

1897 BC: Destruction of Sodom

(*dates estimated)

Chapter One

1897 B.C.

The long, single blast of the ram's horn pierced Eran's dreams, instantly dissolving the gentle oblivion and thrusting her into a harsh wakefulness. It was a warning call, the call of danger. She threw off the hide covers, scrambled to her feet, and had a cloak tossed over her shoulders before the shofar ceased its mournful wail.

Her husband, Shem, gripped her arms, a trembling fear radiating through his touch. "Mother," he said, then spun and fled from their tent. It was a one word command, one needing no interpretation. He would inspect the camp, see that the emergency plan had been followed, then gather with the other men to face the band of raiders. She had one objective. Eran would try to prevent her mother-in-law from stirring the ire of the king's men. Again.

The darkness of the pre-dawn hour was fading on the eastern horizon, the shadows still heavy among the rows of tents. Eran was mindful of her footing, ignoring the grinding in her knees as she stepped, working through the stiffness that came with each morning sun. Scuffling sounds came from within the tents she passed, the sound of hasty preparation, of protecting and preserving what little remained in the encampment of Hebrews.

Hooves pounded on the road beyond the tent city. Closer with every beat. Five raiders? Twenty-five? They would know soon enough.

Jael's tent was on the perimeter of the camp, on the back side nearest the rocky hills. The position of relative safety meant nothing to her mother-in-law. Given the choice of any tent, she chose to remain as near her husband's grave as possible. Noah's bones were sheltered in a cave a stone's throw from her dwelling, and it was his remains she would fight to protect.

A young man emerged from his tent, darting from the arms of his wife to join the men in the courtyard. He held no spear, no knife. The few they had left were hidden from the eyes of the invaders so they wouldn't be taken, and so there would be no bloodshed. Opposition to King Amraphel's men would not end favorably. If one band of raiders was defeated, the retaliation would be brutal, annihilation of the tribe not beyond possibility.

The man's weapon was prayer to the heavens, strengthened by discipline to stand aside as his possessions were ransacked. Eran patted his arm as he passed, praying for his safety, knowing he would fight with bare hands if he had to, if his greatest treasure was threatened. He would use whatever means possible to keep his children from the clutch of the raiders.

Jael's tent flap was still closed. Eran stopped and listened for sounds coming from the cave. Hearing nothing, she breathed in relief. She hoped the blare of the ram's horn bounced from the woman's aging ears. They had turned to stone over the past year and for once, Eran was grateful for the deafness. Perhaps she still slept. Perhaps she could escape the terrors trespassing into the camp.

Most of the terrors anyway. The king's men would invade the old woman's tent as all the others in search of tribute. Eran had to be nearby when Jael realized what was happening. She had to stop the woman from clawing at the soldiers, and kicking them in her fury. She had to prevent Shem's mother from going to the cave and hurling stones at the raiders when they searched the grave and dug up the bones in their quest. She had to keep Jael from getting herself killed.

Calming herself with a deep breath, Eran lifted the flap and peered inside.

Startled eyes looked back. Jael was awake, her tidy braided hair of yesterday a wild mess from the night's rest. An oil lamp spurted to life in her hands. "Eran?"

Eran attempted an easy smile but could tell it fell short of reassuring Jael that all was well, that she came to visit in the early hours for some good cause.

The lamp fell to the earth as her mother-in-law's face registered understanding, then set into a determined mask. Eran braced herself as the woman stepped toward the door.

"No. Don't stop me," Jael said and pushed on Eran's shoulder to move her aside.

For a woman over nine centuries old, Jael possessed amazing strength. Eran planted her feet and held up her arms, struggling to block the doorway as Jael shoved her with both hands. When she couldn't get her to budge, she took a handful of Eran's hair and yanked.

Eran grabbed the woman's wrists.

Her bony arms twisted free. "Don't stop me. I have to save him," Jael said.

Eran wrapped her arms around Jael's waist and pulled her into her own body, trying in vain to subdue the elbows jabbing her ribs. "Please don't fight me, Mother. Please. Stay here. I can't let you attack those men again." Jael couldn't hear her, of course. She understood what was happening though. She knew Eran was keeping her from protecting Noah, and for that she would keep fighting her own daughter-in-law.

No one expected the ancient woman to be sound-minded. Her outbursts were forgiven, even by the raiders. The last few times they invaded the camp, they permitted Jael's aggression, her senility evident as she dug yellowed nails into their flesh. Sagging skin and gnarled bones saved her from their immediate wrath. Mocked and tormented as they scattered Noah's remains, she was pushed aside and forgotten when the search was over.

But her assaults were escalating. The last time Noah's bones were disturbed, force was required to prevent Jael's continued thrashing on the men of Amraphel. She didn't stop even after she was slapped across the face. Two men held her back when she refused to acquiesce. Their patience would not be indefinite.

Abruptly the woman's fighting stopped. Jael exhaled loudly. "I'm sorry Eran," she said, but her shoulders didn't relax. Eran knew better than to release her hold.

The old woman rammed her heel onto Eran's knee.

Eran flinched from the fiery pain, her hold loosening long enough for Jael to wriggle free. "He's my husband," she said over her shoulder as she hustled toward the cave.

The woman's ears were as dull as the old tools they had left. Not so her heart. It understood what her ears did not. Love defends. Love endures. Love defies all reason, even to the point of death. It didn't matter whether or not Jael understood that her husband was dead, that the man she adored was gone from the earth and living with his fathers beyond the expanse of sky. Jael would fiercely protect Noah, whatever remained of him.

And Eran was supposed to stop her.

♥

Shem glanced back at his tent. Eran pushed past the flap, shuffling in the darkness towards his mother's tent. He whispered a prayer of protection for them both. His wife would do her best to keep Jael from harm, a task growing more and more difficult. With each raid, his mother's persistence gained strength.

He couldn't bear for the old woman to be tormented again, her emotions tossed about and trampled, her soul laid bare beneath a barrage of insults. It was a pain beyond the pain of flesh and bone. A spear to his heart. How could men be so cruel to the one mother of them all? And when would Jael's defiance provoke a turn for the worse? The raiders would be pushed beyond the limits of their patience one day, and he feared his mother would find the tip of a spear in her own heart.

He stopped at the first tent on his route, needing to see for himself that the preparations were followed as planned. A soft glow from an oil lamp lit the interior. A young mother and two older women huddled against the wall on the right side, three baskets of grain in front them. Simple bedrolls, cooking utensils, and the remainder of their meager possessions were tossed in the center of the tent. To the far left side was nothing but a scratchy old goat hair rug.

Shem fixed his gaze on the rug, stiff and riddled with dirt, a poor man's possession of no interest to a King. It didn't move. No one would suspect the hole beneath, or the treasure of young lives hidden within the packed earthen walls. With a quick nod of approval he left the tent and moved down the line, stopping at the dwellings with similar hiding places. The women had done well. None of their little ones were detectable, no toys or tiny blankets carelessly exposed. Shem's heart beat rapidly anyhow. If one hiding hole was discovered, they would all be uncovered and stripped of their contents.

The children. It was all they had left. Their greatest treasure, their future, had to be protected. King Amraphel had taken others away by the dozens to serve in his temples. They would have only brief memories of the ways of the Hebrews under the dominion of the One True God as they bowed at the feet of man-made idols. Shem stopped to peer into the sky. "God of the heavens. We need You. Don't let the babies cry."

Chapter Two

Jael stood at the mouth of the cave with a rock in her fist. Three raiders on horseback reined in beside her, torchlight reflecting from their copper helmets and bouncing off the stony embankment. Derogatory comments poured from their lips, aimed at the ancient woman, her people and her God. They spoke in the tongue of Aram, the common language of trade.

Eran winced as she put weight on her right leg, her knee burning from the blow, her gut churning. Her mother-in-law was prepared to fight. She understood enough of the men's language to understand the intent, but Jael wouldn't fight against mere words, no matter how crude. The rock in her hand would be used to stop the men from entering Noah's burial cave.

"She means no harm." Eran couldn't control the quiver in her voice as she limped closer to the men. She shouldn't stand before them in fear, they were of her lineage. Yet she did, trembling with uncertainty. The raiders held little respect for their blood ancestors, choosing to give it to their King instead. To them, she was merely another old woman to be disregarded, not the mother of their Semitic tribes. "She only protects her husband's bones."

The men laughed in unison. "We were warned to watch for

this old woman," one said. "We know she hides her riches beneath the pile of stones."

"There is nothing hidden in the cave. There has never been anything hidden in there, as you well know. It's just the bones of Noah. Leave his widow in peace. Please, leave her husband's grave alone."

Two of the men dismounted and stood before Jael. The other rode toward Eran, waving a spear before her eyes. "Stay here," he said. "Don't interfere."

Eran did as she was told as the man joined the others, aware for the first time of the voices rising from the center of the camp.

The raiders on the ground stood on either side of Jael, poking her arms with the tip of their spears. Jael's feet remained solid as she guarded the cave, her upper body shifting away from the weapons nipping at her flesh. "Stop! Leave him be!" Her cries were filled with resolve.

The tempo increased. Her right side was poked, then the left, then the right again, this time on her leg. Jael's agitation grew, her arms slapping wildly at the weapons while the men deftly pulled them out of her reach.

Eran swallowed hard against the knot tying up her throat. She searched again for Shem, for anyone in the shadows, or in the pale swatches of ground where the morning light was removing the darkness. There was no one to help her.

The third soldier dismounted, danced his way around Jael and entered the cave. He planted his torch and pulled the first stone from the pile covering Noah's bones, tossing it effortlessly behind him.

"Leave him alone!" Jael's voice was hard and shrill. She raised her arm to hurl the rock in her hand.

"Stop! Jael, no!" Eran ran toward her.

The two raiders seized her mother-in-law and thrust her to the ground. Jael screamed in anger then latched both hands around the nearest calf, digging her nails into the flesh.

The raider yanked his leg from the woman's claws and kicked her in the abdomen, showering a new strain of curses over her crumpled body.

Eran fell at her mother-in-law's side. Jael scowled and gripped Eran's arm, trying to rise before clutching her belly in pain and falling back to the ground. Her brilliant blue eyes sent daggers of fury to the men as they tossed the memorial stones aside. She breathed hard and fast, but she breathed.

"Be still, Mother." Eran positioned herself between the men and Jael, pinning the bony shoulders to the ground with little effort.

The shouting from the center of the camp had diminished.

Where were the Hebrew men?

Where was Shem?

♥

Two dozen raiders entered the camp on horseback, fully armed and holding flaming torches to the morning sky. They drove their horses in a tight circle around the Hebrew men, shouting praises to their King.

Shem looked over his shoulder at the fifty or so men gathered in the center of the camp. Old ones, and those barely into manhood, shoulder to shoulder with the young and strong. They were fine men, devoted to the ways of their fathers. They didn't deserve the persecution from King Amraphel.

As Priest of the One God, he took position in front of the group, standing beside his great-grandson Eber. This was Eber's tribe, the Hebrews. The men were his responsibility, his to protect and preserve. Shem gave him a reassuring smile, himself finding strength in the leader of the camp. Eber was wise and would not act rashly, clinging to faith in Noah's God while adversity fought to destroy his generations.

Japheth, Shem's older brother, stood behind him, whispering prayers in earnest as they waited for the raiders to stop circling, for hooves to stop stirring up the earth and confining them in the dusty cloud. When their leader raised his arm, the horses stood still, their riders taut in their saddles, awaiting instruction. The leader tossed his torch to the ground at Eber's feet. "We're here to collect the King's tribute. What do you offer?"

Shem grit his teeth and kept a steady gaze into the man's eyes as Eber spoke. "We are children of the One God. We don't pay tribute to kings claiming authority over their brothers. We honor only the Creator."

The leader smirked. His request was always the same. The answer was always the same. The proceeding search, the same. His men would take whatever they chose as the tribute. "You are fools," he said.

Amraphel's man nodded to the other raiders. Most of them dismounted, splitting into groups of two to search the camp. Three of them left the courtyard, guiding their horses towards the cave. Shem groaned, not realizing he did so out loud until Japheth's hand squeezed his shoulder.

Low rumblings filtered through the young men, shushed by their fathers and grandfathers. Initiating violence was prohibited in the camp and Eber demanded discipline of the tongue as well. Other camps had been decimated when they dared raise a knife in defense of their possessions or made threats to Amraphel's men.

Shem longed to draw a knife. The raid wasn't right, it wasn't fair. He couldn't though. It was hidden in his tent as Eber had ordered. And he wouldn't. He would restrain himself too. No one would die if they could control their venom.

Beyond the tents, his mother's angry voice ricocheted off the embankment. Shem grabbed Eber's arm to steady himself. There was one in the camp who couldn't control the fury in her heart. The oldest person alive, the mother of them all, would not submit to the invasion in peace.

Shem forced himself to remain with the men, praying for the women at the cave as he watched the raiders enter the tents. They exited with only baskets of grain and simple rough-hewn possessions. Nothing living. No little ones were found.

The stolen tribute was piled onto carts at the camp entrance. The leader grew restless as the stack of simple belongings rose, his expression darkening. "Where are they?" he asked.

Eber turned his head slowly, looking to his left at a small patch of cleared land on the perimeter of the camp. Small mounds of stones lined up in even rows. Forty of them. "Our dead," he said. "Buried there."

Two raiders went to the burial site and rapidly kicked through rocks, lifting the uncovered bones for the leader to see. His eyes narrowed. "You'd sacrifice your own offspring rather than submit them to the King?"

Shem held his tongue. Eber's lips pinched together and he stared at the sky.

"You truly are fools to-"

"Stop! Jael, no!" Eran's voice rose from beyond the tents, interrupting the raider.

Shem turned and bolted toward the cave, discipline overrun by the fear of what he might find.

Eran was kneeling over Jael. There was no blood that he

could see and his mother's verbal threats rose above Eran's pleas for silence and the raiders' gruff laughter. They were alive. Eran exhaled audibly as he dropped beside her and put a protective arm over her shoulders.

Several raiders followed him on foot, joining the three already there. The leader trailed behind on his horse, sauntering up to them, chuckling. "So this is what you hold dear, old man of the Hebrew tribe."

Shem stiffened his spine and pulled back from his wife and mother.

The raider smiled with his lips, his eyes remaining fixed and cold. He nodded to his men, pointing at the women. "Take them," he said.

Chapter Three

"Take them."

The man pointed at her. Eran latched onto Shem's arm and tried to hold on. Three men pried them apart, dragging her husband back and restraining him.

Another man scooped Eran into his arms. She tried to twist from his grasp, finding only a tighter hold against the rigid muscles of the raider's chest.

"Bind them if they fight," their leader said. "And load them onto the cart with the rest of the garbage."

"Shem!"

Her captor's grip tightened, his fingertips delving deep into her arm and thigh. "No screaming, woman."

Eran swallowed a cry and craned her head to find Jael. Her mother-in-law's arms draped around the neck of one of the raiders who had followed Shem to the cave. Jael leaned into him as if she were a child in the arms of her father, no longer yelling or fighting. The young man held her gently, tenderly almost. His expression wasn't the mask of derision his comrades wore and he intentionally carried her close to Shem.

"Don't let Noah get cold," Jael said as she passed her son.

"Cover him back up so he won't get cold."

"Moth-" Her husband's words ended with the tip of a spear thrust in his face. He turned to Eran, eyes glistening and desperate as she was carried off between the tent rows and he was held back.

Eran closed her eyes and took in a deep breath, slowly exhaling. She opened them again, in the courtyard, where the Hebrew men stood, eyes widening and horror emerging as they grasped the nature of the King's tribute. Not just grain this time.

The thought quickened her heart rate. What else was found? She lifted her head to search the carts and Amraphel's horses, seeing possessions only. No children. God had heard their pleas and kept them safe.

Abruptly Eran was dropped onto the cart amidst baskets and hides. Jael was placed beside her, gently. "Thank you," she whispered to the young man as he lifted Jael's arms from his neck and placed them in her lap. He wouldn't look up, chuffing at Eran's gratitude and striding away.

Jael leaned against Eran's shoulder, arms enfolding her waist, and her knees pulled up into small bundle of new frailty. She rocked slowly. Denah, Japheth's wife, had done the same thing years ago, as pain tore through her body and took her unborn child. Eran had given her sister-in-law medicines to help her rest, and heal. She could do nothing for Jael's pain. Her pots of medicines lay hidden in a tent.

"Does it hurt, Mother?" Jael's groans answered the question. Eran wrapped her arm around the woman's bony shoulders and stroked her head with the other. Jael's hair was silver, still thick as a horse's tail and braided into one long rope. Had she ever worn it otherwise? From the time Eran was purchased for Shem, she could recall seeing it fixed only the one way. It was consistent as the sunrise.

There was security in the old woman's familiar patterns. God had been with Jael Before, before the Great Flood, and God followed her through the years of struggle on the new earth, during seasons of wealth and those of turmoil, and God was with her now. To be near the old braided head was to be near the One God himself. Eran pulled her in close.

The cart jerked into motion, turning right, toward Nineveh, rather than left to the city of Haran. Eran exhaled the breath she held inside. Beyond Haran was land of unspeakable evil. Nineveh was riddled with its own sin, but at least it was in the land of the two great rivers, the Tigris and Euphrates. She would remain in the land of her offspring.

Eran rocked in rhythm with Jael. Flanked by raiders on horseback, she watched the tent city of the Hebrews slip behind a dusty shroud.

♥

Strong hands propelled Shem's face into the dirt and held it there while he fought for air. The invaders laughed before releasing him and heading toward the courtyard. Shem scrambled to his feet and ran after them, feeling the acute absence of a sharp weapon in his grasp.

The tribe was no longer maintaining peace, shouting at the raiders from behind a wall of spears. The wall opened to allow his wife and mother to be carried through and placed on the cart, then sealed shut again.

Shem pushed his way to the front. They were taking old women. Surely they would take him instead. He wanted to believe it, yet knew the men had been trained in the vindictive ways of their leader. The king's men understood the power of emotional pain, of prolonged suffering that was worse than finding the escape of death.

"Take me. Leave the women here." Shem grabbed the reins of the leader's horse only to have his knuckles smacked with the hilt of a knife.

"We have what we need." He turned away from the Shem and gave the order to move out. Dust whirled around the retreating party, from horses' hooves and the wheels of the cart that followed them.

Japheth and Eber held Shem's arms, preventing him from running after Eran and Jael, momentarily lost in the brown cloud.

"Wait, Shem," Japheth said. "We're no match for them. We'll follow on the donkeys, out of sight, to see what happens. See if they realize what they're doing and let Eran and Mother go free."

Donkeys? It was all they had for transportation. And only a handful of real weapons remained among them. A pitiful army. Chasing behind them was purposeless. They couldn't overtake them. They couldn't fight against the spears. They couldn't ask kindly and expect to have the women returned.

But they couldn't do nothing. Shem nodded his consent.

♥

Jael dozed in Eran's arms. The few times she had opened her eyes and looked around, there was understanding written in her expression. No fog, no forgetfulness, no confusion. With clarity she saw the raiders, the road to Nineveh, the fact she was clothed only in a sleeping tunic with Eran's coat draped over her. And especially that the two women were the only Hebrews on this journey. Eran watched as her mother-in-law scanned the faces and attire of the men accompanying them. Searching for one of her own, for a face that spoke of reassurance. Jael absorbed the facts before her, then closed her eyes again, knowing the truth, Eran was sure.

The young soldier who carried Jael slowed his horse to ride alongside the cart. He had done so several times each hour, his face composed, as if only checking the stolen bounty, seeing that it wasn't bouncing around and spreading grain everywhere. His eyes found Jael's face, every time, and lingered there, a softness emerging until he kicked his heels and urged his mount forward, away from the two old women. There was compassion in the man, a trickle of hope.

A bump in the road awakened Jael. She didn't try to sit this time, keeping her head on Eran's lap. "I'm sorry, Eran." Her voice was faint, as if she were far away. "I'm sorry."

Eran resumed her easy stroking on Jael's back. What would become of her? Amraphel, King of Shinar, was Jael's great-grandson. He disowned her once, cutting all ties to his parents and grandparents, aunts and uncles. Even Noah and Jael were dead to him. Anyone adhering to the truth of their God was an enemy in his eyes. How would he treat his old relatives now, dropped on his palace floor as tribute?

"Remember Before." It was a command, not a question. Jael continued. "Remember the Beginnings. Remember the One God, who watched our fathers. Always watching. Always. Seeing. Never alone. Never."

Never alone. Yes, it was true. Eran clung to the thought. The hands that led her into Noah's ark and away from the Tower in Babylon, would lead her now. Even in Nineveh. Even without Shem. Eran wiped perspiration from her forehead. God would be there. He wouldn't abandon her after all these years.

Jael winced as the cart pushed through a rut in the well-traveled road. In pain, injured intentionally. Eran pushed anxiety from her mind as best she could, knowing God's presence didn't always guarantee protection from the evil intent of man.

What would they find in Nineveh? She had never been to the city of Amraphel's summer palace. It was a wealthy city, built by the blood of slaves and by her own children's children. Did any of them remember the God of their fathers? Had their loyalty to self-proclaimed kings replaced all trust in the living God? Had the youngest among them even heard the name of Noah?

Eran looked beyond the cart to the road they had traveled, the road leading to Shem. He would come to their rescue. She kept her eye to the roads for signs of him, and her prayers to the heavens for the merciful arms of salvation.

♥

The afternoon breeze brought little relief from the sun. The road was in open land, many trees having been felled away for safety. Robbers could be seen in plenty of time for travelers to draw weapons, and while that was a comfort, it meant there was no shade to break the hot rays. Eran rearranged her cloak to shield Jael despite the warmth it generated. The woman slept restlessly in the nest, her moaning soft and persistent as she breathed. Her skin had taken on a clammy feel, one of illness not related to the temperature of the air.

The young raider pulled in beside the cart and took a quick glance at Jael. He spurred his horse away from the cart, coming back in a few moments and speaking to the driver. The horsemen continued on as the cart slowed to a stop beside a meager stand of young oak trees.

Jael didn't awaken. The man climbed on board and pushed

Eran's cloak aside, intending to lift the woman from her lap.

Eran latched onto his forearms. "What are you doing?"

The man nodded at the trees. "For you. Go and, take care of your needs. Hurry."

Eran released his arms. He eased himself off the cart with Jael tucked against his chest and took her to a grassy patch, leaning her against a tree. Eran watched for a moment then quickly climbed off the cart and ducked behind trees and tall grasses to relieve herself. The thought of running away was brief. She wouldn't abandon Jael and knew she would be caught, or speared, in short order if she tried. Her knees would give out before the first mile toward home.

The young man waited beside Jael. He had taken Eran's cloak and spread it out over her body, tucking in the edges around her like a warm cocoon. Eran put her hand on the tree trunk, intending to kneel in the shade beside her mother-in-law, but the raider grabbed her forearm and lifted her up. "No. We're leaving. The old one stays here. She's dead."

Eran gasped and turned to Jael. The woman's lips were pink, her chest gently rising and falling. "What? No, she-"

The man pulled her by the arm toward the cart, his whisper fierce in her ear. "That's what I told the others. She died and I left her for the vultures."

Eran tried to pull away. "I can't leave her here alone! Don't, please. Please-"

"Your people are coming. I've seen their dust behind us."

Understanding coursed through her mind. He was saving Jael. There was only one reason she could think of to explain his deceit. "Are they your people? Are you one of the children, all grown up, a child of the camp of Eber?"

The man flinched at the name and gave a curt nod. "I was. Not now." He glanced at Jael. "But I remember you, and our old blue-eyed mother." In one smooth motion he picked Eran up and put her back in the cart, then tossed in a skin of water to drink. Back on his horse, he signaled to the driver and the cart jerked to a start.

Eran fell back against the grain, her eyes watching her mother-in-law through a watery haze before the dust obscured her view. Jael would be discovered and taken home to live out her days in the care of those who loved her. The young raider took great risk. Not so much as to leave Eran along the road. She couldn't expect that. It was plausible Jael died from the fright or the blow to her gut. No one would believe they both died or escaped without help.

Jael would return home and Eran would go to Nineveh.

A new fear shook her spine. An unfamiliar one, one of loneliness.

Dark blots appeared in her vision, threatening to merge and block her consciousness. Eran lowered her head and forced herself to breath in and out at a regular rate, fighting the fear within. Shem wasn't there to protect her. She couldn't draw from Jael's well of strength. The tribe of Hebrews was out of reach. Denah, Japheth, Eber – their hands too far away to cling to for support.

For the first time in her life, Eran had no one to lean on.

Chapter Four

Eber led eight donkeys from a pasture that was tucked into the hillside, impossible to detect from the road. There were twenty more, plus cattle, sheep and goats, and four pair of oxen. All but the oldest and weakest were in small pastures away from the camp. When the shofar blew, the shepherds herded the beasts into the narrow canyons and waited until the raiders were gone before venturing out again.

Eight donkeys meant an eight man army would follow the trail of Amraphel's men. Shem sighed, though it was a wise decision. They couldn't risk using all the packing beasts. When they had done so before, when the first of their children were taken, the raiders stopped them on the road and took all forty-five horses. It was an easy victory for them, holding a knife to the throat of a child was all that was necessary for the Hebrew army to surrender. That was some twenty years ago, he guessed.

It had been at least a year since the last child was taken. Hiding them in the ground this time was a success and would work again. They needed to bolster the old rugs to ensure they wouldn't collapse under a man's weight though, and pray for other alternatives. Diversity was key. Hiding the youngest ones in clay pots with false bottoms and sending older ones up nearby trees spread the risk. Fortunately the raiders were less intent on finding the children. They had taken all the golden haired ones for the temples and the dark haired ones were of far less value. There was little of anything of value to them anymore. Harassing the camp was sport, winning guaranteed by the raiders' unpredictable arrival and the chaos they stirred. Finding the little ones was added entertainment, the resulting devastation a bonus to their game.

Shem gathered filled water skins and took them to Eber, remembering he had not thanked the man yet. "You did well, Son. Thank you. You spoke as a man of the One God. Noah would have been pleased with your actions, and your restraint."

Eber stopped a vigorous brushing of donkey flank. "I didn't lie. I promised you no untrue words would come from my lips and I kept that promise."

Shem slapped the man's shoulder. "I noticed the creativity in the words you chose." He looked at the forty tiny graves. A handful of women were sorting bones from stone and reburying them. "Yes, our dead are buried in that plot. Our dead sheep."

Shem read the thoughts behind the man's furrowed brow and dropped his arm on his shoulder. "Misleading those men to spare the lives of the innocent will be forgiven by our God. Don't allow guilt to tear you apart."

"But Jael and Eran. We saved some and lost others."

"It's my fault. I shouldn't have run to the cave. I meant only to protect them. When Eran screamed…"

"Your wife and mother were in jeopardy. You did what any man would do. And you may have saved their lives by intervening."

"It's only a matter of time, isn't it? Amraphel's men will kill our people eventually. Mother was injured. The violence is escalating."

"Listen to your own words and don't allow guilt to tear you apart Father Shem. We'll track the raiders, see if the women are taken all the way to Nineveh, and if so, then devise a plan to get them back. God will show us, if that's his will."

Shem picked up two water skins and fastened them to a donkey. If the raiders would bend so low as to injure and kidnap old women, what was next? When would the first man be killed for allowing a hateful word to slip? When would a torch be intentionally held to a tent? When would Amraphel tire of the non-compliant tribe and order their annihilation? They wouldn't be the first.

The days of protection were gone. Noah's presence had been a safeguard to the encampment, nestled in the verdant hills between Haran and Nineveh. Even under orders from kings in the region, no one dared to harm the ancient one, the man of the Old Earth. He was thought to be immortal, thought to have the power of life and death in his grasp. While wars raged among the kingdoms, the Hebrews were left alone. The generations of Noah revered the man of the ark as a god.

Then Noah died, and the wall of protection crumbled. Persecution began, and continued, increasing especially in the last decades, a time of relative peace in the land of the two rivers. Warring kings had no time for the harassment of irritant tribes. Ones at ease took the opportunity to increase their storehouses from within their own borders. Bit by bit Amraphel ripped Shem's community into fragments.

Eber's small tribe was Shem's only family still speaking the original tongue of Adam. They alone feared the One God. It was difficult to understand why the persecution continued. Did God want his name to be slashed from the memories of the people of earth?

Japheth placed an armload of provisions on the ground by Eber then turned to Shem. "Shall we tend to Father before we leave?"

His brother's spine wasn't the least bit bent with age. Gray curls fell from his head, secured with a tie in back, exposing crinkling skin and the heavenly blue eyes he got from their mother. His hands were gradually taking the form of their grandfather Methuselah's, starting to gnarl and twist at the joints and Japheth rubbed them frequently. He did so now, as he prepared to work them in a task they could easily assign to younger, stronger hands, but didn't.

"Yes. I'm ready." This was a task they chose to do themselves. Shem secured the last of the skins and turned toward the cave with his brother.

Japheth's wife, Denah was at the mouth of the cave. Her eyes glistened and she squeezed Shem's hand without speaking. The three of them began picking through the rubble, separating Noah from the stones.

"They won't be harmed in Nineveh." Japheth's voice was too sure, trying to convince himself as well as his wife and brother. "They'll be recognized and honored."

"Mother was on the ground. I'm sure she was hurt."

"If anyone can tend her, it's Eran. She'll see to Mother's well-being."

Eran had great abilities with her herbs and roots, knowing when to change a bandage and when to leave a wound alone. She could concoct a potion to remedy a headache or dry out a rash. Years of experience taught her how to cure most anything. She amazed him with her skills and he wouldn't trust anyone more than his wife when it came to medicine. Her supplies weren't with her, however.

Shem blew dust off a bone and placed it in a baked clay pot. His father's remains had been tossed about too many times to be whole any longer and easily fit inside the lidded container. "How many families will leave this time, do you think?"

Japheth stopped and ran a dusty hand through his hair. "More than last time. They're tired of hiding their babies, of always wondering when the next raid will come. I don't blame them. As much as I want us to be a strong tribe for the One God, I don't blame them for choosing to leave this place."

"But so many go to the land of Canaan," Denah said. "I know there's open space for the herds, but it still frightens me. Choosing to live in a land where they sacrifice their own children to gain favor for their crops. How can good come of it?"

Shem stretched his back after heaving a large stone aside. "Abram lives in the land of our nephew Canaan and prospers there. The others follow, believing they'll find a safe haven and make their own riches. I'd stop them if I could. We won't be a tribe at all if the migration continues."

Neither his brother or sister-in-law commented. Once, they all had great hopes in Shem's young descendant, the sixth generation after Eber, the ninth from himself. Abram was true to the faith of his fathers, and wise with business. A natural leader, destined to follow in the steps of the maturing Eber. They knew he could bring strength to the Hebrew tribe, knew he was the one to oversee the rise of a mighty nation with his diplomatic ways. Shem believed young Abram could accomplish what he himself had failed to do.

Then Abram's father died. And God spoke.

Abram immediately followed the command he claimed to have been given, the one to pack up and leave his home near Haran and go to the land of the Canaanite tribes. He was promised a nation.

So he said.

The great expectation had waned. It had been twenty-five years since Abram left them, and as far as they knew, his wife Sarai was still without a son in her arms. She was beyond her child bearing years by this time. The Hebrew nation they all longed for, a people raised in the ways of the One God, refusing to bend beneath winds of opinion, had not been fulfilled. Disappointment was still keen.

Japheth spoke after a length of time. "Perhaps now there's a son on Abram's knee. I haven't heard for some time. Last I knew, Abram faired well otherwise. He had not turned to the ways of the local people."

"And others have stayed true, I have to believe." Shem and Japheth locked eyes, perceiving each other's thoughts. They didn't know with certainty that their brother Ham walked with God or if he succumbed to the ideals of the pagan lands after he left them to follow after his sons. They had received no word from him and Naomi in over forty years.

King Amraphel hated his grandfather Ham, blaming him for troubles that began years ago. Naomi and Ham fled from his wrath, but Shem doubted they made it far. Amraphel was persistent, a hunter through and through. Shem suspected his brother was dead. And he wouldn't admit it to anyone, but he hoped Ham was dead, in the arms of his fathers, rather than bowing to the feet of golden deception in the land where sin never sleeps.

The sorting complete, Denah sprinkled droplets of myrrh over the bones. Shem discreetly breathed through his mouth until the pot was sealed and the dark earthy aroma contained. Eran used myrrh for ailments and he knew good came from the resin, but he didn't like it. It was a burial spice, one they had added to his father's bones, many, many times in the hundred years since his death. It was the smell of sorrow, the fragrance of life ending.

He and Japheth stacked stones over Noah's remains again. When they were done, Denah placed a ring of braided grasses and wild flowers on top. A circle, like the life it honored, complete. No more days on this earth to add and none to take away. No more joys, or disappointments. It began and ended, dust to dust, first breath to last.

Shem placed his hands on the mound and voiced a prayer, hoping as always it would be the last time his father was disturbed. He would try again to get Jael's permission to move the grave to a more secluded location. If he had the chance.

Chapter Five

Fran sang all the songs she knew, some of them twice, then made up her own words and melodies. She wished she had her flute, preferring it to singing out loud, never as confident with her voice as she was with the instruments Shem carved for her. The latest one, of ebony wood, gave a deep mellow resonance, unnerving almost, as if it called down the very spirit of God to walk in their midst. She needed the comfort of the flute right now, and the strength of a holy presence.

The raiders paid no attention to her. The cart of tribute trailed the other horses and she was left undisturbed. Eran peered over the edge. She could jump from the cart. Would anyone hear the thud as she hit the packed roadway? The driver rarely turned his head her way. He might not even notice. It wouldn't be simple to land without hurting herself, however. What if she broke her hip? Could she risk it?

Eran kept vigil on the road behind her and kept the option open. If she saw Shem and thought it was her only chance, she would muster the courage. So far there had been no sign of the Hebrew men.

After hours of watching the road unwind, the long strand

connecting her to home growing longer and longer, she allowed her eyes to close. There would be no dramatic rescue. The sun was settling on the horizon. It wouldn't be long until the raiders entered the city gates of Nineveh and they would be sealed in for the night. Shem wouldn't camp in the darkness, risking his life and those of the men with him. There were too many thieves along the roadways. If he really had been following as the young raider said, he had turned back by now.

Eran shivered in the cooling air. Was Jael still warm? She wrapped her arms around her knees and prayed that she hadn't been lied to, that Shem really had been coming and that he found his mother, safe and warm, and alive. She prayed for his safety as well, and that he would find a way to bring his wife home.

♥

She was alive. Shem saw his mother's head turn their direction when his startled cry alerted the others. They stopped abruptly in the shade of the oaks, the only protected place they'd passed for miles. He ran to her and put a hand to her forehead. Cool, clammy. Her eyes disappeared into deep wrinkles as she smiled and pulled a spindly arm from beneath Eran's cloak to pat his cheek. "There you are, Shem. I'm glad you came. I'm getting hungry."

Shem forced a calm smile to his face and tucked strands of loose hair behind his mother's ears. "Are you alone? Where's Eran?" He shouted into her ear, then mouthed the words again where she could see his lips.

Jael looked puzzled for a moment, then nodded as she remembered. "She went to the city. With the grain. She'll be home soon."

"Was she hurt, Mother?"

His mother shook her head. "She's fine, Son. She's fine. She'll be home soon." Again she patted his cheek, her expression the same as it been when he was first married and worried over the health of his bride. Eran was frail, malnourished and so shy he didn't know her eye color until after they were married. Jael reassured him with a pat on the cheek many times in those days. He put his hand over hers then took it to his lips, thankful his mother didn't fully grasp what was happening.

Japheth retrieved a water skin and held it for Jael, making sure she drank several mouthfuls while Shem and the others searched the immediate vicinity. "She isn't here," he said when they returned. "And she wouldn't leave Mother, unless she was searching for healing herbs. I can't see any tracks though, and she wouldn't go too far. Not on her own."

His brother held his gaze. "They abandoned Mother, and kept Eran. If they didn't leave them here together, I have to believe they'll take her to the city."

Japheth eased the cloak from their mother's body. "No blood, nothing appears broken. She's breathing hard though and keeps rubbing her abdomen."

Shem fought the anger in his heart. "She's injured."

"But alive."

"Yes. A blessing." The men could have killed her. "And the cloak, it's a good sign. She was placed against the tree and wrapped up intentionally, not just dumped."

"It is a good sign. There's compassion among the raiders."

Shem peered down the long stretch of road toward Nineveh. "Eran is alone. She must be terrified." He had always been there to protect her. Or someone had. When he hunted with his brothers, Jael and Noah were there. Denah and Naomi, too. Or their sons, or grandsons. Always someone. "She must be terrified."

His brother's hand rested on Shem's shoulder. "We can't catch them by nightfall, not with Mother. The city gates will be locked. And I don't think we should split up."

Shem sucked in a deep breath. "I know. I agree. We'll take her home and, and…"

"Pray. Wait for a solution."

"Yes. There's an answer. We know where she is. We'll find a way to get Eran."

Japheth motioned to one of the younger men to lift Jael.

Shem eased himself to standing and stepped out of the way. He could carry her light frame if she was placed in his arms. Getting her from the ground was all together different. He had lived many, many years with vitality and strength. They were behind him now. He already climbed the mountain to life's peak and was on the down slope, straining to keep from going too quickly to the valley below. The years forced him to reconsider tasks he once did with ease, without a second thought, like lifting a fragile old woman from the earth.

Jael winced and hugged her belly as she was moved. The brothers exchanged a glance, sharing the pain. She groaned as she was placed on a donkey and as Japheth got on behind her. His brother held Jael against his chest and spoke the calming recitations of their Beginnings, words etched on their minds since childhood "In the beginning God created the heavens and the earth…"

Their mother couldn't hear him. It didn't matter. The words calmed Japheth and they would dull the sharp edge of Shem's turmoil for the slow ride home. He secured Eran's cloak over his mother and they turned the donkeys back the way they had come. Away from Eran. It was a wise decision. It was the only choice.

But it felt so wrong.

How could he leave her? For five-hundred years they had

been together. Through the Flood, the dispersion of their heirs, the persecution, times of doubt and times of fear. She was beside him when hope was all he could cling to, hope in the God who saved them and hope that he would save them again. His life was linked to Eran. She was solace to his trepidation, laughter in his weariness, peace amid the chaos of an earth once again distorting Truth and pursuing its own pleasures.

Choosing Eran was the one thing he had done right.

He would find a way to bring her back. He had to. Half his heart was torn away when the raiders took her from him. How could he live without her?

Chapter Six

More and more men appeared on the road as they neared the city. Most were soldiers on horseback, carrying an arsenal of weaponry. They greeted the raiding party enthusiastically and with great guffaws of laughter as they circled the meager load of stolen tribute, discovering Eran's shivering frame with astonishment.

She hunkered as low in the cart as possible, hugging her knees to her chest. Her long hair was uncovered and the thin tunic inappropriate outside her tent, but there was nowhere to hide. Preventing the gaze of the men was impossible. She tried to bury her head against her knees to block them out, yet found herself unable to keep her head down, needing to see the faces of those laughing at her plight. Would she recognize any of them? Would any recognize her and intervene? She hadn't seen the compassionate young raider for hours, and so far no one offered even a smile of reassurance.

Heat climbed up her neck and filled her cheeks, doing nothing to still the chattering of her teeth. Another pair of soldiers pointed at her and stared, as if she had three heads with a horn sticking out of each one. There was no animosity, just amazement and curiosity.

They spoke in the tongue of Amraphel, one unknown to her, yet she understood their amusement by the tones and gestures and expressions. No one anticipated finding an old woman among the bounty.

A trumpet sounded in the distance, from the wall of the city. Eran felt her heart beating quickly as the unknown drew closer. King Amraphel despised the Hebrews. They refused to honor him as either a king or a god, but it was more than that. Noah and his three sons held fast to the words of the Creator, to the light of truth, exposing Amraphel's dark heart. He blamed them for the fall of his kingdom in Shinar, his first attempt to rule, his first outward attempt to exalt himself over God.

Then there was Abram, another reason to hate the people of the One God. Her young Hebrew relative outwitted the King and his allies in battle once, with a mere 318 men. It was a humiliating defeat for the Kings of Mesopotamia, one that increased the persecution on Eber's camp. That was fifteen or so years back, and no number of raids appeased the trampled pride. Amraphel held his grudges.

Would she be taken before him? Would he treat his great-aunt with respect or would he have her tossed into one of his dungeons? It was impossible to know. She hadn't seen him in years. He was kind and humble in her presence once, an inquisitive child with never-ending questions about the earth and ways of mankind prior to the flood that took it all away. His pride knew no limits, however, and he had become a man who lived up to his first given name. He Will Rebel had indeed turned his back on the truth of his fathers.

After the majority of Noah's descendants left the Plain of Shinar, Amraphel reconstructed the tower that God judged. It stood on the bank of the Euphrates, his defiance pointing in the face of God and claiming superiority. Afterward he set about building cities. Babylon, Erech, Akkad, Calneh and Nineveh were all fortified places, anticipating war, and filled with temples to made-up gods. He was one of them.

Eran consciously breathed evenly, suppressing the anxiety that clamored to overwhelm her. She had never set foot in Nineveh. Shem and others had come, searching for the golden haired children. Always he returned home without them and spent days in quiet reflection afterward. The crowds, the ungodliness, the lack of reverence to the ways of their fathers troubled him. She had never found reason to go there, never had a desire to see the golden city for herself. Now she had no choice.

The cart began a gentle climb up the bridge leading to the main city gates.

A blurred spot developed on the periphery of her vision.

They passed sentries, lined shoulder to shoulder, helmets and chests covered in metal.

Her stomach churned and the black spots multiplied.

To her right and to her left, the rushing torrent of the Tigris River stormed beneath the bridge. Eran put her hands to her ears to block the sound and squeezed her eyes shut.

It was too late. The darkness converged and Eran succumbed to its grip on her consciousness.

♥

The rhythmic clip-clop of hooves brought Eran back to awareness. A cobbled street passed beneath her, the flank of a sweaty horse rubbing against her cheek as it bounced her ribs against its spine. She was lying over the animal like a sack of grain. A soldier put a hand on her back as she tried to move. His spear made the same clink–clink rhythm as the hooves.

A cacophony of sensations swarmed around her. Foreign words in her ears, pungent smells in her nose, the sight of feet ornate with jeweled bands stepping away from the horse as it grew close. The flesh on her front side felt damp from heat while her backside, with nothing but the thin tunic between her and the evening air, was chilled. She tasted the brine of her own fear.

The cobbles turned to cut stone, then mosaic tiles before she was lifted from the horse and placed on her feet. Above her head, a brick fortress rose to the sky. Carved panels in the vivid hues and intricate patterns of an artist circled the walls, depicting warriors and conquests. Strong arms caught her from behind as she tipped backward, taking it in. "Steady now," the voice said.

Eran looked at him, and the others standing beside her. Four of them were soldiers, armed and dressed in the short tunics and leather boots that allowed quickness of movement. The one holding her had no weapons. He was draped in a long blue garment, trimmed in golden embroidery. Shaved clean, his oiled head shimmered from the torchlight. He still had her by the arms. "Do you speak the tongue of Aram?" he asked. "Can you walk on your own?"

She nodded, understanding his words, though not sure her legs would stop quivering enough to allow her to move without wobbling. The man took her arm on one side and led her through a set of massive doors, past more soldiers into an open chamber. It was covered in tiles, and columns, and more soldiers. Scarcely seeing any of it, she was led from room to hallway to courtyard to hallway to even more rooms. The structure could contain the entire Hebrew camp. They finally stopped outside a door and the man knocked.

A woman answered, dressed in similar clothing. She was in

her middle age years, the paints on her face thick and creeping into the fine lines of her skin. Her eyes opened wide as she looked Eran over. "This is her?"

The man chuckled. "She's yours to tend now." He turned and left.

"Eran, wife of Shem, son of Noah." The woman tipped her chin and bowed slightly before resuming her inspection, her eyes absorbing the details of Eran's appearance. "You really are an old one," she said. "I'm called Fatimaa. I just received word about you an hour ago. The messenger said we wouldn't believe who was coming. One of the ancient ones, he said. The wife of Shem."

The woman led Eran into a room three times the size of her tent at home. It was furnished elegantly with a raised bed, two stuffed benches and more rugs and pillows than she could count. She simply stood and stared, too tired to care about the finery.

"Do you know where you are?"

She shook her head.

Fatimaa looked at her quizzically. "Do you speak?"

Eran looked into her eyes. They were not unkind. "Oh, I'm sorry. Yes. And no. I'm in Nineveh. That's all I know."

"You are in the palace of the King," she said. Her voice was proud, as if this were a good thing. As if that should make Eran's fears dissolve. Instead she shivered, once again aware of her meager attire.

Fatimaa clapped her hands and two guards entered. "We'll go straight away," she said to them. She took Eran's arm in her carefully manicured hand and started for the door.

Eran drew back. "Where? To the King?" Her voice was high pitched and her knees suddenly felt unstable.

The woman signaled to the men to help Eran stand. "No," she said. "Not yet. Not looking like you do. We'll make you more presentable. And feed you. But first to the baths."

The dark of night covered the sky outside her window by the time Eran's skin had been thoroughly scrubbed then massaged with almond oil. Her long hair was washed and combed and coiled, then she was dressed in a simple pale blue tunic. A tray of food was delivered, then taken away after Eran dozed off after only a few bites of the rich fare. When she was finally allowed to crawl into the bed, exhaustion was held off as her mind spun. She had not been killed or forced to see Amraphel. She was clean and fed and provided a room. But there were guards beyond the door. For all the pampering, she was still a prisoner.

♥

Jael breathed raggedly, her heart rate speeding up and slowing at unpredictable intervals. Denah mixed another blend of willow bark and hemlock oil to add to the honey. Shem took the concoction when she finished and dipped his finger in it, then placed some inside his mother's lower lip. When that absorbed, he would add more, until he was certain the medication was sufficient to ease her pain.

His mother was dying. He knew it. There was nothing he could do to prevent her life from leaving her body and traveling to be with her beloved husband. Even Eran, with her ability to mix the herbs for ailments, wouldn't be able to keep Jael among them.

Japheth paced the perimeter of the tent, his hand repeatedly running through his hair. He wanted to fix the situation, desperate to undo the wrongs yet there was nothing for him to do, except to pray, and pace. Shem understood his brother's frustration, the hurt welling up inside him too and threatening to explode.

What was done was done. There was no going back, no

restoration. He focused on the honey ointment, a task that wasn't really necessary. His mother was beyond the realm of pain by now, her body continuing through the motions as they had for centuries in a last grasp to the life she had been given.

Noah's death wasn't like this, wasn't tied to violence. Their father lived to a ripe age of 950, his last decades peaceful. Bit by bit his body gave in to the effects of time, like their grandfather Methuselah, until the last breath was released. Noah was surrounded by family, by his generations who existed because he dared to believe in the One God's words. He built the ark, the crazy mammoth structure, before rain ever fell from the sky. In the face of ridicule, he persisted. He saved his children, the beasts of the earth and the birds of the heavens. Because he believed in the unseen, the earth once again was filled with man and all nature of living creatures.

They prepared for Noah's death, knowing it was coming, seizing every opportunity to be at his side and feel his heart beat to the sounds of the children's laughter. He had opportunity to tell them again and again the words of wisdom he heard from the Lord and every firstborn among them had been blessed beneath his hand. His face reflected contentment when at last he left them.

Jael's death was handed to them on a plate of spite. She was ripped from their care and would be gone before the day was out.

Shem welcomed the rise of numbness in his spirit. It would carry him through the moment. Anger would come again, he knew. And sorrow, profound sorrow.

His mother breathed easier as the medicated honey dissolved in her mouth and coursed through her blood. When the bowl was empty he stood, allowing Japheth room to rub scented oil into her hands and on her face, then Denah formed his mother's hair into a neat braid. She adjusted the covers on the pallet so they were neat, placing Jael's hands on top. Japheth waited until she finished before lifting the tent flap. One by one, Jael's descendants tiptoed in, kissed her hands and her forehead and said their farewells.

Jael gave no last words as the evening gave up its light and darkness descended. When they found her by the road, she reassured him that Eran would be home soon, and had not spoken since. Her eyes had drifted closed on the ride home and her vessel of life had been drained.

By nightfall, Noah held his bride once again.

Chapter Seven

Morning was gone and the sun nearly overhead by the time Eran woke from a night pocked with dreams of Jael's cries. Automatically she reached for Shem in the bed. He wasn't there. She was in Nineveh, alone.

Fatimaa rose from the couch when Eran stirred. She helped her rise from the pile of pillows and soft covers. Eran's hips and knees and spine protested the movement, the usual awakening stiffness compounded by yesterday's bouncing in the cart. Fatimaa took her straight to the baths.

She tried to relax in the shallow pool so the warm water would ease the ache in her joints. She tried to enjoy the massage on her scalp as her hair was washed and rinsed and combed. She wanted to appreciate the fragrant oils rubbed into her skin and deep into her sore muscles. She couldn't. Today she would stand before the King and the anxiety trumped all other sensations.

Fatimaa pulled an inner garment of fine woven linen over Eran's head. It was green, the color of barley sprouts first rising from the soil. It draped about her thin frame in loose waves, ending at her ankles. A second tunic covered the first, knee length and of the same color only darker, and trimmed in blue embroidery. Her hair was curled and coiled, and color added to her eyelids, lips and cheeks. Fatimaa chattered pleasantly as she transformed Eran, disguising the woman of the land as one raised in nobility. When she was finished, she triumphantly handed Eran a mirror.

Eran cringed at her image. It was not the face of an old Hebrew woman. Her thin line of lips was an unnatural pink, like her cheeks, with tiny fingers of the color already seeping into the surrounding creases. Blue shimmered above her eyes, filling in the entire space below her eyebrows and golden hoops dangled from her ears. Her hair, faded and dull, wasn't draped with a veil. It was styled and exposed, pinned to the top of her head with a strand of jade beads draping her forehead. She thrust the mirror back into Fatimaa's hand and forced herself to smile. "Thank you. I don't recognize my own face."

The woman beamed.

"What will he want of me?" Eran asked.

"I don't know. Usually I'm given girls to prepare for the goddess, for service in the temples. I've never been given an old woman."

"The girls. Are they Hebrew? Have you tended to the Hebrew children?"

"I have. They're one of many tribes committing their chosen ones for Ishtar. The King prefers ones with hair like the sun's rays, of course, and there used to be more from your people. It's been a while since I prepared a Hebrew girl. The newest ones have come from the north."

Fatimaa couldn't hide her pleasure in her duties for the King. Didn't she realize the children were taken from their parents? Ripped from their homes and carried off, screaming, crying for mothers? Fathers, helpless, unable to protect them, standing beneath the spears of Amraphel, seeing their sons and daughters for the last time.

"Do they fight, or try to run away?"

Fatimaa stopped painting Eran's toes with paint and looked at her with surprise. "The children? Of course not. They're frightened at first, in the King's palace, in the city for the first time. But it's an honor to be a chosen one for the temple. They learn quickly how to obey and serve."

"Do they resist worship of Ishtar? What happens if they choose to serve the god of their fathers?"

"I don't know. I only prepare their bodies for service, not their hearts. I can't imagine any of them choose another god or goddess, though. They are in a position of greatest honor. Ishtar is the chosen one of Nineveh. Besides our King, of course."

Eran leaned forward and grasped the woman's shoulder. "Can I see them? Can I speak to the Hebrew children?"

Fatimaa mopped up the paint Eran made her spill. "They reside in the temple. When you go to pay homage, you'll see the priestesses." She looked up suddenly with wide eyes. "Any in particular that you hope to find? Did you give your own little ones to Ishtar?"

"They were-" Eran started to explain then stopped herself as tears collected in the corner of her eyes. "No, Fatimaa. I didn't give any girls away."

Eran slumped back down on the overstuffed bench. Even if she found the taken children, there was nothing she could do to return them to their parents. If any wanted to return. Most were snatched away so young they wouldn't remember the tribe they were born to and those that did had been in Nineveh for years. This was home to them. Only the unseen blood coursing through their hearts remained Hebrew.

She couldn't see them, regardless. There were standards that could never be crossed in homage to the True God. Stepping foot in the temple of a false god was one of them. She could not go inside the houses of worship, not even to see the distant offspring of her womb. The children taken from her people were behind a wall she couldn't scale.

♥

The tiled floors all merged into one long walk from the room in which she slept to the ante-chamber into the King's throne room. Four guards accompanied Eran, silently escorting her with muscles tensed and at the ready. She wanted to believe they were there to protect her rather than preventing her escape. One glance at their fierce expressions nullified the thought.

The guards led her into a long narrow room lined with benches, and left her there, the tall double doors clanging shut behind them. Four other men protected the doors at the opposite end. There was no one else waiting to see Amraphel. Eran dropped onto the nearest bench.

The tiled mosaic on the wall in front of her was of the King. He stood with one foot on the neck of a dragon, a bloody spear held aloft in triumph. The great lizard's heart was in his right hand, still oozing crimson drops onto the soil. The image sent a shiver up her spine. He looked so much so like his grandfather, Ham. If she didn't know it was King Amraphel, she could have believed it was her brother-in-law in younger years. He was a hunter too, but not of men. Ham had not trained his grandson to destroy the lives of others. The King chose that path on his own.

The length of the room, both sides, presented scenes of similar conquests. Some beasts. Some human. The King triumphed in each image, his prey defeated soundly and he without a scratch.

Eran caught herself wringing her hands together. She pulled them apart and laid them flat on her knees, drying the moisture and reminding herself to breathe. When the door opened and she was summoned, she wished she had chosen a seat at the far end. It was a long walk to the door, all the men watching her. Her request to cover her hair had been denied. There was no veil to hide the fancy coils on her head or the awful face paint. Or her fear.

The throne room was a long rectangle, similar to the one she left, with windows occupying the spaces of the murals, lush gardens replacing records of his conquests. King Amraphel was on a massive throne at the end, flanked by a dozen guards on either side. Other than them, she was alone with the man who hated her people, hated his own fathers.

Once again, the solitary walk. She watched the floor tiles as she willed her legs to move, stopping before she reached the gilded steps to his throne.

How long since they last spoke? Three hundred years at least. Soon after God divided them by tongue, Amraphel proclaimed himself the ruler of Shinar and began the rebuilding of his tower. Shem, Ham and Japheth tried to control him, tried to sway the people back to the One God and his ways. After a time the King refused all direct contact with the sons of Noah. He had men by then, many men who followed his every command.

"Lift your head." His voice was the same, reverberating in the nearly empty space like the call of a jackal in a canyon. The command was meant to be followed.

Eran looked up, into the eyes of the man on the throne. This was no simple self-proclaimed ruler. He planned and oversaw the building of large fortified cities in the Plain of Shinar, ruled over many thousands of people who worshipped him as a god. His armies were loyal, known to be brutal, and the mere mention of his name stirred fear in the villages. His heart was cold and dark. Amraphel would kill a man rather than give him bread to feed his children. But he was still her kin, one she rocked as an infant and prayed over as he grew. Her eyes watered.

"Nimrod," she whispered.

Dark eyes flashed for an instant. "Don't. Call. Me. That." His voice didn't rise. It didn't have to, the tone alone quaking her spine. Eran looked at her feet and waited until he spoke again.

"Eran, wife of Shem." He said her husband's name like a foul taste in his mouth.

Lifting her chin, she dared to look into the deep brown eyes, the handsome face of Ham's grandson. Black curls fell to his strong shoulders, onto a robe of deep cobalt. The long sleeves stopped short of his wrists, encircled with gold and gems. He didn't hold a weapon. She exhaled.

Nimrod changed his given name when he declared himself king. He chose Amraphel, meaning Keeper of God. It was rebellion in his heart he had never excised. It was meant as a challenge to the One God, whose authority he spurned, and Eran didn't want to voice the name. Nor did she want to stir his animosity. She tipped her head before lifting it again. "King, King Amraphel."

"I wasn't expecting this sort of bounty. Interesting." He paused. Eran didn't fill in the void. "You've become an old, old woman, haven't you? Do you still play the flute?"

The question surprised her. She nodded.

"Speak."

"Yes. Yes, I play. I'm surprised you remember."

Amraphel leaned back into the soft padding of his throne. "I remember. I remember many things."

Again the tone that made the hairs on her neck stand at alert. Eran stayed on the topic he initiated. "I tried to teach you to play. You preferred the sound of arrows striking targets to the sound of melodies."

"Indeed. I chose the greater skill to master. Now, I wave my hand and an orchestra appears. It seems I made a wise decision. Many wise decisions."

Eran stared at the jewels on his fingers, unable to meet his eye and comment. His decisions led to the loss of lives, and tribes, and innocence. Families were torn apart, cities plundered, and fear of war ever-present. Deciding to place himself over God gave him riches and power and a hunger for more. Never satisfied. Amraphel would never have enough.

"So, they tell me you Hebrews took the lives of your own children rather than give them to me."

Eran bit down on her lip. Amusement tinged the edges of his comment.

"No response to that, Eran? I think you people of the One God cleverly hid them again. Well played. Japheth and Shem are stubborn old goats but they play an intriguing game. No matter. Look what I received instead."

Anxiety prickled up her throat. Eran automatically put her hands to her neck, as if to push it back down.

The king rose to his feet and stepped down beside her, slowly walking around and looking her over. "Shem must be miserable. Not knowing what I'll do with you." He picked up a curled lock of her hair then let it drop. "Hmm. And what shall I do with you, Eran?"

Pleas for mercy ran across her mind but Eran kept her mouth closed. His nearness increased the firm beating of her heart and she couldn't stop her hands from winding together over and over again.

Nimrod lifted a manicured finger and gently ran it along the wrinkled creases of her forehead, making the beads tinkle together. His eyes smiled. "One of the old ones. Old, old, Eran, who walked the earth before the Flood. Age may be your asset, wife of Shem. My asset, as well, now that you belong to me. A celebration is in order. Tomorrow. Tomorrow we'll honor your presence in my great city."

The King returned to his throne, lifting an arm and summoning guards from the doorway to her side. "I'm pleased with the Hebrew tribute for once. You'll indulge me, of course? Be my guest in a tour of the city?"

"No!" she wanted to scream. "I don't belong to you. I won't be your amusement. I demand to be released!" The words stayed on her tongue. Eran nodded then dropped her head, confused. Her treatment in the palace and the King's words didn't match the tone of his voice, the tone of his heart. Celebration. Honor. Guest. The favorable words removed none of her anxiety.

Guards flanked her on either side, turning her away from the King. She was escorted down the long pathways, back to her room, and left alone. Dropping onto the bed, she cried for Nimrod, the little boy who chose pride over humility. She cried for Jael and Noah, believing the unbelievable only to witness their descendants fortify cities with high walls, squabble over land, kill without remorse. She cried for Shem and for all the Hebrews and the unjustness of their persecution.

She cried for herself too, praying for strength to stand firm, resilient, not crumbling beneath the tyranny of the King, or anyone, anything, opposing her and the ways of righteousness. Alone in Nineveh, only God could equip Eran with the courage to reach down deep into the soul of fear and yank out its heart.

Chapter Eight

The scrap of metal had a sharp edge and blood dripped from Shem's finger before he realized he cut himself. He lifted his tunic and wrapped the injury tightly, his immediate thought to fetch Eran, so she could add the correct herbs and such to stop the wound from festering. As soon as he thought it, the pain hit him again. Eran wasn't here.

Was she even alive?

Eber sent three men to Nineveh to see what they could find out. They carried items to trade for information and to disguise their purpose if stopped by soldiers. That was two days ago, after their farewells to Jael. They were told to return when they uncovered any information, or in two weeks if not.

"Need some help, Brother?"

Japheth appeared at the mouth of the shallow cave, their brother Ham's old workshop. One look at Shem and he reached for a dusty clay jar, pulling out a thin length of linen. It was one of many kept in the cave for the nicks and gashes that accompanied Ham's creative endeavors.

Shem peeled his garment from the cut and took the cloth to make a bandage. "Thank you. Eran wouldn't be happy if she saw this, would she?" Shem indicated the fresh stain on his clothing.

"No. Better give it to Denah right away. She'll clean it good."

Yes, Denah would see that his garments were clean. And his belly full. And his mind occupied on any number of tasks that had long ago been delegated to other men of the camp. She asked him to repair a tent with a patch of goat hair, then speak to some children who were still not sleeping well since the raid, even asked him to check on the health of an injured lamb in one of the more remote pastures. If a task needing attending and Denah caught wind of it, he was first on her list. He'd barely had time to think, which was her intention, but he needed to rest now and then too.

"Are you hiding here in Ham's cave to escape my wife's list of chores? She expects a tilled patch of land by sunset, you know."

Shem laughed. "Denah worries over me like a-" He almost said 'a mother hen,' then stopped himself. His mother was gone too. "Like a good friend," he said. "I appreciate it, really. But, you're right. I can't lift another stone out of that field. Thought I'd see what was left in here."

The cave was lined with flat topped stones and simple tables. Bits of various objects were scattered about on top, remnants of Ham's projects. Japheth picked up a bit of wood, one end carved into a handle, the other smooth, unfinished. "She does it for herself, too. She fills her mind with all sorts of concerns so she won't think about Eran. Or Jael. There won't be a speck of lint anywhere near this camp for awhile."

"I wish I could ease her mind and tell her Eran is fine, or will be fine."

"We'll know soon. Hopefully the scouts will be back in a few days." Japheth put the carving down and picked up another object, a bowl made of copper, tiny holes punctured in one side. "I don't even know what this is." His blue eyes crinkled at the corners when he looked at Shem. "What would our little brother have done, if he had been here, do you think?"

"Would there be any Hebrews left if he remained? He would fight for the camp regardless of any direction from Eber. He wouldn't allow one child to be taken while he still breathed."

"Were we wrong? Are we wrong? Not to fight?"

It wasn't a new discussion. There had been many similar talks over the years, and always the same. No bloodshed if it could be prevented. Still the question was asked, all of them needing the reassurance from the others. "We do as we believe our God demands."

Japheth stared at the bowl in his hands. "I miss that brother of ours. Times like this, especially. I miss his laugh. I need it. Now Mother, gone too." Japheth put down the bowl and examined another odd bit of their brother's creation, this one designed to fit over his useless right hand and be used like a hammer.

Shem had the same empty place in his heart. Ham and Naomi left the camp as the persecution escalated, hoping it would cease when they were gone. It did for a time, a short time. The raids began again, Amraphel's appetite for vengeance not appeased by his grandfather's disappearance.

His brother didn't tell them where they were going, or when. He talked of leaving, and why he felt it was for everyone's benefit, then the issue was forgotten. At least, that's what Shem thought. One spring morning Ham and Naomi were gone, and no degree of interrogation could force Shem to reveal the destination to Amraphel's men. He didn't know. Not for certain, anyway. Ham had mentioned following the path of his son Canaan, of starting over in the fertile lands where the hum of bees rode the breeze and a single cluster of grapes filled a basket. If he survived, Shem felt certain his brother had traveled that direction, but he had no proof.

"He would storm the city and try to haul Eran back, tossed over his shoulder if he had to. And he'd avenge the brutality against Mother."

Japheth agreed. "He'd ensure the destruction of the camp."

Shem looked away from his brother, uncomfortable prongs poking his conscience. He was doing the same thing. Not by violence. By failure. Failure as a father, as a leader, as Priest of God. If all his sons had remained faithful, there would be many strong tribes of Semites who stood for justice and men like Amraphel would have no ability to put fear into the hearts of their children or to take their women away.

Where had he gone wrong? He raised all his sons and their sons in the way of truth. He was quick to discipline the rebellious and quick to forgive the repentant. They worked hard, slept hard, and married well. Why had so many chosen to abandon the One who created Adam? Now the sons of his sons had nations of their own, truth mingling with fabrication in a drink sweet to their lips and poisonous to their hearts.

Only his third born son, Arphaxad, remained true. Arphaxad's grandson, Eber, followed the path of his fathers too and his tribe was a fine testament to the ways taught by Noah, but the Hebrew camp was less than 300 strong.

He failed. Shem's responsibility to his fathers, to raise up a people of God, was a dismal failure. The Hebrew tribe was unraveling. The young families were moving to the cities and marrying into other tribes. He couldn't blame them. They did so to protect their children.

How would the camp survive? How would Truth be carried throughout the generations? Who would remember the One God?

The younger Hebrews were aging at a faster rate than ever. Each succeeding generation ripened to manhood more quickly, matured, and died in fewer years than the one before. Noah lived 950 years. Shem was well over 500 and had outlived all of his sons and most of his grandsons. His great-grandson Eber still thrived, but after him, five generations were dead and buried. None of those men saw a three century mark and the last few were old and worn by their two-hundredth year.

Shem didn't even know who would lead after Eber. Abram had been his choice as Priest for the One God and leader of the tribe. He had been everyone's choice at one time. The young man had shown much potential to lead and govern, but he was one of many now gone from the homeland.

So few of them left. Too few to stand up as a mighty force against unrighteousness. They would all be dispersed if the pattern of raids and exodus from the camp wasn't stopped. He fully understood why Ham left. His brother was trying to preserve the people of the One God. Shem needed to do the same.

He held his gaze steady on Japheth. "I'll decide what to do when the scouts return. If Eran is, is…," he couldn't say the word. He licked his bottom lip. "I have to leave."

Japheth stopped examining a shard of hinged metal. "Leave? The camp?"

"Yes. The raids will stop if I'm not a thorn residing so near the King."

"He won't stop. Amraphel won't stop because you're gone."

"He might. There's nothing left here that he really wants. I'm Priest of the God he despises. That's enough for him to show his strength against me, against us."

Japheth frowned. "If you leave, the ire will fall on Eber. He despises us all."

"Ham and I more than you and the others, though. You know it's true."

His brother's eyes glistened. "No quick decisions. Promise me Shem? Don't pack and leave in the night as Ham did. I couldn't bear it, and Denah. She would never recover."

"I promise. I'm not certain where I would go, anyhow. My offspring have kingdoms in all the land of the Tigris and Euphrates, and they all fight against one another."

"Loyalties among them change with the tides. You would always be in danger."

"Your sons have made nations for themselves to the north. I could go there."

Japheth dropped his arm over Shem's shoulder. "You would be welcomed among my generations. Denah has talked of going too, but not while Jael still lived. The journey is many months over the mountains. It would not be an easy one but we could manage it I believe."

There was another solution. One Shem thought through in his mind but had never dared say out loud. Until now. "Or, I could submit to the King. Pay the tribute."

Japheth pulled back and faced him, the oldest brother demeanor fully evident, down to the finger pointing in Shem's face. "No. None of us would agree to it. Your possessions mean nothing. You know that. He wants your worship. And if you give in, he'll expect it from us all. Nothing will be gained. Nothing."

Shem took his brother's hand and squeezed it in his own. "What will become of us, Japheth? Who will carry on the name and ways of our fathers when we're gone, when Eber and the others are pushed to disband the camp? How can the Promise be fulfilled?"

The Promise. God told First Woman Eve that a man would rise from her offspring, the Seed of her seed, and would crush the head of the Evil One. Man would be freed from the clutches of sin. It was the hope of his people. But it couldn't happen if no one believed in the God of all creation, in the One who set the standard of right and wrong, who judged and who saved. If no one believed in righteousness, if no one fought for truth, sin would reign forever.

In the nations around them, history was distorted, the many gods and goddesses praised for all that the One God was and did. The origins of the earth, the creation of the waters and the beasts and mankind told and retold through lying lips, tweaked to meet the newest demands of the culture. Even the history of the Flood was perverted now, and Noah's faith twisted in the tales among the children of his children.

How could the Promise be fulfilled? He, as priest, should have known how to answer that question.

He did not.

Chapter Nine

Henna was blended with other ingredients to make a rinse. It brightened Eran's hair, the faded strands taking on a deep chestnut hue. It still didn't disguise her age. Not even a heavy application of color to her face helped. It migrated into the furrows and made them more apparent rather than making them disappear. After wiping most of it away, Eran turned to Fatimaa.

Fatimaa sighed. "You look so, well, so old. And your hair is more brown than gold. I hope the King is satisfied. I don't know what else to do." She put her hands on Eran's cheeks and stretched the skin away from her face.

Eran pulled away and smiled at the concern on the woman's face. "I *am* old. You can't turn back the years. No fuss will make me someone I'm not."

"I can still put a style to your hair. I can't allow it to just hang there. It's too stringy."

Eran sat still and allowed her to braid the hair and tuck it into loops. "I'm not sure what to expect today. I don't know what the King is planning."

"He said you'd be his guest, though. How special you must feel!"

"I don't know if special is good. I don't like fanfare. I wish it were over already. I wish Shem was here."

Fatimaa patted her arm. "Don't fret. It makes the wrinkles stick out more on your forehead. It will be a glorious day, I think. You feared the King would kill you at first, remember? It seems you have found his favor instead of his wrath. Try to enjoy his blessings. I wouldn't be able to sit still at all if I were you."

"I'd trade places with you if I could."

"Nonsense. Now here, stand up so we can put this robe on." Fatimaa unfastened the long row of pearl closures then held up a deep green robe.

Eran slid into the garment, mindful of the smooth hand of the finely woven fabric. Golden ribbons looped around the pearls to hold the garment closed. It fell to just below her knees, the paler green tunic from the day before peeking out the bottom. New leather sandals were tied to her feet and gold bands secured around her wrists.

"One more piece to add."

Eran tried to find reassurance in the pampering. Peace wouldn't come. It was impossible to shake the feeling she was being prepared for something more than a simple celebration to honor her, long-lost kin of the King. She felt more like a sacrificial beast, despite Fatimaa's opinion. Amraphel had an objective to this charade and she doubted it in was in her favor.

Fatimaa draped a heavy chain over Eran's head then repositioned the large pendant on her chest. "It's beautiful. You, well you look as good as possible. I did my best."

Eran ran her fingers over the golden medallion. It was an eight pointed star, the symbol of the goddess Ishtar. She held the offensive symbol between her thumb and one finger, as if it would burn her skin. Lifting it, she saw a smooth stone in the center, a teardrop of black onyx. She caught her breath.

First man Adam carved a similar stone to pass to his descendants, to the man designated as the leader, the priest of the One God. The original belonged to Shem but he no longer had it. Amraphel stole it years ago, back when they knew him as Nimrod. Forged to the star of Ishtar, he mocked the God of Adam, marrying the false to the true. Eran's hand shook as she pulled the necklace over her head and tossed it to the floor.

"What's wrong?"

"I can't wear it."

Fatimaa put her hands on her hips. "You must. The king sent it specifically."

Eran shook her head. "It's an offense to my people. To my God. I can't."

"The star of Ishtar? It's an honor to wear her symbol. Only the priestesses wear them."

How could Eran even begin to explain? Merging the One God with the false goddess of fertility and warfare was open hostility to Amraphel's fathers. And to her. How could she wear it and not be struck down by her God?

Fatimaa took Eran's hands and held them. "Wear it. He won't be happy if you don't."

Eran sighed. The woman had no idea what it represented. She saw generosity and favor, not animosity and mean-spirited pride. She saw goodness in Amraphel, not the rebellious heart lurking beneath his display of fine clothing and gaudy trinkets.

Wearing the star would please the King. Eran stared at it, not wanting confrontation. Inducing the King's ire was avoidable. Inducing her God's ire was avoidable too. "Fatimaa, I can't. I can't."

The opportunity to explain was squelched by a knock, and the entrance of guards. Eran stepped over the pendant and followed her escorts from the room.

♥

A light flick of a switch and the elephant's front legs folded beneath him, then his back legs. Eran's own knees groaned at the thought of it having to lift its weight up and down from the ground, and at the thought of her own knees trying to climb upon its back. She stood at its side and tried to find a foot hold before the guards intervened. In one smooth lift, she was hoisted onto a padded cushion, a rope thrust into her hands. As the beast rose, Eran clamped onto the reins for balance.

She had not been taken to the King and he was not here, in the noisy courtyard. It appeared her tour of Nineveh was to be on the back of the great beast. It was draped in fine linens as she was, with tiny silver bells along its neck that tinkled with every motion.

Around the animal, the priestesses of Ishtar chattered like a flock of sparrows. Their pale green garments were similar to her own, the star of the goddess gleaming from their chests. Some were little girls, five or six years old. Others were many decades old, with all ages in between. There were blue eyes among them, and greens and browns, and some as dark as night. Pale skin stood next to cinnamon colored next to rich earthen hues. One feature was the same. All the priestesses had hair the color of the golden sun, braided and looped like flower petals on their heads.

Eran peered into the curious faces below her feet, hoping to recognize the ones from her tribe. They were rounded, happy faces. She saw no haunted eyes or vacant stares, no bruises on their limbs or forced smiles. They looked up at her with open awe. Eran smiled at them and in return was drowned in a flood of giggles.

Did they know who she was? Did any remember?

These were Amraphel's chosen ones. He took only the fair haired Hebrew children in the first of the raids, girls and boys. The girls were raised to serve the goddess in the temples. The boys kept for breeding, for producing an endless line to serve Ishtar. In later raids, any children found were taken. No one knew what became of the dark haired ones. Now Eran had seen one of them, the compassionate raider who saw to Jael's rescue. Those children were alive too, somewhere in the city. The thought gave her hope.

A whistle sent the girls scrambling to line up in front of the elephant. Three rows of twenty stretched out to lead the procession, the smallest girls in front and the older ones behind. The last three women in each row held censors of burning incense, the smoke rising and settling around them in an aromatic cloud.

Eran held tight to maintain her balance as the parade moved forward from the enclosed courtyard to the open streets of Nineveh. The girls chanted in unison, a tongue she didn't know, one resonating with worship, and awe and majesty. The perfect harmonies drew the attention of patrons on the street.

All activity ceased, every head turned their way. Eyes first looked at the priestesses, then up to her. Jaws dropped and eyes widened.

Then heads bowed and knees hit the earth.

Eran slouched as far down as she could and lowered her head, mortified. The people of Nineveh were bowing *to her*.

"Sit up!" The flick of a switch zipped against her leg.

Eran flinched and sat straight. The elephant trainer stood beside her. "Why are they doing that? Why are they bowing to me?" she asked.

The man looked at her with a sneer on his lip. "Why would they not honor the immortal daughter of Ishtar, come in the flesh herself to bless them?"

"I'm not-"

"You are. Act like it." He snapped the switch a hair's breadth from her face.

Eran sat rigidly on the elephant, staring above the heads of the men and women gawking at her, falling prostrate to the ground and calling out to her in their many languages. Her gut churned. Her heart ached. Her mind sought forgiveness from the God who had the power to wipe the city clean.

♥

Ishtar was favored among the Ninevites. She granted protection in battle, victory assured for the proper sacrificial offerings. The blessing of many sons came from her as well, and the health of the babies she granted. Besides her grand temple, many shrines were carved into the walls of homes and shops in her honor, her image found on every corner.

Eran was her daughter, the product of the goddess and a man from the old earth, a gift to save mankind from complete annihilation after the Flood of Judgment. She and a few others were placed on a boat and allowed to live, and breed, and fill the earth. That's what the chants of the priestesses proclaimed. That's what the people believed.

The Ninevites knew the tales of the Old Ones, the Immortal Ones who aged but never died, the ones who survived the flood in a boat and dwelled in the land of the two rivers. Every Semitic child had heard the stories of their beginnings, of the three mothers who lived on and on, their children populating the earth. Now here in their midst was one of them, an Old One, an Immortal herself. Ishtar's temple overflowed with offerings.

It was morning, the tenth morning in the palace and Fatimaa had not yet arrived for the morning ritual of bathing and dressing. Eran sank into the luxurious cushions of her bed and prayed, asking God to save her from the daily parade of worship. The generations of her womb kissed the earth as she passed. How could God allow it to continue?

It was an abomination in his sight, she knew. Yet what could she do to stop it? The whip cracked against her flesh when she slouched, when she cried, when she tried to refuse. And the threat had been voiced by the man with the whip. "Think of your people."

If she refused to participate, the ramifications against the Hebrews would escalate.

Was it a risk she should take? What if her rebellion against the King led to the destruction of the camp? It wasn't a decision that affected her life alone. She didn't know what to do, except to pray daily for forgiveness, for wisdom, for the strength to do what was right. Then she waited for directions. If none came from God, she followed Fatimaa's directions, obeying the King's commands. Every morning so far it had been Fatimaa guiding her path. God had not spoken.

For all her years trusting in the One God, knowing his presence followed her, she realized it wasn't God who led her through life. It was Shem. She relied on his wisdom, his understanding. He knew what actions to take, when to wait, when to hang on in faith and when to strike. If not Shem, Noah led them, and before that, her father made the choices that governed her life.

No one had ever leaned on Eran for direction in times of crisis. Not even herself. She had never been the light in the darkness. Now, there was no one else.

She squeezed her eyes closed and prayed again for God himself to speak, straining to hear the voice of wisdom in the silence of her heart. Eran needed God to point the way.

Fatimaa opened the door.

Eran opened her eyes and threw off the covers, resigned to her fate, allowing herself to be purified and presented to the city on the back of the elephant again.

♥

As soon as the beast stepped forward into the city, Eran scanned the crowd for Shem, as she had each day. So many expectant faces, but not his. Where was he?

The latest embellishment to the entourage was a gilded cage of lions. Ishtar's favorite beasts, three of them, were caged, riding on a cart behind the priestesses. Amraphel added them to spike interest, and keep the tributes flourishing. The roaring cats attracted attention for the past few days but already the novelty was fading. They would be replaced. She would not. She had a steady following in the city from those seeking a blessing on their wombs.

A young woman pushed her way through the stalls of a fruit merchant and came alongside the elephant, placing her hand on its hide. She rubbed it for a moment as if the action assured her that contact with the Immortals had been achieved. Her lips repeated a prayer of fertility and homage to Ishtar, her eyes finding Eran's and seeking the blessing of new life.

Eran turned from the woman's gaze, not wanting to give false hope by smiling or acknowledging her pleas for a son. As the parade ambled forward the woman fell back, her face bright with anticipation, her place filled by another seeking Eran's hand. And so it was every day. Prayers filled the streets, never reaching the ears of the stone goddess. They stopped with Eran and she had no powers to fulfill their desires. The hope of Nineveh was founded in lies.

The day did not end like the others however. Near the end of the route, a boy stood by the roadside, straining against his mother's hand. His face brightened at the sight of lions and he pulled away, dashing toward them. His mother screamed. A guard stepped forward and intervened, preventing the boy from reaching the cage, but not before claws lashed out from between the bars. The guard jerked away as the lion caught his arm, raking down the flesh.

The parade stopped abruptly as the priestesses screamed and broke rank. The man fell, clutching his injured arm. Eran dropped the reigns in her hand.

Someone yelled for water, the request rippling over the crowd to the back, where an urn was passed to a woman standing by one of the trickling canals that irrigated the city. She bent and filled it, then handed it back. The water was passed hand to hand toward the street.

The water wasn't clean. Refuse was flushed from the homes and businesses in its current. The man would die of poisoned blood. Eran had seen it too many times in her many years of tending the sick, the putrid rinses then the festering wounds, the fevers, the death.

Eran rolled onto her belly and slid to the ground, wincing as her feet hit the hard surface, the impact racing through her knees. She limped towards the injured man, pushing girls aside, until she reached the ring of guards. They parted, as she neared, wide-eyed.

"Don't use that water," Eran said.

The urn stopped its travel, held by a merchant nearby. He looked at the guards, then set it down when no one took it from him.

The man was on his back cradling his arm. "Get bandages," she said to the men as she eased herself to the ground to examine the wounds. They were bleeding profusely but they weren't deep to the bone. A length of fabric was placed in her hand and she secured it loosely around the man's upper arm, then wound it over the wounds in a dense layer. "It will soak through in no time. Add more as it does, then carefully remove it when the flow diminishes."

Eran looked at the guards hovering over her, catching the eye of one to make sure he understood. "Take the binding off when the flow diminishes," she repeated. "Don't clean the wounds in the canal water. Use strong wine to flush it out instead. Mix an ointment of myrrh and olive oil to coat the open flesh, then wrap it with clean cloth and change it daily. Make sure he eats and drinks and rests, even if he doesn't want to."

How many times had she spit out treatments like that in the past centuries? Many, many times. Always, her words were followed. The Hebrews respected her knowledge of healing. The Ninevite guards nodded understanding, whether they followed through was out of her hands. It was all she could do.

Eran struggled to a standing position, unaided, and with a generous amount of crackling in her joints. The man was placed on a woven rug and carried away, but the crowd didn't dissolve. She stood encircled by them, a silent gathering neither angry nor grateful for her intervention. They stared at her with questioning expressions.

Eran wiped her hands on her garment. It was saturated already with the man's blood. Heat climbed up her neck under the scrutiny of the crowd and spread to her cheeks as she grasped their confusion. Why had the daughter of Ishtar not healed the man?

Couldn't she wave her hand and make the gashes close? Why weren't prayers lifted to the goddess on his behalf? Where was the explanation for the lion's behavior? Was it providing justice for some hidden sin in the man's life?

Where was the magic, the power, the spiritual? Where was the something unearthly that rose beyond the ordinary?

Understanding replaced confusion, face by face, and with it came disappointment, betrayal, and sorrow as the city lost the solution to all its woes. The daughter of Ishtar had no healing powers. She had no ability to change the course of events. Standing among them drenched and stained, she was just an old lady with wrinkled flesh and tired bones.

The guards rallied and sent the girls back to their lines. A cloak was taken from someone and wrapped around her to hide the blood and she was lifted back onto the elephant. In moments the parade moved onward, the fanfare diminished as word traveled like smoke in the wind.

No one sought her blessing. No one bowed in homage.

The people of Nineveh saw through the charade, saw her humanity.

She saw something too. Lifting her head as they approached the palace, a cluster of men caught her eye. They were Hebrews from the camp.

Chapter Ten

The ark was complete, fully pitched and stocked. Every known kind of beast on the earth and creature of the air was housed within the gopher wood walls. Shem couldn't take his eyes from it, despite the whirling smoke that burned his eyes.

Everything around him was on fire.

He was desperate to stop the flames, to make the ark safe, but he could find no water. It would all be lost. He had to act quickly, but he didn't know what to do.

His father appeared beside him, unfazed by the acrid fumes or the debris circling around him in plumes of purged landscape. "Stop struggling, Son," Noah said.

Shem searched his father's deep brown eyes for reassurance. They disappeared into crinkled ravines as he smiled, the weathered cheeks rising to meet the line of snowy eyebrows, prickly, independent strands that followed no particular order. Snowy curls framed his calm face.

"What am I supposed to do?" Shem grabbed for his father's hand, clutching nothing but air.

Noah turned away from him, moving toward his ark, growing smaller and disappearing into the smoke-filled clearing. His voice penetrated the darkness. "Remember the Promise."

Shem pulled his eyes above the gray whorls, back to the vessel. Everything around it was burning.

The ark stood unscathed.

♥

The cry of a hawk startled Shem from sleep. He automatically checked in every direction for raiders. There were none. The bluff overlooking the road below was vacant. He leaned back against the rock where he had fallen asleep, the image of his father still sharp in his mind. It was the dream again, the same dream he'd had for years.

"Within Shem's grasp, the Pledge cries out, the Promise awakens." The words from Noah were spoken to Shem alone, when his father was only days from his last heart beat. They had given him an element of joy during the sorrowful time. It was a positive message, one predicting a successful transfer of leadership, and the fulfillment of the Promise that put yearning in the heart of every God-fearing man since Adam.

Now the words plagued him in his dreams. He was responsible for that Promise. What once humbled his soul now carried an element of unrest. He couldn't save his own tribe from the hands of men. His wife was carried off in his presence. The task was daunting and he didn't even know what it was, not exactly. God had not given him instructions and benchmarks. Other than to raise up a nation of men with righteous ambitions, he was at a loss.

He didn't want to fail. If God told him to find gopher wood and clear acreage for another ark, he would. He wouldn't question the voice of his God, and for many centuries he longed for just that, for the Almighty to speak. The older he got, the more he craved the communication, the acknowledgement that the God of all creation truly dwelled with him as his father had once prophesied.

The older he got, the more he feared what would be asked of him, too. He didn't know if he had his father's spiritual stamina, at least not anymore, but he would prove himself obedient, he would give his all to follow his God's commands. He would build an ark twice the size of Noah's if required.

It was mid-afternoon, nearly two weeks since the scouts left for the city. Shem sighed and scanned the horizon toward Nineveh. He expected them back days ago. Would they be lost too? Would he ever know what happened to his wife?

One thing he knew - he needed to leave the camp. It was a chance for the Hebrews to find peace. A slim chance, but one he needed to risk. Eber could take over as Priest. Shem would hold a simple ceremony, here in the camp since there would be no traveling to Havilah for the transfer of position. That was where Noah took him, to the outskirts of Eden itself, to say the blessing. It was gone now, the Garden of God's Presence, buried beneath the waters of the flood. Like the life he knew in the Hebrew camp, it had to become a memory.

He had to leave the region. But how could he, not knowing about Eran?

The only solution was to move to Nineveh. Move to the seat of Amraphel's domain to watch and wait and listen. He would find her bones, if that's all that remained, and bring them back to be with Noah and Jael. Then he'd leave again. Somewhere, if he could. Or he'd meet his death in the city. It was better to die in Nineveh than abandon the light of his soul, wherever she was.

His sister-in-law Denah was lost to Japheth once. His brother prayed for her to be returned to him. God delivered. Shem lifted his arms to the heavens and asked him for Eran.

"Shem! Look!"

The scrambling of rocks drew his attention to the path leading up to his rocky perch. Eber huffed to the top and pointed to the horizon.

Dust. A dust cloud low along the road meant riders were coming.

♥

The scouts collapsed in the shade, having no time to rest as the Hebrews filed in around them. Eber ordered food but no one moved, no one wanted to miss their story. The scouts had seen Eran.

Denah wrapped her arms around one of the young men and squealed. "You saw her! Tell us everything!"

Shem couldn't stop his eyes from tearing. His wife was alive.

The men described the parade, Eran on the elephant and the adoration of the people. They hadn't realized it was her on display for several days, choosing not to attend an event for Ishtar's worship. Once they realized, they followed her for three days, staying in the back of the crowd. They were there when the lion attacked, and Eran helped the man. They heard the change in attitude afterward.

"There was no parade the next day. We waited for it, hoping to catch Eran's attention and perhaps even speak with her. We wanted her to know we were there. She looked our direction on several occasions the day before but I don't know if she realized who we were. And we had to be careful, we couldn't just push our way in front of her. We were being watched." The scout looked down at his hands.

Shem gripped the young man's shoulder. "You did well. You were smart not to draw attention to yourselves. You men did very well."

"The mood changed after that. It was obvious Eran lost favor because she didn't heal the injured man. They said she lost her powers because she dared to touch human blood, and that she couldn't help anyone anymore."

"Not that she was merely human?" Japheth asked.

"No. She's still viewed as an Immortal because the King said she was. His word would never be questioned."

"She's of less value to him now." Shem said. "Perhaps he'll let her return."

Eber nodded. "The wheat will be ready soon. After the harvest, we'll take all of it and see if he'll make a trade."

Shem closed his eyes and thought about his course of action before responding. "Thank you, Eber," he said once he knew the plan in his mind was the one he would follow. "That's generous. But it isn't enough, it won't appease him. I need to go to Nineveh. Alone. I'll go to Nimrod and ask for her. That may be what he's waiting for, what he'll take in trade. Me."

♥

Hebrews! If there were scouts, then Shem knew she was alive. Eran stood in front of the window again and looked out onto the city below. He would come soon. He would find a way to take her home.

Fatimaa sighed in the corner of the room. There would be no fuss, no fine clothing, no extravagance again today. The parade was cancelled for the third time. She was disappointed. "I still don't see why you thought you had to be the one to help him. If you'd stayed put, nothing would have changed."

Eran explained again. "He was injured because of me. I couldn't sit there and do nothing."

"He's alive still. That may give you favor with the King again."

"It had to happen, Fatimaa. When the barren women remained barren, and the sick babies died, the people would see that I am no child of a goddess. You can see it. I'm old, that's all. The daughter of Ishtar talk was all foolishness to garner tribute. The King used me to make a profit."

"I don't know what will become of you now." Fatimaa spoke candidly.

"I'll be alright. Shem will come."

The woman bit on her lip and turned away. Eran heard the unspoken words. "What good would it do?"

The thought sent chills up her spine. She was right. What could her husband do to persuade the King to let her go? What if the price was Shem's life for hers?

Chapter Eleven

Shem paced the long room, down and back, no longer looking at the mosaic images of the King lining the walls, images of him as the great hunter, the victor over man and beast. One by one the men seeking audience with Amraphel had come and gone and he alone waited. And waited. And waited. The King had not forgotten him. That he knew.

Many hours later a guard entered and pointed at him. It was time to face the man who spit in the face of everything he'd been taught as a child, who feared no one, not even God.

For all the praying he had done, Shem's heart still thundered in his chest as he passed through the door into the throne room. He had no idea what to expect.

The King sat on an elevated throne and said nothing as Shem walked the distance to stand before him. He didn't bow, or even lower his eyes. He forced himself to look calm, pleasant as he approached. No animosity. No fear. He hoped Amraphel couldn't tell that his heart was pounding.

"Shem, son of Noah."

"Amraphel. You're looking well." Nimrod was clothed in finery, gold on every limb. He had the fat of the land at his disposal yet remained strong and trim. Shem had forgotten how much the man resembled his grandfather Ham and it was as if Shem stared into the face of his little brother. Almost. The eyes were wrong. The ones peering at him were cold, uncaring.

"The gods are good to me."

Shem ignored the intended barb. "Your wife and sons?"

"All healthy. Enjoying prosperity, the best the world has to buy. Or take. Your family?"

"My mother died recently." He watched for a sign of remorse. He saw none. "And my wife. She's in your care I understand."

"She is. An interesting item for my men to acquire."

For all the practiced speeches in his head, Shem blurted out the cry written on his heart. "I want her back."

"Of course. Of course you do. That's why you've come to see me. I knew you would in time." The King leaned back and smiled. The condescending tone wasn't reassuring.

"I'll have her delivered." Amraphel waved his hand and a guard left the room.

Too easy. Sweat trickled down his back beneath his tunic. "You're my brother's grandson. Your animosity towards your family is unwarranted. We don't approve of your ways, but you are yet one of us. We can choose to be civil. We can exist without violence."

Amraphel pointed his finger at Shem. "There is no violence when you are obedient."

"Your men killed Jael. She held you on her knee and loved you. It was cruel. It was wrong."

He shrugged. "I didn't order it. She raised a weapon and the men defended themselves."

Shem took in deep breath, calming himself, controlling his tongue. "Eran is an old woman. Let her be. Let the Hebrews live in peace. You know they'll never raise an army against you. They just want to raise their crops and cattle and children, and die with happy memories."

"No army?"

The King referred to Abram. "I can't control what our men do when they leave," Shem said. "They follow their own hearts. They follow God as they understand his commands. Those in the camp listen to me, and I won't permit hatred against you. Let's be at peace with one another."

Amraphel raised his hands and clapped. "Very moving Shem, priest of Noah's God. I might even agree to your words. I might even give you back your wife. It's all a very simple matter."

Shem felt his spine stiffen. "What is it you want?"

"The same as I expect from everyone in my land. Pay your tribute."

"You've taken it all. There's nothing of value remaining to add to your storehouses."

Amraphel's lip curled. "Not your worthless possessions, Shem. You. Give me the homage I am due."

♥

Eran was summoned to appear before the King. It was late in the day, and Fatimaa wasn't with the guard sent to escort her to the throne room. She wasn't required to wait this time. She was ushered into the King's presence as soon as she arrived. He wasn't alone. The man standing before the King of Shinar turned as she approached.

"Shem!"

Her husband's eyes opened wide and he started toward her.

Amraphel lifted his arm and both he and she were stopped by

his guards, long spears blocking their paths. "A happy reunion," he said. "Too soon. We aren't finished with our business, are we Shem?"

Her husband closed his eyes and drew in several long breaths. When he opened them, she could read resolution on his face. And fear. His eyes caught hers and held them for a long moment before he forced his attention back onto the King. "I can't comply with your request." His voice was soft, but set.

Amraphel raised his eyebrows and shook his head. "A shame." He pointed at Eran. "Shall we let her know what it is we haggle over?"

Shem pressed his lips together and didn't respond. Eran shifted from foot to foot. It was her freedom, she knew.

"A simple gesture of homage is all I ask of him. Bow to me once. Kiss my hand. Who of your illustrious tribe would even know? But he won't, Eran. This son of Noah won't bend his knee to save you. He'd rather allow you to die."

"Die! What? No!" Shem tried to free himself from the guards, unsuccessfully.

She clamped her hands over her mouth, feeling the quiver in her legs increasing. The guards grabbed her arms and held her upright.

The stakes had been changed, she guessed. Not her freedom, but her life.

Amraphel rose from the throne and stepped down to Shem, circling him slowly. "Generous man that I am, I'll allow you another chance to think about your decision. You are old, and old men don't always think clearly, do they?"

Her husband looked at the ceiling, his lips moving slightly. He prayed. Prayed for wisdom, for deliverance, as he had done so many times through their years together.

Amraphel chuckled. "That's good. Ask your God what to do. And if he has no answer, ask the daughter of Ishtar. Surely she'll provide you with sound advice. Isn't that right Eran?"

Shem lowered his head and addressed the King without looking her direction. "Take me. Take my life. Let her go."

Eran fought the dark spots threatening to cloud her vision. No!

The king laughed and shook his head. "That's not part of the bargain. Too easy for you." He leaned into Shem and draped his arm over his shoulders. His words were directed into Shem's ear but loud enough for Eran to hear. "I'll put the choices before you one more time. Bow to me, Shem, and you both go free. Back to your little camp with your little lives and your little god. Refuse, and only I will know what becomes of your bride. You'll wander this earth never knowing when, or how your wife meets her end. The lions? The dungeons? The temple of Ishtar?"

"No!" Eran tried to wrench her arms free only to have them pulled behind her back.

Amraphel ran a finger along the tip of a guard's sword. "No? Then perhaps I will kill you, Shem, and let your poor old bride live with your screams reverberating in her head. I have options. So do you."

Shem found her eyes again. His glistened and he choked back a sob as the King screamed in his ear. "Choose!"

Eran strained against the men keeping her from Shem. Her own tears were flowing freely but that was all she could move. The men held her firmly, away from him, the blade of a dagger pressed against her throat.

Shem jerked his eyes away from hers. He was trembling and his voice came out in a stuttered response at first, then he stopped, took a labored breath, and started over, his words dissolving any doubt. "I will never bow before any man. It is the One God whom I serve, the One God whom I worship."

The King slapped Shem's cheek.

Eran screamed.

Amraphel laughed. "So predictable. So stupid and so predictable." He turned to the men holding Eran and flicked his wrist. "Take her away."

Shem collapsed to the floor. "No! Eran, I'm sorry! Eran!"

His voice filled her ears as the men drug her out to the ante-chamber and dropped her on the floor.

♥

Shem couldn't control his sobs as Eran was ripped from his sight. What had he done? He ensured the death of the only woman he had ever loved, ever held in his arms. The realization tore through his heart.

The King left him in a heap on the floor until the tears diminished.

"I can't understand you, Shem, son of Noah," he said.

"Please don't hurt her. Please. Kill me. Take me instead." Shem could only whisper.

"No. I've made my decision. You are free to go. Free to live with the foolish choice you made."

Shem tried to rise but found his legs too weak. He started again, getting to his knees.

The King put a hand on his shoulder. "One more item of business before you return to your Hebrews." He lifted Shem's chin with one jeweled finger. And smiled.

A guard stepped forward. He held a metal rod, the end radiating a heated glow.

"Just so you don't forget who owns this land, and your life."

Strong arms held him in place as the brand seared into Shem's forehead, then the room dissolved into darkness.

♥

An anguished cry penetrated her sobs.

Shem.

Eran flung herself against the throne room door, beating it with her fists.

The painful wail stopped, replaced by Amraphel's hollow laugh.

Eran slid down the door and lost the contents of her stomach, welcoming the suffocating descent of blackness.

Chapter Twelve

Eran opened her eyes, anticipating the confines of a prison cell. She was in her room, alone. She pulled herself to the edge of the bed and sat up, pressing her fingers to her temples to ease the throbbing. Her husband's cry rang in her ears. Was he dead? Was she next? Was she waiting for execution?

The thought didn't frighten her. If Shem was gone, it would be alright to join him with his fathers who had died already. She was old, and life had been so very good at times and others, filled with turmoil and heartache. She had had enough. Already she had outlived many of her generations. It was no wonder Amraphel portrayed her as immortal. To the children born in recent years, it appeared so.

But it wasn't true. She would live her years and die as all mankind was destined to do. Some as old men, some full of disease, riddled with illness. Some at the hand of another.

Eran stood and moved to the open window. The end of her long life might be today and she wanted to feel a cooling breeze on her cheeks, one carrying the scent of roses and lavender and mint.

The air was hot and still. She braced her arms on the ledge and looked down to the street several stories down. It would be a quick fall and her old bones would shatter. Death would follow, the heartache ended. The image made her dizzy and she pulled her head back in. She wouldn't do it, couldn't do it. What if Shem was still alive? What if-?

The door opened and Eran turned, hoping to see Fatimaa. Instead, the guard was back. For the second time that day she followed him through the corridors. This time he didn't go to the throne room, but outside.

Hope poked its head out of a shell. Was the King letting her go? Would she find Shem?

She was led away from the palace to a side street where a long caravan stretched out in both directions. Brilliant white and yellow striped awnings covered carts and donkeys brayed incessantly as they were tied to loads or loads were strapped onto their sturdy backs. Men in short loincloths packed, stacked and secured crates of all sizes. Local spices made a fragrant haze over the bustling swarm, and no one seemed at all interested in her presence.

The guard took her to a man, a very tall man, a foreigner with pale blue eyes that peered at her from beneath a turban. They spoke in Amraphel's tongue, gesturing at her and bantering back and forth. The turbaned man put his hands on his hips and ran his eyes over her, then shook his head.

Eran shivered. She wrapped her arms around herself, as if to make herself small enough to disappear. They were haggling. She didn't need to understand the words to realize the King's man was selling her to the foreigner.

When the bargain was agreed upon, the tall man gave the guard silver pieces and slapped him on the back. The man of Amraphel left, leaving her with the trader. He turned back to Eran and spoke the common tongue of commerce. "Do you ride?"

"Ride?" She couldn't grasp his meaning.

"Donkeys. Can you ride a donkey or do you prefer to be carted?"

She was to be taken away. Eran quickly looked in every direction, seeking Shem or Hebrews or anyone to help her.

The tall man caught her chin between his finger and thumb. "No running off. I paid for you. I'll bind your feet if need be but it will be a long enough journey as it is and I'd like to deliver you without injury. It's your decision."

A line of boys filed past her. Their feet were shackled to the same chain, their heads shaved bare and a metal loop inserted through their noses. Men with whips stood on either side of the slave chain.

Eran ran a dry tongue over her lips. "Ride," she said. "I can ride."

The man nodded. "I am called Tolo."

"Where?" Eran felt the churning of fear in her gut. She knew where the tall men of the caravan brigades dwelled. "Where are you taking me?"

Tolo hoisted her onto an animal and put reins in her hand. "To the Land of Canaan."

♥

Shem stumbled from the edge of the roadway where he'd been dumped, beyond the city gates. Nausea rose again in his throat, though there was nothing left in his gut to come out. He made his way to a stand of trees and collapsed against a trunk, trying not to move any muscles in his face. Every last twitch sparked pain from the burn on his forehead.

The Seal of Amraphel, stamped permanently on his flesh. The eight pointed star with crescent moon in the center, was his signature, his mark on sheep and cattle, donkeys and horses. And men. The mark of a slave, or of one who rebelled against the King or stirred his anger. Outside Nineveh and the other cities of the Shinar kingdom, only escaped slaves had the mark. To feed such a man, to provide him shelter, to assist him in any way was prohibited. It meant death to the provider.

To injure a man with the seal was also prohibited. This was the King's property and no man dared destroy what he owned. A sealed man was left to fend for himself, hoping he wouldn't be hunted and returned for some imagined bounty. Hoping to find the means to survive.

Shem slid down the tree, sinking into the ground and resting his head on a root. Amraphel could have killed him. He chose not to, choosing instead to prolong the agony of Shem's existence, not knowing what would become of Eran, not able to seek the comfort of his people without risking their lives, now that he was sealed.

It was Amraphel's pattern. He did the same to his own grandfather, back when no one fully understood the rebellion hidden in his heart. When he thought Ham deceived him, Nimrod maimed his grandfather's right hand. Ham suffered greatly, more than if he had been slain. That was Nimrod's intent. Death was too easy.

What had the man done to Eran?

Shem made himself get up, and sit. What had *he* done to Eran?

Guilt wrapped its arms around his soul, ugly and tenacious. He couldn't bow to the King. Right? Or should he have? It would have meant nothing, just a simple gesture. No one would have known. He could have rescued his wife.

No. His God would have seen. Amraphel would have won.

He had no choice.

Had Eran been tortured? Was she dead already, or locked in a prison cell?

Guilt clung tightly. It would always be there. As long as he breathed, he would never get Eran's tormented face from his mind. He could have saved her and didn't.

Yet he couldn't. So he didn't. No matter which direction he chose, he would have lost.

Amraphel had indeed won. He could see it now. The King would have triumphed in any scenario. Shem was a pawn in rigged game.

A rustle in the weeds caught his attention. He had no weapon, no possessions to steal. And no strength to fight. He remained where he was.

"Oh. No. Shem. No." Japheth fell to his knees beside him, his eyes fixed on the ugly blistered wound.

"You followed me."

"We did. We've been watching the gates."

"Don't help me. Don't make it worse."

His brother whistled to signal the others. "Since when do we obey orders?" He poured water from a skin onto a cloth and placed it tenderly on Shem's forehead, then secured it with a long strip of linen. "That will have to do for now."

"Leave me here. I have to get back into the city. I don't know if, if…"

Eber appeared in the weeds and ran over to help Japheth lift Shem up.

"We're going home, Brother."

"I can't leave her. Again."

His brother paused and allowed him to give a brief account of the meeting. "What if she's waiting for me? I have to go back. He may have set her free."

His words fell unheeded. Japheth and Eber helped him stand. He didn't miss the look they exchanged. They wondered as he did, if Eran was even alive.

♥

Eran kept a watchful eye on the road as the caravan left its campsite and moved out for the third day. Tolo refused to allow her to ride the donkey again, not after she fell off the first day as they were leaving Nineveh. The steady clomping of hooves, the water rushing beneath the bridge, the aching for her husband, the unknown ahead, had been too much. There was no stopping the darkness that swallowed her.

A striped awning covered the load of merchandise, protecting the contents from the harsh rays of the sun and the rains that occasionally sprang up this time of year. Eran leaned back and looked beneath the edge, where the canvas met the walled cart. She rode in a cart again, taken against her will for the second time, without knowing what to expect, first as tribute and now as a slave.

Her conditions were better than the last time. A full flask of water and soft blankets were within reach, and room to stretch out fully if she angled her legs around the crates of amphorae.

As far as she could tell, she was the only woman purchased, the only person other than the band of young boys. They could be trained to work in the mines, or in cutting the stones for the pyramidal tombs of the rulers in Egypt. They could be raised to think as the people who owned them, could fight as soldiers. She couldn't do any of these. She prayed she wouldn't be another goddess in disguise.

Tolo paid a hefty sum for the right to take her from the land of Shinar. It wasn't for her body at least. She was far too old to be desired in that way, except by her husband.

Shem. She pictured him in the throne room, bold before Amraphel. Was he dead because of it? Had the King maimed him somehow, like he did to Ham? Selling Eran was a means for profit. Would he do the same with Shem?

No, not likely. What would be the sport of having his enemy disappear in the far off lands? Her husband was dead or he suffered somehow for his unwillingness to bow.

The image of her husband finding strength in his God under the King's threats was etched on her mind. She would have crumpled in fear. Her husband's devotion to the One God surpassed hers and this brought more fears of the days to come. How could she stand without him?

Amraphel thought he defeated Shem. He was so wrong. Her husband defeated him soundly, despite the cost. Shem would have given his life for hers, given anything except what belonged to his God. He did what was right. She had never been more proud of the man she wed. But she knew her husband. He would carry the burden of her death on his shoulders. If he was alive, he suffered in spirit. Guilt would destroy him before anything Amraphel could do to his flesh.

Eran surveyed the hills and valleys as the caravan advanced. The trade route led to the city of Haran, then turned south to Damascus, then into Canaan. It was many weeks to get there, and unless she was traded again in Haran, she would leave this land of the Tigris and Euphrates. Forever.

One hope remained. The road connecting Nineveh to Haran was the same she had taken a few weeks before. The Hebrew camp was on this stretch of hilly terrain. It was approaching, its position hidden from view by a bluff, a shield of stone. Lookouts kept watch from the top, ready with the shofar to sound an alarm. Her husband often sat there, too, finding solitude among the rocks to seek wisdom from above. Would anyone see her?

Eran leaned back and watched the hills pass, waiting for the right time to lift the flap of canvas from the cart.

♥

The misting rain passed overhead, long enough to cool his skin before it was gone, not long enough to calm the dust stirred by the latest caravan. Shem leaned against a rock on the bluff, mindlessly watching the string of camels and white robed traders pass by on the highway, heading toward Nineveh. The camels came from lands far away, exotic places he could scarcely imagine, where stone structures rose to the sky in giant memorial pyramids and seas of sand stretched out for days and days. His brother Ham's children settled those lands, forming powerful nations of their own where no one remembered the God of Noah.

The stories told from travelers beyond Haran made Shem's soul sick with grief. Many idols were worshipped. Children were given in sacrifice and life given no more value than beasts of the field. He doubted any truth remained in Canaan's lands, or in Egypt, and Ethiopia, and the regions across the seas where Ham's generations lived. He doubted they knew of the Flood and of judgment and salvation.

Shem scraped up a handful of stones and sent them skittering over the edge, one by one. The earth was no different than before the Great Flood. Man, made in God's image, chose rebellion. He didn't know why the mighty hand of judgment was withheld this time.

He sighed and started to rub his forehead when the bandage stopped him. Cleaned, dressed and wrapped by Denah, it would heal, leaving him with the scar, Amraphel's claim of ownership. The mark that jeopardized the entire camp. For now, he promised his brother he would remain nearby, minimizing the risk by living in the caves where they hid the livestock from raiders. He wouldn't jeopardize them outright by living among them and, though he didn't say it to anyone, he couldn't stand to be in his tent without Eran.

How long would he stay? He didn't know. Not indefinitely. It was time for him to move away from Eber's tribe. If the persecution diminished, it was worth it. He owed it to them, to give them a chance to succeed.

Dust remained clouded on the horizon above the road. Shem watched it progress, another caravan, this one inching toward him on its way from Nineveh, heading to Haran, the great city of trade. It traveled slowly, a long line of carts and donkeys, flanked by armed men on horseback.

He could reach it, if he hurried. If he left his perch and scurried down the hillside, he could be to the road by the time it came near. He could hop onto one of the carts and hide beneath the yellow and white striped awnings and go away, leaving the Hebrew camp. He could join the traveling band of merchants and be gone from the land of his youth.

Shem stood, keeping his eye on the line of men, beasts and merchandise. His legs trembled. There was time to get to the roadside.

His feet didn't move. He couldn't leave yet. He promised his family he wouldn't disappear as Ham and Naomi had done. The resulting emptiness of their actions remained carved out in his heart with no means to fill the void. It was business unfinished, a tale with no ending. He wouldn't do that to Japheth and Denah.

As the caravan neared, Shem sat back down and shielded his

eyes from the rising dust, drawing up images of Eran as she laughed at his jokes and played her flute in the moonlight and walked with him through fields of wheat, marveling at the harvest. There was strength in her gentle presence. She stirred the breeze that whisked away his fears and lifted him to the heavens, away from the turmoil, where he could look down and see clearly the road to travel. As the voice for the One God, he could only whisper without her in his shadow. Eran's unyielding devotion to him, and to their God, filled his lungs with shouting. How could he lead his people without her?

No, he couldn't leave. Not while she was in Nineveh. Not while there was still a chance they could complete their lives together.

♥

The bluff was in view. Eran's heart pounded as the armed horsemen passed by on their rounds. She untied the awning on one side and gripped it to keep it from blowing aside too soon. If she could draw attention to herself, long enough for the lookout to see she was alive, and heading toward Haran, it would be enough.

With a deep breath, Eran let go of the awning and stood, bracing herself against a stack of crates. She turned her eyes to the hillside. A white cloth against the pale stone? Dust climbed the air between her and the rocks, enveloping the view. Was someone there? Shem? Eran raised her arms overhead and waved, screaming her husband's name.

♥

The irregular marching of hooves and creaking of wheels rose from the dust of the caravan. Indistinct voices traveled among the sounds of braying beasts, along with pots that clanked and crates that groaned. It was the loud din familiar to any caravan, a rumble of thunder on the overcast day. Shem kept his eyes closed as it passed, the sounds melting together into one tone. Sometimes it seemed as if his own name rose from the cacophony. A call to follow. He tuned it out.

The traders would go to Haran or beyond, then one day come back, going the other direction. Back and forth, a monotony he wondered if they grew tired of. Life unchanging was good, he wanted to tell them. Be grateful for rising in the morning and falling to sleep at night in your own familiar pattern, your own familiar place. Change was not always in a man's favor. In a moment, the best portion of his world can slip away.

♥

"Be careful," the man said. "You need to sit. One bump and you'll fall out." He maintained his balance on the horse while leaning sideways to secure the awning, blocking her view, until the bluff lay behind them. He thought she yelled because it had come undone. He and his companions were attentive, more so than she realized. They would have seen her had she decided to jump. They would not have allowed their merchandise to escape.

Eran crawled on her hands and knees over the crates to the back where she could lie on her belly and peer under the awning at the bluff. It was lost in the dust. The road behind her was filled with more yellow and white covered carts, laden donkeys, and horsemen. No one followed the caravan.

Had anyone seen her?

Shem thought she was dead, given to the lions or some other

fate at the hand of Amraphel. He had no reason to suspect she was so near. He had no reason to question the caravans. There was a chance though, a chance he saw her, or heard his name above the noise. He could barter for her in the city of Haran when the caravan stopped to trade out the tired donkeys for fresh ones. If he was even alive.

"Please be there, Shem. Please."

Chapter Thirteen

No one came for her in Haran.

Eran watched the stream of faces around the caravansary as donkeys were exchanged, goods bartered and carts re-arranged, desperate to see familiar faces as she had in Nineveh, the day she fell from the King's favor. There were none.

No one would take a message on her behalf to the Hebrew camp, either. Not without payment.

No one knew she was there. No one knew she was alive and she had no means to make it known.

After two days they moved out again. The route turned south, heading into arid country. They would travel from oasis to oasis until they reached the fertile lands of the Salt Sea, where rivers and springs fed the cities of the plain, the cities of her nephew Canaan. It was land that sowed iniquity, harvested immorality and feasted on the destruction of their fathers' God.

Eran shuddered. Did her God turn his righteous eyes towards the land of Canaan? Would he even know she was there?

♥

There were only five raiders stirring up the morning routine, and none were interested in taking tribute. They looked for Shem. They looked for reason to bring charges against the camp, wanting to release the mayhem due a tribe harboring a slave.

Shem stayed hidden in a narrow crevice of the cave, behind the oxen, and under a hastily formed blanket of rocks. Still he could hear the shouts, calling out his name. Then he heard the horses, venturing away from the tents, towards the hills where he and the livestock were hidden. They had come close. Too close.

Japheth and Eber came to get him when the men had gone. The welt on Eber's jaw from the fist of a raider was already turning purple.

And Shem had already decided what he had to do.

He sat with Eber and Japheth, coughing out dust inhaled in his rocky hide-out. "I can't remain here. It isn't safe for any of us. The raids won't stop, or the violence."

"No one will feed you in Nineveh, or Haran or any city in the region of the Five Kings, Brother. We can wrap your head in turbans but you'll be found out eventually, and they'll return you to him."

"I know. I'm better off alone in the wilds than among men with loyalties to Amraphel."

"But-"

Shem interrupted Japheth. "I won't do that either. I've decided to leave the land of my fathers and follow our people to the west. I'll go find our relative Abram."

He allowed the men to absorb his words, knowing they would speak their minds and hearts, knowing he could trust their wisdom as well as their devotion.

Eber nodded. "He'll welcome you, and protect you, risking the safety of his own camp, if I know him. He'll be loyal to his ancestors, to you Shem."

"I won't stay any longer than necessary. Long enough to form a new plan once I see what the land is like, what the people are like. He can help me acquire sufficient weapons and tools to make it on my own. There are caves there as there are here."

"I don't want you to leave us, but I understand. It's a wise decision. If you must go, finding Abram makes the most sense. He and Sarai are far enough from Amraphel to minimize the danger. His seal holds power, but there won't be as many men to back it up. You'll still need to be cautious. Always. Loyalties are far-reaching and ever-shifting."

Japheth looked past Shem's shoulder toward the road. "What about Eran?"

"If she is alive and the King finds me in his city, who knows what he would do to her, just to spite me. I can't save her there. I can only try to protect her by leaving. I don't want to abandon her, but…"

Eber squeezed his hand. "I'm not moving this camp Father Shem. We'll send scouts and listen to the street gossip. We'll watch for Eran and find a way to bring her home. I promise you that."

"Tell her I'm sorry." Shem swallowed the grief rising in his throat. "If she is alive, tell her, tell her…"

Japheth interrupted. "Tell her we are with Abram. And send a messenger to inform us."

Eber turned his head sharply toward Japheth. "Us?"

"Yes," Japheth said. "Denah and I. We'll go with Shem."

Shem stared at his brother, unable to find words.

Japheth smiled. "That is, if he wants us to go."

Shem slapped him on the back. "I do! Of course I do. I want you with me."

"You'll need resources to pay your way on a caravan," Eber

said. "We'll tan hides over the next few weeks. You'll wait that long? It will give the rest of us time to adjust to the thought of you leaving, and time to see if Eran comes back to us. Maybe time for you to change your mind, see if God's plans alter your course."

Shem arched his spine back, crackling the bones as he stretched. "We'll wait. Then we'll step into the land of Canaan's children. I pray there is wisdom in this decision. I can't shake the feeling that it's the direction I'm supposed to take. I can see no other alternative."

"Our God will not abandon you there."

Shem knew it in his mind. God was there, always watching. He wanted assurance in his heart as well, that the Creator was holding a lantern to the path ahead. He was too old to make the wrong choice about going into the darkness of the lands of Canaan. If he wasn't supposed to go, and God didn't intervene, it would be disastrous.

Chapter Fourteen

The night and day cycle held little variety. When it was light, the caravan moved. As darkness approached, it stopped. Forward progression and keeping the merchandise from thieves were the objectives. Eran was finally allowed to ride a donkey when she asked, needing the change from the monotony of the cart. Her tolerance for sitting on the back of the beast was limited, adding new pains to her body after only a handful of hours. Then it was back to the cart. Cart, donkey, cart. Cart, donkey, cart. When they stopped for the night, she was allowed to walk about, and freshen up, then back to the guarded cart to eat and sleep.

Only the landscape changed as they headed south. The verdant hues of lush fields were gradually replaced by sparse, yellowed vegetation and air that was dry and hot. Gentle hills grew taller, rolling toward craggy mountains on the horizon, and water no longer followed the roadside in narrow streams. Dense groves of trees thinned and separated, dotting the land rather than covering it, the forests decreasing in number like the small walled towns.

After several weeks of sameness in routine, the men were eager to get to the Oasis of Damascus. Eran heard the anticipation in their voices, even when she didn't understand the words. The caravan always stopped there, Tolo explained, and he allowed the men to swim and relax, and enjoy a meal prepared beyond the usual fare of dried fruit and breads. The oasis was well protected by the local men, who reaped generous profits from travelers eager to lay their weapons aside for a night of feasting.

Eran found herself longing for a pot full of clean water. Weeks-worth of dust clung to everything and scrubbing through it to find her own skin again would be a simple pleasure. Maybe she'd be allowed to wash her garment too. She lifted the corner and watched the cloud of particles fly away. The tunic and sandals no longer qualified as finery fit for a goddess. Her hair was pulled back in a simple braid and covered with a scrap of fabric. Both held more dust than an urn of burnt incense.

Canaan, she'd heard, was green and vibrant with life. Water flowed over cliffs and filled lakes, then reached into the plain with nourishing fingers. The fields gave abundant harvests. Honey poured from hives and a single cluster of grapes was all a man could carry. Its merits were exaggerated, surely. Why would God bless a land so intent on ignoring him?

The caravan's final destination was Zoar, a small city, one of the five Cities of the Plain of Canaan, near the coast of the Sea of Salt. There Tolo would sell his merchandise, buy spices, trinkets, and dyed fabrics from the Egyptian merchants, then turn around and go back to Nineveh.

He would take the same route, past the Hebrew camp. Eran tucked the information into her mind. With each step of the donkey's hooves she was further from Shem, but there was a final destination and from there, the path could be retraced.

Leaning back onto a crate, she closed her eyes, trying to envision the oasis ahead. She could find no joy in the anticipation, as the horsemen did. As much as she wanted this journey to be complete, to stand again on an unmoving surface, the unknowns ahead kept her wary of change. Tolo led the caravan but it was financed by another man, and it was he Eran belonged to now.

♥

Denah's hands deftly wove strands of hemp into a rope two fingers thick. She secured the ends together to form a circle, then poked sprigs of lavender, mint and wild rose into the weave. A fragrant aroma filtered into the stale air of the cave surrounding the grave.

Japheth and Shem watched her make the wreath in silence, wiping perspiration from their brows and drinking thirstily from a skin of cool water. The last mound of soil had been heaped and packed into the deep hole they dug, their parents' remains now resting below the earth, with only a simple stone to mark the site. Hopefully the two could rest in peace at last.

Shem felt the burn of tears in his eyes. This was the last time they would be with Noah and Jael. Already he felt a keen sense of loss. He never imagined he would be buried somewhere they weren't. Home was always in the vicinity of his mother and father. He assumed he and Eran, and their children and children's children would lie in death together, their bodies sleeping on the same soil, beneath the same moon. Leaving Noah and Jael felt wrong. But he couldn't take them to Canaan. His mother was still covered in flesh and never, ever would he separate her from Noah. They would remain in the land of the two rivers and he would be the one to walk away.

None of the sons of Noah would rest with their father. He and Japheth would die in places their father had never seen. Maybe in Canaan. Maybe before that, along the way. Maybe this journey would carry them to lands across the great seas and they would be buried there. His heart knew they would never return to this land and it ached at the thought. He wanted to go back to the remnants of the ark first, to see it once more. And the little village where he raised his sons, and the hillside where he watched the sunrise over the Euphrates, and the graves of family already gone. Every place would be just a memory once he left, like those of the old earth.

And Eran. What would become of her? Who would weave the wreath to place on her grave?

Denah placed her creation on the flat stone resting over the burial site. The fragrant wreath represented life, from dust to dust, from dependence to dependence. It honored the deceased as God's image, fragrant with the breath of the heavens giving his body life, and fragrant with hope of living beyond this world. Eran made most of them for the graves in the Hebrew camp since they were the people of her lineage. Her slim fingers wove the fragrant stems into the design rather than adding them separately as Denah preferred.

The women of the camp trained one another in their skills, adding flair and variation. Shem was glad their work wasn't identical. He liked seeing Eran in his belongings, items fashioned by her own hands. He was mindful of it as he packed, choosing essentials that bore her finest handiwork. With reluctance, he took none of her personal belongings. There was a chance she would make it back to their tent among the Hebrews. The meager collection of possessions he bundled for the journey would be little burden for his pack animal.

Tomorrow, he, Japheth, and Denah would join a caravan as it passed.

Tonight, the camp would dance and feast, sorrow put on hold

for the night while the sons of Noah were still in their midst.

For now, Shem needed to be alone. He climbed the hill to his spot on the bluff and sat with his back to the stone. He prayed. For the Hebrews. For the journey. For his wife, wherever she was. And mostly, for the Promise. "Bring us redemption from Evil, God, our Creator. Bring to pass the words you gave to Mother Eve."

Chapter Fifteen

Rot saturated the morning air, clinging to the winds, masking the woodsy aroma of old cedars along the roadway. Eran identified the stench long before the men on horseback began sniffing the breeze and casting questioning glances at one another, long before they realized vultures were circling overhead.

The carcasses were heaped and smoldering in a wall in front of the caravan.

There had been an attack. The sheep had been slaughtered and positioned intentionally to block the roadway. The caravan was instantly on high alert and all men had weapons drawn as they were forced to come to a stop.

Eran wrapped herself up in a blanket and watched from the cart as the men searched the forested grove flanking one side of the road, and the grassy clearing on the other side. When no bandits were discovered, part of them grabbed long handled picks and started the grisly process of yanking the top carcasses from the stack, dousing them with water and hauling them into the open space where they had pastured. The others kept guard, Tolo himself circling the long line of merchandise with a dagger in hand.

They were well-protected, but a caravan at rest was an invitation for trouble. Someone went to much effort to destroy what wasn't theirs already.

A flash of movement in the clearing caught Eran's attention. It was a woman, on her knees struggling to roll a stone along the ground, trying to get it to a low mound of others nearby. She buried someone. The shepherd? Her husband? Her son? One death that meant nothing to the men responsible, perhaps everything to her.

Leaning over the edge of the cart, Eran pulled up handfuls of the long grasses growing in thick clumps there, then quickly wove them together to form a simple burial wreath. There were no flowers nearby, no aromatic herbs to add. It would have to do. As Tolo made his rounds, she handed it to him. "For the grave," she said, pointing to the woman.

Tolo nodded and took it without speaking. He rode to the woman and gave it to her without dismounting. If he was the kind of man to assist a grieving woman bury her dead, he had no opportunity to reveal it. One of his men screamed.

Eran jerked her head around to see the commotion rising near the dead sheep. Bandits dropped from the trees, dressed and covered in paints so they could disappear in the shadows of the branches. They held curved swords and ran toward the caravan. Quickly she covered herself with blankets. Beyond her, men shouted and anguished cries pierced the air, and more shouting. Weapons clanged upon weapons and donkeys brayed in the sudden swarm of chaos.

When the eruption diminished she peeked out, reassured by the nearby sound of Tolo's voice commanding his men. As quickly as it started, the thieves had been routed. There were only a handful that she could see, stupid enough to take on the thirty or forty defenders of the caravan. Now there were none. And no one would see that they were buried.

♥

The mood was jubilant by the time they reached the large oasis. They were delayed by the road block yet still managed to arrive before nightfall. The intensity of the day filled the men with drive and they pushed the beasts of burden as hard as possible. No one wanted to remain in the open country when there was relaxation around the bend.

The waters of the Baruda River fed the area plentifully, the smell of vegetation and feel of moist air only adding to the buoyant feeling. Numerous caravans were scattered within the lush haven, each having its own position near the river. Tolo's group was led to the shade of large palms, short grasses making a cool rug for the outdoor room where they would camp. The animals were led to water that lay a short distance away by men already stripping off garments in eagerness.

Eran let her bare feet slide in the grass, staying near the perimeter of the trees. The local men had already taken up the guard post and fatigue was settling into her bones. She was ready to lie down on the cool green carpet when Tolo asked her to see to the injuries sustained by his men. They lost no one in the skirmish, and that was a rare occurrence, but several had been knifed.

She was handed a small selection of supplies: needles made from acacia thorns, thin linen fibers, rough bandaging, and wine so fermented it made her eyes sting as she pulled the stopper. Tolo hovered nearby as she soaked the old bandages and peeled them off, cleaned the wounds with the wine, stitched them closed as best she could and re-wrapped them. He supplied his men with painkiller in the form of the strong beer made by the locals. Actually, all his men seemed to be enjoying the medicine, injured or not. Tolo, she noticed, kept himself sober.

Stars covered the night sky by the time she finished. And stains covered her only garment. The last time she tended to an injury and ruined her clothing was in Nineveh. It seemed so long ago.

"Thank you. I usually have to do that sewing part myself. Looks much finer with your hand." Tolo handed her a fresh tunic from his crates of merchandise. He nodded toward the palm trees. "The water is over there. I'll place a guard for your safety while you bathe. The men are grateful for your kindness. They'll stay away until you're finished."

Eran gripped the garment in one hand and steadied herself on a tree with the other. The confidence she found in the work of healing was suddenly gone. Churning in her gut replaced the calmness.

"I, I can't." She stared at her feet, breathing in and out to keep the darkness pushed away.

"I guarantee your safety. And your modesty."

Tolo didn't understand. No one understood. "May I have a jar of water, instead?"

"Well, yes, if that's what you prefer. The river is cool and I think you'd prefer it. It isn't deep on the edges. The current is only strong in the middle. Stay close to shore if you can't swim, and you'll be fine."

Eran forced herself to look up, straining her neck to find the eyes of the tall man. "Thank you, but the jar will be fine." Her voice quivered.

Tolo looked confused, then shrugged his shoulders. "As you wish. I'll have some delivered to the cart."

Eran nodded, anxious to escape his scrutiny. Anxious to lie down until the queasy sensation passed. Anxious to turn her back to the open water that made her limp with fear.

Tolo let a rare smile find his lips. "I'm pleased with you. King Amraphel's man said I wouldn't regret the purchase and I see he was right."

"I'm just an old woman. Why did you buy me? What need could anyone have of me?"

Tolo lifted an eyebrow. "Old or not, you're a Healer. The land of Canaan never has enough of them."

♥

A Healer. Amraphel sold her as a Healer. Eran worked her way to a private stand of trees and sat on a stone. As a little girl she had been trained to help the sick and injured animals of her father's herds. No one had to ask her twice to assist with difficult births or congested udders. She couldn't bear to see the beasts suffer. Showing compassion and easing their pain came with its own reward.

She had never been strong and hearty, never been able to work in the fields as her siblings had done. She learned to cook and sew and tend to chores under her mother's protective wing, and while they were good skills to master, her mind wanted more. Seeking new remedies for ailments had come naturally, and led to treating people as well. After walking the earth for centuries, she had learned a head full of treatments.

She used her skills without question. It was her gift, the helping of those in pain. Was that the right thing to do? The men she stitched up today, of course. They protected her. But Amraphel's man? Did she save the life of a man who would later turn a sword to one of the Hebrews?

Eran soaked a cloth in the water jar and scrubbed the filth on her skin. She had never questioned how she used her knowledge. Now she was going to Canaan for that purpose. Her remedies would prolong the lives of those who disregarded truth and gave their own little ones to the fires in homage to golden idols. She might have to treat the wounds of warriors and the diseases of vile men. What was she to do?

Would she have the courage to refuse? Was she wrong to even consider it?

Shem would know. But he wasn't here. Neither was Noah or Jael or Denah. Or her father, or anyone.

The washing took up both jars of the fresh water Tolo provided. Eran pulled the clean tunic over her head and stayed in the isolated grove, away from the rowdy men enjoying their night of roasted meats and fresh fruits. Cumin and mint saturated the grove and her stomach rumbled. She would eat after she prayed.

Lifting hands to the heavens, Eran sought her God. "Show me what to do. Don't allow me to anger you, to work against your will. Remember me in the foreign lands and please, please, if Shem still lives, guide him to my side."

A long time later, her heart emptied, she gathered the soiled linens and headed for the bonfire, to add them to the pile and to check on her patients. Her God had not revealed himself. Not audibly, not visibly. There was quiet on the rivers of her soul, though. No turbulence. Unless he spoke up later and told her otherwise, she would use her abilities to help the hurting, even in Canaan. They were the children of Noah and Jael, the generations of their sons. How could she not?

Chapter Sixteen

The six donkeys merged with the slow-moving string of camels, carts, a few oxen and more donkeys. The caravan appeared to be a conglomerate of merchants, nomads, and families, the safest sort to join. The wealth it carried would be negligible compared to one with a high merchant component, but would be well protected all the same. There were children and wives among them, and the men would fight for their protection. Shem had actually chosen it because of the mixed personage. They wouldn't stand out in case the King's men decided to go man-hunting.

The leader was brusque, guiding his horse alongside Shem and the others as they took position in the back of the line, where they were told to join when the arrangements were made. He eyed them with a look of doubt, questioning their age and ability to ride. Japheth responded with equal bluntness rather than showing desperation. Gaining favor, they were permitted to pay the fee and join.

In motion, the caravan stopped for no one, they were told. If they fell behind, they fell behind. All men were expected to be armed and ready to defend the group. All women were to help with food and routine chores at night. No fighting, no unapproved slave trades, and no questioning his decisions. Illness was to be reported immediately, and if he decided the sickness might spread, that person would be left at the nearest safe location. No refunds.

Shem and Japheth agreed. They, with Denah and the pack animals, officially became part of the group.

Japheth fell in beside him after lagging behind with his wife. "She'll cry for a long while. I wish there was something I could do."

"She'll miss the camp. They'll miss her."

Japheth sighed. "Yes. And Eran. Denah feels as if she's abandoning her best friend."

"I know." Shem felt for the turban on his head, ensuring it came low enough to conceal the burned image. "I have to leave. You don't. She doesn't."

"I do, Brother. My place is with you. I've felt that we were to leave this place on other occasions, after the raids especially. Then with what happened to Mother, I knew it was time. God prepared me, and Denah. He whispered to her heart that we were to pack our things and not question. She's grieving but she knows this is a journey we're meant to take. To be with you. I hadn't considered going to Canaan however. Can't say I'm eager to head that direction."

"Not a destination I've dreamed of either. If God is going to send a sweeping arm of judgment again, it will be on Canaan. I'd rather not be a part of any of that again. I don't want to witness another great turmoil. I'm too old."

Living and living and living, surpassing generations and still living was not the blessing it seemed. Not when man repeated his sins, learning little from the ones who lived before. Not when he could see the repetitious nature of rebellion, of pride, of selfishness. As marvelous as it was to hold the tiny infants of the successive generations, it was difficult to hold onto hope that this new life would choose faith over the follies of its ancestors.

And there was no end to the remembering. Each wrong choice, each word said in anger, each opportunity missed for no good reason. Remembering, and feeling the aches of more than five hundred years wasn't something he would wish for anyone. Stacked high in his head, Shem tried to dismantle them at times. They came back, and new ones were added.

There were the good memories too, of course, and they made it possible to rise each day. For all the ones he wanted to forget there were those that he could pull to the forefront and find joy, and hope, and a reason to keep walking a path of faith. Most of them included Eran, the wife he was leaving behind. Forever, he was sure. Unless the King was dead, he couldn't go back, wouldn't risk endangering the Hebrews.

"Thank you for coming, Japheth. I pray we find our God in Canaan."

♥

The string of camels and donkeys came to a complete stop. Several weeks on the road and it had happened during the day only twice before. The smell in the air was rancid. Shem's pulse quickened, knowing it would be no simple rock slide to clean up this time.

Tying a scarf over his nose, he made himself breathe through his mouth. He and Japheth handed the donkey reins to Denah and went toward the front of the line with the other men to see what was happening.

Rotting carcasses lined one side of the roadway at the head of the caravan. They appeared to be sheep, appeared to have been stacked at one time. Wild animals had amplified the grisly scene by spreading the foul carnage into the narrow strip where the carts could pass. Stark bones, stripped of meat, were scattered everywhere among the larger pieces of beast. Black flies were thick like bees at a hive, and the sound alone made his skin crawl.

Jackals claimed ownership of the road, snarling, baring teeth at the intrusion. Shem turned his head as bows were drawn, the beasts swiftly counted among the dead. The sights and sounds made his gut heave, but he couldn't leave. There was work to do. He and his brother were handed shovels. Shem scooped a load and carried it from the road, starting a pile in what used to be a small pasture. Japheth and the other men followed, adding to the pile until it was waist high, them starting a new one. They were nearly finished when he noticed a grave a short distance beyond.

The mound of stone stood above the grasses in the trampled pasture. Bandits don't stop to bury their dead, and the memorial stones were the work of a woman, he guessed, by the choice of small rocks when there were larger ones to choose from. At once, his heart was saddened. Death was everywhere. Life uncertain. Pain guaranteed.

For no reason he walked to the grave, paying his respects to the unknown person beneath. Since he was there, he voiced a prayer to the heavens for the woman left behind. He lifted his head to leave, then stopped. A circle of desiccated greenery lay atop the mound. Simple woven work that he had seen many times before.

♥

"You think she was here?" Japheth sounded skeptical. He was a man who liked the tangible, drawing conclusions based on many facts rather than just one. But even he had to admit, this was a good one. The putrid air of death had not made Shem delirious or filled his mind with desperate visions.

Shem held the wreath up again. "I know Eran's handiwork."

"Anyone could have made that, Shem. It looks like her pattern, but I don't know. I want to believe you..."

Shem couldn't stop smiling. "It would be like her, honoring the graves of strangers. And Amraphel sending her away on a caravan makes sense. He couldn't kill her. He couldn't even kill me and I'm the one he despises." Shem automatically checked the position of the turban. "Dozens of caravans routinely take the route from Nineveh. It's a possibility, you have to agree."

"Yes, it's possible. He may have sent her off with traders. She might be alive."

"We might be able to find her." His heart beat steadily, his mind whirling with the possibility. It was a sliver of purpose, one he grasped with all his might.

Maybe it was false hope.

Maybe not.

Chapter Seventeen

Zoar was the smallest of the Five Cities of the Plain, the furthest south, below the Sea of Salt. The caravan passed Sodom, Gomorrah, Zeboyim, and Admah before finally terminating in a guarded lot outside the city. Both donkeys and men were given freedom. Other men arrived to load Tolo's merchandise onto smaller wagons, taking them away when they were full.

Eran stood beside the cart she had ridden for over a month, not sure what to do as men buzzed around her to empty it. She was part of the ware but no one loaded her up to haul off. When they finished and moved on, she climbed back in and waited, amazed at how weary she was from doing nothing but ride for the so many long days. Tolo found her later, as the last of the carts rumbled away.

"There you are. Come with me."

Eran tried to stand, stooping halfway as her knees groaned. Tolo gave her his hand and helped her to the ground. "It isn't far to Master Okpara's home. Can you walk?"

Eran nodded. "Okpara? A strange name. Does he speak Aram?"

"Of course. He is well traveled."

"Do you live there? With Okpara?"

"No. He hires me to guide his caravan. He doesn't own me."

"He owns others? Has slaves? I suppose he will consider me his property."

Tolo nodded. "Yes, you are his and yes there are many others. Servants and slaves."

"He is a man of means then."

"Your Master is a wealthy man. Sees himself as King of this city."

Eran shivered at the thought of being owned by a King. "Is he kind? Do I have reason to fear?"

Tolo hesitated. "He is kind to those whom he favors. He will treat you well if you adhere to his rules. He isn't a bad man."

Eran gripped the man's arm, not wanting to be in the new land without him. He was the only person she knew, and her only connection to home. "When do you return to Nineveh?" She tried to make it sound like pleasant conversation, not a fearful plea.

Tolo looked down at her, reading the hope in her eyes. "Very soon. But not with you. Forget the land of your past. It will only bring you pain."

♥

Okpara was three quarters the height of Tolo, and twice the girth. His eyes were lined with kohl and he stood bare-chested in the doorway, a long white garment falling to the ground below his ample belly. He was not impressed with Tolo's judgment.

"You spent how much for her?"

Tolo put his hands on Eran's shoulders and inched her forward. "She *is* old, yes, but I've seen her skills for myself. She has the finesse of a physician, trained in the country of another land though. She'll know of roots and herbs and potions your latest medicine men knew nothing about. She's worth the silver from your coffers. Worth a try at least. Trust me."

Okpara laughed at Tolo's exuberance. "Alright. Alright. Your decisions are always in my favor. I'll take her, put her to the test."

Tolo tipped his head and took a step back. "I'll see you tomorrow then?"

"Yes, come for dinner and share the travel details with me. Tonight, forget about the caravan and find some entertainment."

Tolo grinned and nodded again, then turned and walked away, his long legs separating them in moments. Eran was left with Okpara, her Master. He looked her over as if deciding whether he really wanted to keep her, then finally led her inside the spacious open foyer.

The two-level home wasn't the size of Amraphel's palace, but it was the largest private home she had ever seen. As a bride in Noah's home, she thought he was surely the wealthiest man alive, living in such splendor, and it had been a quarter of the size of Okpara's residence, she guessed, and far less ornate. Tapestries and mosaic floor tiles gave color to the white walls, which were lined with evenly spaced niches. Golden urns and animalistic figures occupied the spaces. It took her a moment to realize the strange creatures were idols, so she turned her gaze to the floor. There were many vacant eyes peering back at her.

Okpara gave instructions to a servant girl waiting in the background. She left and returned moments later with another woman, whom he summoned to his side. "She's called Eran," he told her. "Our new Healer. Show her to a room and get her settled. And see that a guard is posted."

♥

The glare of the sun was as oppressive as the shade of the palms was up-lifting. Reaching the oasis in the early afternoon was a blessing. They could swim and relax and allow the beasts to drink their fill of the cool water. The caravan wouldn't leave until morning. None of them were expected to stand guard here and he could sleep the deep slumber of the weary.

Shem stood with the caravan guide and studied the map. It was only a few days until they would part ways, the caravan following the main route, on the east coast of the Sea of Salt, while he would take the smaller road on the west. The well-traveled King's Highway was easier for a caravan, and could loop around the Sea from the southern end if it needed to reach the cities there. The western route was rockier and riskier, but quicker, a more direct route to his destination. Abram last lived in the region called Hebron, in the hills west of the Sea, and Shem prayed he still did.

The man tapped a stubby finger on the map, in the area Shem intended to travel. "That's Amorite territory. Don't go there unless you want trouble. Them giants live in those hills." He looked at Shem, squinting his eyes so they were just slits. "Ever seen one up close?"

The Amorites were his brother Ham's descendants, through his grandson Amori. Many of the east-bound caravans they passed were protected by the tall men from Amori's loins. Several heads taller than his own people, they were difficult to miss. They had strength to match and reportedly enjoyed a good fight with little provocation.

Shem nodded. "In Nineveh. With the caravans. I bumped into one once. He didn't give me any trouble. You can bet I got away from there fast as I could though."

The leader laughed and punched him in the arm. "I would've too. Here, even more so. This is their land and they don't like to share, don't like outsiders. They marry their own kin and keep breeding more and more tall ones. I've heard they keep getting taller, making a whole tribe of giants, they are."

"And here," he pointed at the etched leather map again. "This is where the road splits to either side of the Sea. Some of the people will be going their own way from there. You stayin' with us?"

So far no one had been overly inquisitive as to where they were headed. It was better that way. They didn't want to be tracked, if they could help it. "I'd be safer if I did," he said. It didn't answer the man's question but it wasn't a lie.

The man looked at him with the squint again. "Hmmff. Well, that's right. No one here's going to make you choose."

Shem just nodded and studied the map, putting it to his memory. Sweat trickled from beneath his turban as he did, dripping onto the surface. He pulled back and wiped his brow while checking the cloth wrap on his head.

"Didn't you swim yet? Take that thing off. You won't get scorched by the sun in these trees."

Shem did his best to look calm. "I will soon. The women are in there now."

"Well, water'll still be there when they get their fill, but they won't be in any hurry to be done. I'll chase 'em out so we can get the meats cooking before too long."

"Good, I look forward to it." Shem nodded to the man and went to find Japheth. His brother was half asleep in the shade.

"There are giants in the land where we're headed."

Japheth opened his eyes when Shem spoke, looked around half-heartedly then closed his eyes again. "I don't see any here,

Brother. Let's worry about them later."

"Worry about what?" Denah flopped down beside her husband, wet hair still dripping on her clean tunic.

Japheth pulled her to the grass beside him. "Nothing. No worries for now."

She laid her head on his chest and closed her eyes. "Good. No worries. For now."

Shem felt a fresh stab of loneliness. He also felt the need for a cooling dip in the water.

The women were gone and only a handful of men were back, swimming in the deep middle section. Shem quickly undressed, leaving the turban for last before jumping into the wide stretch of river. A taste of Eden as the heat and dust were washed away. A bit of paradise before the final leg of the journey. The worst was behind them and he hoped to be in the safety of Abram's tents before the next full moon.

Abram knew the territory. He would help them find Eran.

It wasn't wishful thinking, that she was still alive. Surely his soul would feel the agony of her death. The emptiness without her would be the edge of fine-hewn flint blade, not the throbbing, hollow ache he carried. Eran was alive. He just knew it.

Shem took a deep breath and dove into the depths of the water, pushing his lungs until forced to surface. He sucked in a mouthful of air and shook the hair from his eyes, and found another pair staring back at him.

Squinty eyes.

Locked onto his forehead.

Chapter Eighteen

Denah handed him a second dish of grilled ibex before sitting down with her own generous portion. The meat was smothered in a rich sauce of garlic and onion and exotic spices Shem couldn't identify, from lands to the south. It was probably delicious. He ate the first serving without tasting it, his mind too pre-occupied with other matters.

His sister-in-law picked out moist bits with her fingers, eating this dish much slower than the first. They were all three doing their best to appear nonplussed, stuffing themselves with the freshly prepared feast as the others were doing, trying not to reveal the heightened anxiety stirring in their minds. "Eat up, Shem," Denah said. "This meal may need to hold us for awhile."

The caravan leader had said nothing about the seal of Amraphel. Shem saw him talking earnestly with one of his men though, pointing to his own forehead. He wasn't keeping the information silent. Would one of them seek a reward for reporting the whereabouts of the King's property? If not around here, when the caravan returned to the land of Shinar? Shem berated himself again for allowing the mark to be seen. He endangered them all.

For the most part, everyone kept to their own groups,

monitoring their own supplies as they traveled, steering away from personal conversation. It was one of those unspoken rules. Each man's business was his own as long as they were on the road. Shem didn't know how that played out once they disbanded. Loose tongues could mean trouble. Men everywhere used one another for personal gain and even here beyond Amraphel's kingdom, one never knew where loyalties were tied.

"I'm sorry," Shem said.

Japheth put a stuffed grape leaf in his mouth and wiped the oily dribble from his lips. "You don't have to say it again, Shem. And Denah's right. Eat up, even if you don't feel like it. We needed to make the decision when to pull away from the group and now it is decided for us. If we go before the road splits, no one will know for sure which route we've taken."

Over his brother's shoulder, Shem caught the eye of the leader as he poured himself another mug of beer. It was expected that each person pay generously for the drink, prepared by the locals, an added bonus for the men providing their protection. Shem paid his share but drank little. He could not afford the luxury of the deep sleep it induced. The other men of the caravan didn't appear inhibited, fortunately, and as long as the rowdiness stayed friendly this evening, it would make their exit easier at the first hint of morning.

The man looked away after his drink frothed over the top. He took a few steps toward them then turned and went back to a game of some sort. Shem exhaled in relief.

"You think they'll just let us ride out, alone? Won't we look suspicious?" Denah asked.

"Two old men and a woman? I don't foresee a problem. We only have minimal provisions for them to search if they think we're stealing from the others. We aren't doing anything wrong, remember. We're allowed to leave." Shem forced himself to eat the savory meat. Their own provisions wouldn't last indefinitely.

"There are cities all over this region. No one will know for sure where we went. Of course, Amraphel knows Abram's camp is near the Sea of Salt. It wouldn't be too hard to connect us to him." Japheth licked sticky pomegranate sauce from his fingers. "But no one in this caravan will know at least."

Shem waited until they were finished eating to draw out a map in a patch of sand. He made sure the other two knew the terrain as well as he did, just in case. Hebron was just south, and they would stay near the King's Highway as long as they could before veering off to the west. The caravan would take the same route until the split, so they needed a head start. Traveling alone would be faster than with the large group, but for safety they couldn't be on the open road any longer. They would follow its path from a distance.

As the sun dipped below the earth, they organized their belongings and attempted to find a few hours of sleep. The oasis remained alive for hours, laughter and splashing in the river reverberating into the star pocked canopy over head. Shem couldn't relax his mind at all, giving up after a while. He sat on a stone and waited for the dark deep quiet of the camp, when the sun was still hidden and the men were lost in the midst of their dreams. There he waited, and prayed. When he could stand it no more, he got up to wake his brother.

Japheth was already awake, sitting with Denah, sandals tied and possessions bundled. They rose when they saw him and prepared the donkeys in silence. It was a simple matter, leading the beasts from the river, between the slumbering groups toward the check point by the road. The first strokes of light were brightening the sky but the late night revelry ensured an exit without a fuss of farewells.

Japheth and Denah led the way, leading three of their donkeys. They hoped Denah's smile would assure the men everything was alright. Besides, his brother was better than him at coming up with answers to probing questions in case it came to that. Shem followed, the three other beasts trailing behind on lead ropes.

The guards sat beneath a stand of trees at the only place along the road not protected by a stone fence. They were drowsy and barely acknowledged Japheth and Denah as the packs were inspected briefly. Theft inside the oasis wasn't really their concern. They kept bandits out in the night and had received their payment. Leaving customers made room for more.

The grasses behind them rustled. A meaty hand gripped Shem's elbow.

"Leaving so soon?" Squinty, bloodshot eyes looked into his face.

Shem cleared his throat and put on an easy smile. "We, yes. We'll be on our own way from here." The man didn't release Shem's arm. His foul breath filled the air between them. "Thank you for allowing us to join your group."

Time crept slowly as the man peered into Shem's face, his eyes periodically looking at the turban covering his forehead. When he finally let go, he nodded and stepped back. "Well, then. Safe journey to you."

Shem nodded his head in a brief bow of gratitude, then followed Japheth to the road, his heart beating strongly. He glanced back as he mounted. The man stood by the entry gate, arms crossed over his chest.

"Watch out for giants," the man said.

♥

The main house was a large rectangle. Off either side, a long hall of rooms had been added on, one for Okpara's male servants and one for the females. These rooms were for the household help. The field hands and guards had quarters in another portion of the large estate. There were fields to the east and storage barns and stables on the west, and a winepress, and a whole array of buildings for purposes Eran could no longer track. She tried to pay attention as the servant woman led her through the halls describing her Master's ventures, but gave up and focused on keeping pace behind her.

She was taken to a small room, furnished with a bedroll and little else. A long curtain covered the window. Eran pulled it back. The women's annex faced a garden courtyard. Not a sculpted formal affair, but one with vegetables and herbs among the flowers, and pathways circling around the various beds. It was peaceful, and unexpected. She let out a tired sigh.

The woman still stood at the door. She had a hard face and had yet to ask Eran anything or even give her own name. She pointed at the chamber pot on the window ledge.

"There are no rooms for such necessities in the annex." The woman had an impatient tone. "I collect the pots early in the day. Don't put yours outside the door after I've gone. And don't dump anything in the garden. If it needs emptied after my rounds, you do it yourself and I'll show you where later."

Eran nodded, not sure she should speak. The woman was young, twenty or so years old, yet bore the facial coldness of someone much older, one who had seen her share of misfortune. Her fair skin contrasted with rich chestnut waves of hair, the shoulder length locks held back by a band over her forehead. She wore a simple shin length tunic, white as Okpara's had been. Her eyes had the same black outline, narrowed to parallel lines as she spoke.

"For now, you don't leave your room unless you have permission, and you don't. You'll earn it when we see that you are compliant with your duties." The woman walked past her and lifted the lid on a plain wooden chest. "Here are some clothes." A faint odor followed the woman, one of things old and soiled. Eran made sure her face didn't reveal the revulsion.

The tunics she pulled out were white, short sleeved, mid-calf length. "I can find smaller ones if these are too loose," she said, tossing them on the trunk. "I'll see that food is delivered, then show you where to bathe."

The woman turned to leave.

"Wait." Eran found her voice. Her mind was foggy from the journey and for all the information she wanted to know, she could think of nothing specific to ask.

"Well?"

The brusque tone made Eran cringe. She needed a friend in her new home. "What are you named?" she asked.

The servant paused. "Malina." With that, she left and closed the door behind her.

Eran leaned onto the window ledge, resting her forehead against the ornate grill. Beyond the comfort of the gardens, a high wall rose around the property, thick enough for guards to hold post on top. She turned and eased down onto the pallet. Once again she was a prisoner, once again, alone. This time in the land of Canaan. "God, don't leave me,' she prayed.

Chapter Nineteen

Eran woke to the sound of a rooster crowing, a familiar and comforting sound. Roosters kept a regular vigil around the Hebrew camp and the morning call was as sure as the sunrise itself. Only on the ark had they been an annoyance. The torrential rains obscured the light of morning inside the vessel and the poor thing they brought along knew he was supposed to crow, just not when, so he crowed whenever he decided it was crowing time. And that was every few hours for the first week, until he found his routine like the rest of them.

It was a gift to hear his announcement of another day. Eran sighed and tried to find good in her situation. She was alive, not bound in a prison cell, not injured. Her joints ached from the inside, but this was nothing new. She wasn't suffering unbearably. Not physically anyway. Her heart ached for home, for Shem, always there to help her rise with the rooster's call.

Using the wall for support, she got to her feet. Not knowing what the day held, she changed from a sleeping sheath to one of the draping white garments, then put on her sandals that had been cleaned and repaired while she had bathed. She had nothing for her hair so ran her fingers through it and left it down.

A rattle down the hall grew louder and closer. Remembering the chamber pot, Eran opened her door to set it outside. A man stood there, dressed in the short tunic of a guard, a sheathed dagger strapped to his waist. His strong arms were crossed loosely, and he looked her over without a change in expression. His blond curls were cropped at his shoulders and he bore the same proud jaw line, locked in defiance, as she had seen on Malina the night before.

"Oh," she said, feeling the heat climb her neck as he looked at her hands. She set the pot down and faced him. "I'm Eran."

He nodded curtly, turning from her toward the source of the rattle. Malina pulled a low, walled wagon behind her. It contained two squat vessels with wide mouths. He and the woman made brief eye contact before he turned his face away. She stopped the cart by the door, took Eran's pot and emptied it into one of her vessels. Then she dunked it into the other one, filled with water, and sloshed it about before drying it off with a towel and placing it back on the floor.

All this Malina did without looking at Eran. The resentment on her face was as ripe as the load she hauled.

"Follow me," she said.

Eran walked behind her down the hall. Malina stopped at every room and cleaned pots, speaking to no one. The guards turned from her cart, turned from her, as if she had a contagion they would catch by showing her kindness. The woman was anything but gracious herself yet Eran felt a twinge of compassion. Before the Great Flood, she had been mocked and shunned because of Noah and his unwanted preaching, and the memories of it still caught at her heart. They were days of self doubt.

In her younger years, Eran would have put a wall between herself and Malina, a means of protection from the animosity. She had clung to those who showed her kindness and avoided all others. It was simpler then, to be what others needed, did what they expected in order to have a place of security. She had lived too many years for that sort of nonsense now. She would not allow herself to be mired down with Malina's negativity. The woman she followed needed a compassionate ear as much as Eran did.

Malina showed her where to take her own pot to empty, and where the food was delivered in the women's annex, once she was permitted to leave her room without an escort. There was a large open space where the younger girls lived together with their tutors, and private quarters for bathing. The long row of rooms ended at a door. Malina pointed back down the hall. "You have to go back now. You can't come out here."

"Does it lead to the garden?" she asked.

"No. It goes to the dump. It's guarded all the time so don't think about trying to escape."

Eran traced their steps back to her room, aware for the first time that her guard had been following at a distance. Escape? Where would she go?

♥

Okpara came to her room mid-morning. He wore the same white fabric it seemed everyone in the household wore, only his had purple trim along the bottom edge and on the swath that wrapped over one shoulder. His ears had gold rings this morning, and there was a jeweled snake coiled on his upper arm. Both eyes had a thin black line of kohl that extended outward at the corner.

"So Tolo bought me a Healer from over by the Tigris River. It was a surprise, but the man knows his business and I trust you can be beneficial to my household. The latest physician didn't work out as I hoped. You may have knowledge of illnesses no one in Zoar seems to understand."

"I'm not trained except by time and experience, Master Okpara."

"Nevertheless, you appear to have had plenty of both. How old are you?"

Eran hesitated, winding her fingers together. She did not want to be worshiped again. Nor did she want to lie. "Over five centuries now. Halfway to the sixth one, but I assure you I am only mortal. I have no life extending powers and I will die and turn to dust as all the rest."

Okpara smiled. "Not too soon, I hope. I've just obtained you."

Eran relaxed her hands. "No. I'm not quite that old yet."

"Good. I've heard about you old ones. Didn't know there were any left. A shame you don't have any secrets to share that I could utilize for myself. That's a shame, yes. I'd like to live five or six centuries. Of course-"

Okpara stopped himself. Eran waited for him to continue. He had a sadness to his face for a moment, then it was gone. "About your responsibilities. You will train girls whom I've chosen to assist you. As you said, you will die, and I want to have ones to take your place and learn these skills Tolo believes you possess."

"I understand."

"And you will tend to my daughter. She has bouts of illness. None of my physicians can make them go away. See that you figure it out."

Eran swallowed hard.

"You can leave your room in the daytime. Only to the garden and in the women's wing. Not beyond. The guard, Rez-Nahor, must always accompany you. Understand?"

Eran nodded, her mind already curious what illness his

daughter had, and what would be the consequences if she got worse under Eran's care.

♥

Shem examined the size of the footprints in the dried earth near the brook. He could fit his own foot entirely inside them with ample room. He shivered and stepped back into the foliage, hoping his thumping heart couldn't be heard by anyone nearby. They were in Amorite territory. They were a tall tribe, getting taller by some accounts, and a mean tribe, getting meaner. If anyone referred to giants in the land, it was usually a reference to Amori's descendants.

He hadn't seen Amori in years, didn't know if this grandson of Ham's was still alive even. He hoped so, in case they were seen, or detained, or worse. They were on friendly terms when they knew one another in Shinar, and had parted so. The old connection might grant them favor.

Shem checked the wrap on his head. It would not bode well if the Amorites saw the seal. Nimrod and Amori were first cousins. Shem didn't want to test all the cords of family loyalty if he didn't have to.

Picking his way through the trees, he stopped behind the last one before it met the open trail. Jiggling a branch to signal his return, he waited for the bird call from his brother, the signal that the trail was clear, then quickly climbed up among the rocks to where Japheth and Denah were hidden.

They rocky outcropping above the trail was sufficient to conceal them and the beasts, and from there, they could see it as well as the valley ahead. It was a routine they developed, finding high points to see what came next so they could plan a route to negotiate in order to remain safe and find water. Four days on their own, they had avoided unwelcome contact.

The trail they followed paralleled the road, which followed the western coast line of the Sea. Both showed more and more evidence of recent wear and from their vantage point, they could see a community of some sort in the valley below. It was situated in a protected cove of cliffs to one side, the road along the Sea to the other. They would have to skirt the area by scrambling over the rocky terrain above the village, keeping behind rocks to avoid detection.

"Is it safe to take the animals to the stream?" Japheth handed him a skin of water, nearly empty.

"If we take them one at a time, I think we'll be alright. We can fill the skins while they drink." He opted not to mention the footprints in front of Denah.

Denah frowned "That will take awhile. It's nearly sunset."

Japheth squeezed her hand. "We're here for the night. The cliffs are too steep to attempt in the dark. And the road is too exposed, day or night. I couldn't find an alternate route. We have to wait until morning to move on."

"I'd rather not be near this place."

Shem agreed but they had no choice. "We're safe up here. No one can sneak up on us."

Japheth stood and untied a donkey. "I'll take the first one then."

Shem hesitated. Denah was already anxious, and he hated to add fuel to her fear of the Amorites. Ancient Nephilim blood coursed thorough their veins, and she'd had her taste of their kind before. Enough for a lifetime, even a long one such as hers. "Be careful," he said to his brother, catching his eye.

Japheth nodded, understanding the unspoken details.

Denah sat so she could watch the homes below. Shem sat next to her and did the same, peering between large boulders. Built of stacked stone, they were simple and not of an unusual height, that he could tell. There were enclosures for livestock and barrels for water and tools strewn about. It was a not a warring community, and in fact had a peaceful nature to it. If they were traveling anywhere else, he might have ventured in and asked for shelter. He wouldn't of course, willingly trading a bed of fresh straw for the stones beneath his head.

So far, they had seen no one, but the crops were thriving in tidy rows and a few garments were strung up on a line in the nearest house. It was inhabited for sure.

The cool of evening was descending. Shem handed Denah a cloak then stood to look again up and down the trail below them. Japheth had to cross it to reach them, the tree line hiding him only to a point before the land had only low brush for coverage. He had only a short hike up the hill to the rocks, but once he left the trees, he was visible to anyone rounding the last bend in the trail.

There were empty sheep folds in the valley, and that meant there were shepherds who could return at any time.

Shem caught his breath, hearing the low rumble of hooves before seeing the small flock and the men who followed. His eyes immediately turned to the point where his brother would emerge. There was a slight movement of the underbrush.

Hands gripped his tunic and pulled him down. "Duck Shem. They'll see you." Denah pulled away from the crevice and covered herself with her cloak, her lips praying constantly. Shem did the same, masking his scent beneath the dirty garment. From there all he could do was listen to the bleating of the animals as they passed, and the conversation of the men. It was light, jovial, and in a few minutes dissipated down the trail to the village below.

Peeling back the cloak, he looked for his brother. Denah's face was pressed into the stone, searching as well. A low branch trembled. Shem checked the path again before providing the sign that all was clear, whistling like a hoopoe, three sets of three calls. Japheth's face appeared amidst the foliage.

Denah's arms were around her husband as soon as he got back. "You saw them?"

He nodded. "Yes. Tall, but I wouldn't call them giants. We'll be secure here for the night. They didn't see us and fortunately there were no dogs to come sniffing around."

His brother's voice was calm but Shem wasn't fooled, and either was Denah. She ran her fingers on his temple, over the pulse beating out a fast rhythm.

"My turn, then," Shem said, picking up another of the empty skins and untying one donkey. Locals nearby or not, they had to have water.

Chapter Twenty

Malina led Eran to the open doorway of a large room on the upper floor. The room was ornately furnished with carved chairs and tables, thick rugs, colorful tapestries and a bed with columns on the corners reaching nearly to the ceiling. A woman reclined on a couch, blankets draped across her lap despite the warm day. She beckoned for them to enter.

Malina went in first and bowed slightly before crossing the room. Eran followed her example, tipping her head in deference to Khepri, Okpara's only daughter.

"So this is Eran, my newest Healer," she said. Her smooth voice was tired, as if she had already talked the entire day and had little wind left. She scanned Eran's appearance. "You are old. Old and wise, Father says. He hopes you know more than all the others who have failed to help me."

She was young, perhaps twenty years old, with sleek, raven colored hair that hung below her chin in dozens of tiny braids. Her slim body was covered in a white tunic, gemstone jewelry on both upper arms and circling her throat. Eyes green as emeralds were centered in thick frames of black kohl, a darkness beneath them that paints couldn't conceal.

"I offer my abilities. I trust I can help."

"What have you been told about me?"

"Nothing, except you have an illness that comes and goes."

Khepri sighed. "Every time, I have to repeat it. I wish Father would let one Healer speak to the next before he-" She stopped herself, her hand covering her lips for a moment. Her eyes flashed to Malina then darted away just as quickly.

Before he what? What happened to the last Healers?

"Before they left our employment. Anyhow," the woman continued. "I'm not always ill. It comes in bouts, every few weeks. I lose my appetite and strength, and have to be in bed for days before I feel better again. Baniti, my intended husband, and of course my father, expect you find a solution. They are anxious for the wedding and an heir."

"When did the episodes begin?"

"A few years ago."

"Had anything changed around then? The foods you eat, perhaps?"

"No. All the physicians ask me that. They tested me with everything, saying it was too much meat or not enough fish or some spice I couldn't handle. Nothing made a difference. It isn't foods making me ill. And you'll have to ask Malina what potions worked and what didn't. I lost track."

Malina stared at the far wall, avoiding Eran's gaze. Her skin was freshly scrubbed, her hair curling into tight ringlets from the washing it received, her clothing fresh. The odor was gone, for Khepri's benefit no doubt. She was pretty, except for the scowl, the muscles around her jaw tensed and not willing to share any information.

"Tell me about the bouts," Eran said to Khepri. "How do they start?"

Khepri huffed and rolled her eyes. "You tell her Malina. I'm tired of repeating it."

Malina focused her attention on her Mistress as she spoke. "She gets tired more easily at first, and has stomach pains but doesn't throw up her food. Headaches are common, and, sometimes, her mood changes."

Khepri's head snapped toward Malina. "So? I'm sure you aren't so pleasant when you feel terrible."

Malina pressed her lips together.

"What else, Malina?" Eran asked.

She shook her head. "That's all I know. I'm not a Healer."

Eran pulled a list of ailments into her head and sorted through them quickly, discarding most, leaving a vague list of potential others. None stood out as an obvious culprit. She needed more information, but Khepri was obviously tiring of the questions and Malina wasn't eager to share. Eran asked the last, critical one. "Are the bouts always the same, or are they getting worse?"

Khepri turned toward an exquisite tapestry depicting a pyramid, an enormous structure in the land of Ham's son, Mizraim. Egypt, it was called now. "Worse," she said. "I'm getting sicker."

♥

The oasis at En-gedi was an emerald in its setting of stone. Fountains of life preserving water poured from the limestone cliffs into deep pools, nourishing palms and vines, feeding flowers and birds, both arrayed in brilliant hues. It also fed vineyards and orchards, herds of beasts and tribes of local residents. Numerous Canaanite families held reign in the sanctuary, each more eager than the next to offer safe rest and fine cuisine.

Denah, Japheth, and Shem weren't the only travelers, the

caravansaries bustled with foreigners and no one questioned where they were from or where they were going. After inspecting their options, they chose to remain on the outskirts, opting for solitude, away from the cooling waters. There was no specific reason to avoid the paradise except Denah felt as if they were being watched with more scrutiny than any of the others, possibly being followed. Neither Shem or Japheth noticed, and they hoped it was paranoia on her part. They wouldn't risk it being otherwise, however.

Japheth released a tired sigh. "What I wouldn't do for a dive under that waterfall."

"It's beautiful," Denah said, "I'm sorry I feel uneasy about being in the throng."

"I trust your intuition. Still, I'd like to stay awhile, maybe sneak in after dark. Cool grass, fruit from the vine, sweet milk."

Shem chuckled. "Knife to the throat."

"Good possibility." His brother chewed on a slice of dried goat, the last of their supplies. After today, food had to be captured or gleaned or purchased.

Shem sat cross-legged beneath a palm on the far skirts of the lush land they admired. The oasis was on the western shore of the sea, halfway down the great body of water. According to the map he had memorized, the region of Hebron lay due west.

He looked that direction, toward the roll of hills leaving the oasis and fanning out to the right and left. It was good pasture land, fertile and spacious. He could see why Abram made the region his home. There was plenty of room to spread your tents and not tread on neighboring camps. Plenty of space to worship the god of your own choosing, too. He hoped Abram sought favor from only the One God, prayed he had not fallen away as so many had done already.

Japheth interrupted his thoughts. "I think we should follow

one of the streams up into the hills. Last I knew, young Abram was doing well, and large herds need large pastures and plenty of water. Let's go look for the sheep. They'll take us to Abram and Sarai."

Shem tossed a twig at his brother. "Yes, my wise brother. Good plan. With one addition. Let's offer sacrifice when we camp tonight. Let's worship the God who has brought us this far and seek his continued favor."

The seventh day ritual was overdue. It would be nice to relax for a full day of remembering, a day without hiding or traveling. He knew they couldn't, not with the dwindling resources and the possibility of being stopped and questioned by the local tribes. They had to continue, another day's journey in the long string they had already done.

Five weeks now since they left the camp? Six?

More than two months without Eran. If Denah and Japheth doubted she was here, somewhere, in Canaan, they didn't speak of it. Both spoke as if she were alive and that they would all be united soon. Shem didn't mind, knowing it wasn't his heart alone they protected. The four of them were as close as any brothers and sisters. They were friends of the truest type.

Before the Flood, it hadn't been so tight. Denah struggled to find her place within Noah and Jael's household, grasping to the ways of her family and not understanding the truth of the One God. And Eran was reserved under Jael's protective care, not reaching out in friendship to Denah for fear of Jael's disapproval. That all changed when the waters rose, however. When everyone and everything was gone. Eran, Denah and Naomi tied cords of sisterhood that would never unravel.

Denah's soul grieved without Naomi, and now without Eran. She tried not to show it, but he could see her eyes tear up as they rode sometimes, her mind remembering, hoping, praying for the sisters of her heart.

Denah turned his way and caught him staring. No tears this time. She smiled and clapped her hands together, as if suddenly making a discovery. "What if Eran is with Abram?"

His God could do a miracle like that. Shem smiled back. "It would be a blessing beyond my dreams." It would give him the opportunity to tell her he was sorry, that he chose God over her. He had to. He had to honor the God of his fathers, above all else. But it cut his heart to do so and although it was the right decision, part of him died when he did. He needed her to know that. He would ask God again to give him the chance, even if it was on his deathbed.

♥

The rabbit kicked and squirmed in Japheth's grasp. He held it by the ears for a minute then set it down, allowing it to dart off into the brush. Someone, or something else could have it for supper. They couldn't afford to light a fire, a beacon to the surrounding hills announcing their presence. The terrain was too open, no caves nearby to conceal the smoke. A sacrifice to their God would have to wait. None was better than one of grains and berries. Adam's son Cain tried that once and it didn't end well.

Shem ran his finger over the scar on his forehead. No one knew for certain how God marked Cain after he killed his brother. It was one of those facts everyone knows in a generation, then is forgotten. He wondered if it looked at all like the mark of Amraphel.

"Nice catch anyhow, Japheth," Shem said. "You were looking mighty spry for someone your age." He picked through the handful of berries he held, tossing the wormy ones to the side.

Japheth flopped onto the cool ground, punching Shem's arm before stretching out with his hands linked under his head. The sky was covered in stars, the moon bright enough to light up the land around them. From their perch on top of a grassy hill, the earth rose and swelled gently in all directions, flattening out here and there into plains of pasture land before rising again. Shem inhaled the sweet air, feeling a peacefulness for the first time in weeks.

"What is it about this place?" he said. "I feel, feel-"

"At ease?" Japheth chewed on a piece of grass as he watched the majestic canopy. "Like we're meant to be here, at this time, this place?"

"Yes. That's it., isn't it? God's covering is here. We walked an entire day without threat of beast or man. We were protected today."

"I'm encouraged by the vacated pastures we passed. The scat wasn't all that old. Sheep and goats have been here."

"I pray they are Abram's. Amorites live in these hills too."

Japheth was quiet for a moment. Denah mentioned several times she felt as if they were being watched, like at the oasis, although neither man had seen anything when they searched. They would sleep beneath coverings of brush and alternate staying awake to listen to the night sounds anyhow.

"If Ham came through here, I think he would be tempted to stay." Japheth spit out the grass and plucked another.

"You don't think he would settle in one of the cities? He always liked the bustle of activity. And where would Naomi find babies to deliver? She'll never get midwifery from her soul."

"Perhaps she is midwife for her husband's herd of goats these days."

"He was restless at Eber's camp. Even before Father died. He got older like we did though, so maybe you're right, maybe he sought a shepherd's life." Shem turned to his brother. "Do you think they're alive?"

Japheth kept his gaze but said nothing.

Shem broke the look, craning his head to look far, far above into the endless sea of lights. They would never know what became of their baby brother. He knew it and yet couldn't quite let it be finalized in his soul. Would Eran's whereabouts be the same? There were dozens of cities on the caravan route, dozens more in the surrounding territory, not to mention the lands beyond Canaan. Traders bought goods here and took them back to their homes in Ethiopia, Egypt, and lands he couldn't pronounce. Phoenician traders loaded cargo onto ships and sailed away to lands he would never see. She could be anywhere.

Would he ever know? Would he always wonder? Always look at each and every face he passed, in case she was there, looking for him in return? Would he forever question his own actions before the King?

Shem dropped his head onto his knees. The impossibility of his quest rising like flood waters, hope sinking like an anchor into depths far beyond his reach. Amraphel wanted to hurt him in his game of vengeance, and he had beaten Shem soundly.

Chapter Twenty-one

Japheth peered into the shadows. "I expected her back by now." There was fear in his voice.

Denah found a pool in the stream, one deep enough to bathe in, and was eager for a plunge beneath the bright night sky. The chance to be refreshed out-weighed her suspicions that they weren't alone, and Japheth reassured her that it was safe. They had seen and heard no one. The stream wasn't far from their makeshift camp, and the men could hear her if she called out.

But his brother was right. She wouldn't dawdle, knowing they would worry.

"Let's go together," Shem said. It was better to go to her than to call out and reveal themselves.

The uneventful day had lowered his defenses. Shem wanted to kick himself in agitation. Why had they let her go? He grabbed a spear and made certain a knife was secured in his belt.

Foliage rustled in the direction they were heading. Shem and Japheth froze.

Denah emerged.

She wasn't alone.

♥

The enclosed garden was a rectangular space divided by curving pathways that led to gazebos and circled fountains and intersected vibrant flower beds. Herbs, vegetables, fruits, and plants she had never seen were set within the manicured arrangement. Carved statues guarded the walkways throughout, some Eran recognized as Canaanite gods and others were new, ones with human bodies below the heads of animals. Eran shivered as she passed the lifeless eyes, the beauty of the surroundings marred by the odd creatures. Most were draped in dried wreaths of flowers and the ashes of incense covered their feet. Or hooves, or talons, as it were. The garden of Okpara was a shrine of many idols.

Malina stopped in front of one of the images, a woman with arms crossed over her chest, a staff in one hand and a sistrum in the other. The thin garment carved over her body concealed nothing. Her head, that of a cat, stared blankly at the western sky.

"She looks to her homeland." Malina's perpetual scowl softened as she gazed up at the feline woman.

"Where?" Eran asked. "Where are these creatures from?"

Malina's eyebrows raised. "Egypt, of course. You didn't know that?"

Eran felt her face redden. "No." The woman was taller than she was, and looked down her nose as if Eran was a child. Her tone was meant to be insulting. Eran took a calming breath before she continued. "I've never been there and only have heard about it from others who have traveled."

"Okpara's household is from the land of the Nile River."

Egypt was beyond the desert, where Canaan's son Mizraim settled. It was a great kingdom, rich in trade, rich in manpower.

The pyramids there were a testament to their strength as a people, and their loyalty to the rulers. Constructed for the burial of their Pharaohs, the massive tombs held the blood of many dedicated workmen. The catacombs were stocked with wealth beyond imagination for use in the next life, the ruler's body preserved somehow, so he wouldn't return to the dust of man's beginnings.

They were nothing like the simple stack of stones covering Noah. The truly great father of them all wanted nothing more than to disintegrate back into the earth. Eran felt the pang in her heart. Was Jael with him now?

"Why is he here, in Zoar?"

"The trade business is good. He's wealthy, getting Egyptian goods for the East and the eastern goods for Egypt. His wife was Amorite."

"Was?"

Malina turned abruptly from the statue. "She's dead." The sharpness of the response ended the conversation.

Eran trotted to keep up with the woman's strides. It was the most Malina had spoken, and all she said until they reached the gazebo, nestled among a bed of herbs. Three young girls immediately stopped their giggling and sat erect on a bench as they approached.

Malina smacked her hands together once to gain their complete attention. The girls looked to be about ten years old. All wore the simple white garment and the band over their foreheads, holding back sleek black hair. Dark eyes watched Malina with apprehension.

"This is Eran. Your new tutor." That was it for an introduction. She walked to the back of the gazebo and leaned against a post, arms crossed.

Eran looked at the girls. She had been teaching what she knew of healing for generations, demonstrating and explaining with every ailment and injury to those in the camp so the skills would continue after she left the earth. Never had she started from scratch, as if a handful of lessons could teach these girls a head-full of knowledge.

"Well," she said. "Let's start with your names."

None of the girls moved, sitting straight with hands folded in their laps, eyes wide and expectant. She looked to Malina. Did they not understand her? The woman offered nothing.

"Do you understand me?" Eran looked at the first girl.

She nodded once.

"What is your name?"

"Hehet, Mistress." The girl's voice quivered.

"Hehet." Eran smiled at her. "I've never heard that name. What does it mean?"

"Goddess of immeasurable, Mistress."

"Oh." She intentionally kept the smile in place. "Are you from Egypt, then?"

"Yes, Mistress."

Eran swallowed hard. Were these taken children? Stolen from their homes to serve in another man's dwelling? Already she wanted to draw them in under a protective wing, ease their fears and send them home to their grieving families.

"Are your parents in Egypt?"

"No, Mistress."

"Where are they?"

Hehet looked confused. "In the field, working, Mistress."

Eran relaxed her shoulders. She turned to the next girl. They had obviously been trained not to speak unless directly spoken to. "Your name, and its meaning?"

"Keket. Goddess of the darkness."

"And yours?"

"Maat. Goddess of justice."

"Are you sisters?" None of the girls answered. Eran looked into Hehet's eyes.

"No, Mistress," she said.

"Their parents were brought from their homeland to work the fields." Malina walked back to the front. "Along with many of Master Okpara's hands. These girls were chosen to learn the skills of a Healer. They are fortunate to be given such an honor. And they need to remember that many others would gladly take their place if they demonstrate laziness or disrespect."

The girls grew rigid on the bench as she spoke, their eyes following her as she moved.

"They are here every morning for instructions, then return to their quarters for tutoring in language and such, after you are finished with them. They have no other duties than to learn."

They reminded Eran of lilies in the fields, white and pure, meant to be cherished and protected from damage, not crushed beneath the feet of the adults whom they served.

They were hers now. Little minds and hearts to love and protect. Precious ones to nourish and train. Eran felt the deep spring of satisfaction bubbling up and spilling over at her assignment. She lost her home and family, and Shem, the man of her heart. But God followed her to the pagan land. He gave her purpose in the land of Canaan.

Lilies. That's what she would call them. Her little Lilies.

♥

A dozen men poured from the foliage behind Denah.

Shem gripped his weapon and widened his stance, his mind

grasping for a solution against the uneven odds. Japheth adopted the same posture. They were in trouble, his heart rate acknowledging the immediate threat.

Denah was dressed, and appeared to be uninjured. She didn't bolt away from the men, though they all walked at a slow pace, plodding up the hill, not rushing with a fury of weapons. He heard his brother exhale. As they grew closer, he realized his sister-in-law was smiling. She held the arm of one of the men, pulling him forward.

"It's him, Japheth! Shem, it's Abram!"

Shem lowered his spear and stepped up to the man to see his face more clearly in the lights of the night. Abram was past middle age for his generation, though only ninety or a hundred some years old. His weathered face had a full beard, still chestnut colored and curly, circling his wide grin. The same laughing eyes that Shem remembered looked back at him.

Abram slapped him on the shoulder then pulled him into a strong armed embrace. "Father Shem. I can't believe it's really you! My household is honored by your presence. We've been anxious for your arrival, the waiting has seemed endless."

"Waiting? For us?" Shem cupped the man's face briefly, days of anxiety slipping away as he looked into the kind eyes of his young relative.

Abram laughed. "For three visitors, yes. The hills have eyes. My men saw you a few days back, and followed you to the oasis. They wanted to speak with you there but lost you in the crowd. 'Two men and a woman, all old like leather skins left in the sun,' they said. They kept watch as you came this way. I never imagined it was you! When I saw Denah at the stream, oh the joy! I'm so happy to see you."

Japheth took his turn in Abram's arms, then Denah linked her arm through his again.

"My tents are close. Two more hills and you would have seen our lamplight. I couldn't wait 'til morning. I wanted to see for myself who ventured unprotected in these parts, and now that I know, my mind is whirling with questions."

"It's been an interesting few months getting here." Japheth started but Abram held up his hand and stopped him.

"Father Japheth, if you tell me now you'll just have to repeat yourself word for word when you see my Sarai. Come, I'll let you get a good night's sleep and tomorrow we'll talk."

Shem collected the donkeys and handed the reins to one of Abram's men.

"It will need to be an easy walk," Abram said. "My men, myself, we are not yet healed from a bit of necessary surgery." His grin was as bright as the moon. "Another good story to tell tomorrow." He laughed at his own words, his men with him.

Japheth looked at Shem and shrugged as they walked beneath the clear sky to an encampment of tents with the peaceful sounds of the night surrounding them. Shem was full of questions himself, yet grateful for the quiet time, grateful to allow all sense of leadership and responsibility fall onto the shoulders of the younger man. It would be a deep slumber, he was sure. He looked up to find his brother looking back at him.

"God is good," he said.

Shem nodded. "God is indeed good."

Chapter Twenty-two

The tent was dark when Shem awoke. He stayed where he was, pulling soft hides beneath his chin and stretching into the pillowed bedroll beneath him. The dark goat hair tent kept the light out and he had no idea how long he had been sleeping. Was it still night? He didn't really care to get up and find out. He was comfortable. No stone pillows or snapping twigs to investigate. No beasts or predators of the human sort. He sighed in contentment. For the first time in weeks, he felt rested.

He luxuriated for a while longer then pulled himself from the stack of pillows. He wouldn't fall asleep again. Curiosity filled his head with so many questions about Abram and his camp that he was ready to be among them. That, and his belly growled for something fresh and filling.

He lifted the tent flap and peeked outside, surprised by the brightness. The camp was buzzing with the full activity of day, the sun midway up the horizon already. He had slept many hours.

Beside the bedroll he found fresh water and clean garments. As soon as he was dressed he stepped outside. A woman squealed and he found himself in the clutches of Sarai. Her intense brown eyes watered and she choked as she tried to speak.

Shem pulled her into his chest and kissed the top of her head. "Sarai. My dear Sarai. Thank you for your hospitality. I slept like a king."

"Father Shem. I can't believe you're here. My husband told me last night we had guests, but he wouldn't tell me who until this morning. He knew I wouldn't sleep, and wouldn't allow you any either. I never thought I'd see you again. The Lord has blessed me. Again and again and again." Her eyes sparkled with life.

Sarai took his arm and gave him a quick tour. There were many tents in Abram's camp, and many people in all shades of color. And height. They were friendly with the local Amorites, Sarai explained, and with any of the tribes showing peace rather than hostility. All the adult men walked as if they were bare footed on sharp stones, he noticed, while the women moved about freely.

Abram's wife didn't say if the peoples among them were allowed to worship their own gods, and he didn't ask. Not yet. He didn't want to spoil the visit, needing to find his own strength restored before adding another rip to his heart.

The hillside above and below them was terraced for crops and beyond them were pastures, and more tents, and more pastures beyond that. Laughter filtered into the breeze from every direction. There was no lack of food here, and no fear it seemed. Children ran freely among them, lots of them.

The little ones weren't Abram's. That much he learned from the man as they walked last night beneath the moon. Only one son from a handmaid existed. The nation Abram anticipated for the last few decades consisted of the one boy.

Shem dropped his arm over Sarai's strong shoulders. Her back was straight, her hair barely gray at the temples, and if she had aches and pains, she didn't show them. She also didn't have the sagging figure of a woman who had born many children. She was past the age for such things now, yet her joy was evident. Her demeanor was not one of a woman hounded by an empty womb, a grief ridden existence. Sarai had made peace with her situation.

"Indeed," Shem said. "God has blessed you and Abram."

Sarai's laughter sprang from a well of contentment, deep and assured. Her eyes held merriment at his response. "Oh, Father Shem. More so than you realize."

♥

"You're going to do *what* to that baby?" Denah's face was red, pinched into an expression that required no interpretation. Her muscles were tensed, ready to snatch the infant from his father's arms and flee into the hills. Japheth wrapped his arm around her, holding her back. His face was as drained of color as hers was filled with fire. Shem braced his arm on the nearest tree trunk, needing support as his mind absorbed what Abram intended to do with the sharp knife in his hand.

Abram set the weapon down and took Denah's hands. He explained the intended circumcision again, this time more slowly and with a large dose of tenderness, trying to ease her mind.

"It sounds barbaric, I know," Abram said. "Believe me, it was the Lord our God who gave us this sign, this marking as an agreement. I'll explain it all to you today, I promise. Trust me for now. This is part of my covenant with God himself. On the eighth day, our boys are sealed unto him. It is this little one's blessing, as much as he'll dislike the feeling for a moment, he will be God's forever. The entire camp has been circumcised already."

Shem surveyed the small gathering of people, unable to find any words. No one was protesting the ritual, the parents presenting the baby before the knife themselves. Those in the camp who could free themselves from chores had gathered in a circle around the sleeping newborn, supportive of Abram's rules for every male under his care.

Shem had an uneasy feeling all the same, and not just because the very thought of the surgery made his head swim. Egyptians practiced circumcision, and it had nothing to do with a command from the One God. Sarai's handmaid Hagar was from that land, and others in the camp. He couldn't help but wonder if the inspiration was truly of God or if Abram made his own rules under the influence of his people, and of the mother to his only son.

Japheth caught his eye, his brow raised in question. Should they intervene?

Shem shrugged in response. The painful incision wouldn't harm the child indefinitely. The boy wasn't to be sacrificed, the first thought that occurred to him when Sarai brought him to the gathering. Ultimately, it was Abram's camp, his decision on the matter. And for the moment, the only reason Shem could come up with for not continuing was the question of Abram's understanding of God. He would not probe the matter and disgrace the man publicly. He grit his teeth and turned toward Abram and the baby.

Abram searched Shem's face. "Father Shem?"

He nodded approval, still unable to draw words to his mouth, then gripped the tree and held his breath.

Their host continued with the procedure, words of blessing, and in minutes the squalling boy was back at his mother's breast. He, Denah and Japheth were led to a shaded grove where they sat, emotionally exhausted, waiting for Abram. Shem was more than ready to search the heart of this man, the seed of his own generations. He was eager for explanations.

"Why would God tell him to mutilate the children?" Denah leaned against a tree and sighed.

"All the men. Even the oldest among them were cut." Japheth winced at the thought.

Shem dropped his chin onto his tented fingers, elbows on knees. He questioned Abram thoroughly twenty-four, twenty-five years back, when God spoke to him. Abram was convinced God wanted him to leave the hill country of Haran and move his household to a foreign land. He came to his people, the Hebrew camp, full of enthusiasm and profound belief in the words he spoke. "I will make you into a great nation," God told him. "All the earth will be blessed through you."

Or so he believed. Shem didn't question Abram's sincerity. The man believed the words he spoke. But had he really heard the voice of the Creator? Or was it his father's voice he followed, and old dream reborn from the grief of Terah's death? Terah took his son Abram and daughter-in-law Sarai from the region of Ur with the intention of moving to Canaan originally. His poor health altered the plan, and they settled near Haran, near their relatives. Shem wondered then and wondered still if it was Terah's dream influencing Abram. Not God's.

The Hebrew camp accepted his decision to move away with sorrow, and with reservation. They felt Abram was meant to be the next leader of the Hebrews. Now he was leaving. If God spoke, Abram had to listen, of course. He had to pack up all he owned and follow the path God pointed to him.

Shem kept his doubts to himself. Who was he to question a man's call from God? He didn't want to be the nay-sayer. No one believed Noah, either. Time would prove Abram's beliefs true or unfounded. But a great nation? Unless many young wives were taken, Abram's own name would soon be forgotten.

But. God told Noah to build a land-locked ark. It was insane, yet it was true. Shem wouldn't condemn his relative outright, not knowing if indeed God had spoken and planned for great miracles. He wouldn't dare err on the side of doubting God's power. He did allow himself doubt as to Abram's motivations.

"Here I am at last," Abram said as he sat among them, along with several dozen others. Ishmael, his son, sat to his right. The twelve year old boy had bright inquisitive eyes like his father, his mother's good natured laugh, infectious in the camp. The beloved son craved the shadow of his father, Shem noticed. Listening and learning, training to lead what would be his to govern one day.

Sarai sat on Abram's left. Beautiful Sarai, a girl wanted by every available boy in Haran at one time. At ninety some years, she appeared half that age. There was no vanity in her that Shem had seen. Simple dress and simple ways, she radiated light when she smiled. Beside her was Hagar, Ishmael's mother. She had the raven hair of her native land, the delicate features of a woman born to high status. There was no face paint on her skin, though, no kohl lining her eyes as he had seen on the Egyptians in Nineveh and she wore the modest striped garments of Abram's camp.

When bowls of food were laid out, Abram smiled warmly at his guests. "Where to begin? Why don't I start, tell you what has occurred in my life over the last few decades. It will help you understand the procedure you just witnessed. Then you can share your story."

"Good. We'll eat while you talk," Shem said, his hand already reaching for a bowl of figs.

Abram gave an account of the years since he left Haran, skimming over parts, like the time spent in Egypt and the skirmish with Amraphel. Shem's hand immediately checked the position of the turban wrap at the mention of the King of Shinar. He hadn't yet discussed his sealed forehead with his host.

When Abram got to the part of his vision, before Ishmael was conceived, Shem forgot all about the bounty of provisions in front of him. He fed on Abram's words, thirsting for more. Like listening to Noah and the plans for the ark, God opened his ears and the doubts slipped away. Abram's message pierced his soul, anchoring it to an unshakable wall of truth.

"The Lord said my offspring would be as the stars in the heavens," the man said. "'Count them,' God said to me. 'So shall your offspring be.'" Abram's eyes filled with tears. He looked at Denah, then Japheth, then Shem, holding his gaze with vise-like intensity. "I believed the Lord, Father Shem. I knew, I just knew that his words would be fulfilled. In that moment, in spite of Sarah's dry womb, I believed what God promised."

Shem's heart pounded.

As Abram described the covenant vision, where he and the One God were sealed in a divine promise, the truth from his lips burned their own seal on Shem, a mark he could never scrub from his own conscious being. From the core of his soul, he knew the words to be the very breath of God, a breath of knowledge spoken for all generations.

God made a covenant with Abram, a lasting, unending commitment. Shem knew it was true. The pact couldn't be undone by anyone.

Chapter Twenty-three

Japheth's sobs equaled his in length and intensity. If anyone stepped back from emotion and demanded evidence, it was his older brother. The sound of his brokenness was reassuring to Shem, confirming they grasped truth together. The Hebrews would not all be scattered and destroyed. Their God would pull miracles from his storehouse and bless a remnant, through Abram and Sarai. There would be a nation. God's name would not be lost.

Their hope remained.

Finding composure after the unexpected torrent of emotions was difficult. He breathed in and out heavily as those around him gave pats on the back and squeezed his shoulder. Everyone had puffy eyes rimmed in red, even Abram. Noses were blowing and honking all around him.

"Abram," Shem started but had no words to say how he was feeling.

"It's Abraham now," he said and gave the new spelling. "And Sarah."

God inserted part of the spelling of his own name into theirs.

"When Father Noah blessed you the first time, Father Shem,

he said God would always live in your tents. As Japheth was blessed and his peoples grew and grew, still the Lord would remain with you. He would be your God."

Shem nodded. It had been a blessing of great consolation, one he would trade for no other.

Abraham continued. "He has confirmed this again. He has promised to be my God and the God of my children and my children's children. Everlasting, God Almighty will be ours."

"A covenant," Japheth said. "The circumcision is a sign of your covenant with God himself. No wonder you cut away with a smile on your lips."

"I'm sorry I fussed about it." Denah bit down on the edge of her lip.

"No need to feel sorry," Sarah said. "Making our little ones wail in pain is never easy. I think some of the mothers suffer worse than their sons."

Abraham chuckled and playfully rubbed Ishmael's head of thick black curls. "Yes. And there isn't much smiling yet for most of us. Babies heal and forget quicker than their fathers and older brothers."

"The Amorites and Egyptians among you were sealed in this way?"

"All the males in my camp, Japheth. By choice. I gave them the right to decide for themselves. Choose the One God and be sealed or choose to leave, without malice on my part. There are eight nations represented in my camp, all chose the knife, and now all feel the agony of it. It would be prime time to be invaded, eh? We would put up little fight at this point."

"God will protect us," Sarah said. "He has plans."

Abraham squeezed Sarah's hand, then lifted it to his lips for a tender kiss. "There's more to tell you." He spoke to them without taking his eyes from his wife.

More? How much more could there be? Shem already heard more than he could comprehend. He needed time to think it through.

"Sarah gave me Hagar to bear us a child. This fine young man was the result." He lifted Ishmael's hand, clasped in his own.

Shem could read the pride on the father's face, and the adoration in the son's. When Abraham let go, he reached across Sarah and placed his hand on Hagar's knee. "And the Lord confirmed in his mother more blessings on my camp. He told her that Ishmael would be the father of many, descendants too numerous to count."

So the boy would be the start of the great nation of God, then. Shem nodded, understanding, but Denah looked at Sarah with a puzzled expression.

Sarah's smile widened as she watched Denah's face. "Tell me what you're thinking."

Denah tapped her finger on her lips, then pointed it at Abraham's wife. "So, Ishmael will bear the name of the Hebrews and the One God? I thought, perhaps…"

Sarah waggled a finger back at Denah. Her eyes were bright. "Intuition," she said. "A gift from Mother Eve for womankind. You've perceived what I'm anxious to confirm in the weeks to come. God hears the echo in an empty womb. He hears, and he fills."

Abraham chuckled and nodded vigorously. "Ishmael's nations will not be the only ones carrying my blood."

Denah's eyes went to Sarah's flat belly, her eyes glistening again. "God has blessed you. Not only Hagar. After all these years, you have a child of your own."

"What!?" Japheth and Shem spoke together.

Abraham rose gingerly to his feet and lifted his hands to the heavens. His body couldn't express his feelings the way his face did. It was saturated in joy. Shem could easily imagine him dancing on the hilltops and turning cartwheels in another week or so.

"God gave me a son!" Abraham shouted the news. "Sarah carries a child of her own! At ninety years old, her womb will blossom with life!"

♥

Eran closed the door to her room and leaned against it rather than going immediately to the garden. Malina had to pass this way to join her there, and Eran intended to intercept, to walk with her, not behind her, and attempt conversation.

Malina's few words were sopped in disdain. She was brusque with the Lilies and cold to the guards. Of course, she had the task of the lowest slave, and wasn't permitted to bathe daily, so the odor followed her. Beyond the scowl and disinterest she portrayed, Eran knew she was embarrassed. What woman wouldn't be? But Eran wasn't her enemy.

The woman's status was a mystery. She moved freely within the household and even went outside the perimeter gates without an escort when she went to the dump site. She was trusted, and was a friend to Khepri. She monitored the women's annex and was apparently assigned to watch Eran during the lessons with the girls. And she emptied the pots. That piece didn't make sense.

Rez-Nahor, her guard, lifted his eyebrows but said nothing. He would be next on Eran's list. He said less to her than Malina. His words weren't laced in acid at least, and it was his position to be alert, not engaged in chatter. They stood silently, backs to the wall, listening to the slap of sandals on the floor as Malina

166 – Rachel S. Neal

approached.

The woman stopped in front of them and Eran smiled, forcing herself not to show queasiness on her face as the faint odor clouded around them. The woman's eyes danced off Eran and found the guard, and just perceptibly, he shrugged.

So, the two had a connection. Now that she thought about it, the man didn't turn in revulsion from the pot-woman as the others did. Not knowing anything about her stoic guard, Eran decided she liked him. There was an element of humanity in him at least, one that could show compassion.

"Good morning," Eran said.

Malina shot her a sharp look. "What's wrong? Why aren't you at the gazebo?"

Eran took a shallow breath through her lips. "Nothing's wrong. I was waiting for you. To walk with you."

"Why?"

"It would be nice if we got along."

Malina snorted and turned down the hall.

Eran fell in beside her. "Where are you from?"

Silence.

"I come from the land of the great rivers. The Tigris and the Euphrates." If Malina wouldn't speak, she would. "My people live between the cities of Haran and Nineveh. The Hebrews, we are called. My husband is Shem, son of Noah."

Eran watched her face for a glimmer of recognition at the names. There was none. A lump formed in her throat. Had Malina even heard of the One God? Of the Flood and the ark of her father-in-law?

"I was taken from my home and sold to Okpara's man, to Tolo. He brought me here with his caravan. My husband-" the lump constricted her throat.

Malina said nothing but no longer walked with such long strides.

The guards, and anyone else in the hall, avoided eye contact with Malina, even without her smelly cart. She felt the woman's shame, felt her aloneness as keenly as her own. The tears welled up. "I just want to go home," Eran said.

Malina offered no consolation, at least not verbally or with a kind touch. There was no animosity in her silence for a change, and for that Eran was grateful. They walked to the garden without speaking, stopping beneath the cat-headed statue.

"What do you call this one?" Eran asked as Malina ran her finger on the idols' hand.

Malina tensed for a moment, then relaxed. "Bastet."

"Why do you worship her?"

"She is a protectress."

"A goddess from the land of Mizraim. She is Khepri's favorite, I presume. There were many carvings in her room."

"Bastet was her mother's goddess."

And the woman was dead. Eran didn't know if that's why Malina spoke of it, or if the connection had occurred to her. "You weren't raised to worship her, though. You are of a Canaanite tribe."

"I am Hittite. I learned of the Egyptian gods when I came here."

"Were you born to this household? You don't seem like a slave, yet-"

The ice returned. "I reek of one?"

"No-"

Malina turned abruptly and headed for the gazebo. Eran followed. It was the start of conversation between them, even if it ended with sourness.

The Lilies sat in their usual places, lips sealed and rods down their spines as the women approached. Malina retreated to the back and leaned against a post.

Eran stood in front of the girls and coaxed responses as they reviewed the benefits of various oils. Their responses were flat and always in question, as if they were afraid of providing the incorrect answer. If they were to spend their lives as Healers, they needed to enjoy the learning. Passion would follow when they put their skills to use, when they saw how the training had impact, but not if fear held the reins.

"On your feet," Eran said.

Six eyes opened wide. Who was to stand? Eran intentionally avoided calling out their names. "It's alright. I want all three of you to stand and come with me." She left the gazebo and headed for a path through the herbs, taking her time, waiting for the girls to follow. When she heard them behind her, she looked back at them. Three ducklings in a line, hands at their sides. Malina trailed at a distance. She led them to a patch of tall thin plants.

"Now, stop and close your eyes."

Three little pairs of eyes closed briefly, then opened again.

"Close them and keep them closed. Now smell the air. Breathe in the plants around you." At this command, Malina stepped further away. The girls wouldn't smell her however. The mint was too strong. "Tell me what you smell."

No one responded. Eran waited. One eye at a time opened under a squinted lid, caught her smile and closed tight again. "It will be a long day in the sun if no one answers."

The girls fidgeted, shifting from limb to limb. "M-mint." Hehet finally squeaked out.

"Good Hehet. Open your eyes, all of you. It is mint. You need to know how it smells and feels and tastes and how it helps sicknesses." Hehet allowed a small smile to creep onto her face.

"Now break a piece off and look at the stem. How is it different from other stems?"

"It, it-"

"Go ahead Maat."

"It has sides. It isn't round."

"Well done. The stem is square, isn't it? Now tear off a leaf and taste it."

The day proceeded with every known activity involving mint Eran could think of. They crushed the leaves for ointments and made leaf tea for nausea. They learned how to extract the oil and how to preserve if for later use, how to harvest the foliage and how to propagate new seedlings. By the end of the session, one essential herb was covered, and four bodies smelled like the mint garden.

As they were leaving, so did a fifth. Eran watched Malina from the corner of her eye, snapping off sprigs to rub into her skin. The intended lesson of the day had been received.

Chapter Twenty-four

Eran stretched out on her pallet, expecting to be alone the rest of the day. The lesson went well. The Lilies would trust her in no time and would learn quickly. Medicine anyhow. What about the truth of the One God? There was no foundation to build on. She would have to begin with the Beginnings, of creation and tell them that God alone must be worshipped. His image couldn't be just another carved being on a pedestal. It would be a stark contrast to what they had been taught already, that there were many gods to hear their prayers.

The ointment they made was in a corked clay pot. Eran scooped some out to rub into her knees. They were forced to bend and extend many times in the garden classes and now a dull ache climbed up her thigh and down her calf. He mind turned to Shem as she massaged the oily substance into her flesh. He used to do this for her, a gift to ease her pain.

He had screamed in agony. Had his eyes been put out? His hand cut off? Had someone made sure he was tended and the wounds kept clean? Was her husband even alive?

"God of the heavens," she prayed. "Please let me see him

again."

The opening door interrupted her plea. "We've been summoned," Malina said. "Khepri has sent for us."

Eran hadn't seen the daughter of Okpara since the first visit a week ago. Her stomach fluttered. Was the illness worse? She struggled onto her feet from the floor, remembering how much easier it was to rise from the elevated bed in Nineveh.

Malina offered no assistance and didn't speak as they walked through the halls. The light minty aroma still rose from her skin, and a fresh layer of make-up was on her face.

Khepri sat in front of a table covered with small bottles and pots, with a large bronze mirror to one side. A young woman braided Khepri's hair, finishing the last of a head full of tiny braids adorned with colored beads. A second woman sat nearby with a smooth wooden stick and a palette of kohl.

"Too tight!" Khepri slapped at the woman's hand, then quickly lowered it as if the simple motion was exhausting. Her eyelids had a green shimmer, recently applied from a pot of malachite and her lips were reddened with henna, but neither made her face appear vibrant. There was an underlying gray cast.

"I'm almost ready," she said, not looking at either Eran or Malina as her hair styling was completed. Satisfied, she nodded at the woman with the eye paint then closed her eyes. The woman dipped the stick in oil, then into the dark powder. The line she drew along the bottom of Khepri's eye was smooth.

"Not thick enough. Do it again."

The kohl was applied again, several times for each eye before Khepri approved her work. The pots were removed and the slaves sent away as she examined herself in the mirror. Finally, she set it down and addressed Eran. "You don't wear the kohl to protect you?"

"Protect? No, I don't. I didn't realize it was more than coloring."

"All my father's people wear it in the lands along the Nile. It stops the evil from invading our souls. And it keeps the Nile flies away." Khepri picked the mirror up again and admired her reflection. "Malina wears it because I asked her to. She understands."

Malina looked away. Nile flies were not an issue in Canaan.

"What does protect you then? What are the gods of your people?"

Eran clasped her hands together. "There are many in the land of the Two Rivers. Only One that is true. The Lord Almighty, our Creator is my God."

"One God? That's so primitive. I thought we bought you because you were educated." Khepri waved her hand at Malina to summon her over.

"Why am I ill sometimes? Have you figured it out?"

"No. I'm not certain," Eran said.

"Hmpff. Do you play Senet?"

Eran looked at the game Malina set on the table, a rectangular board with a grid of squares. There were six flat sticks, white on one side and black on the other, and pawns in the shape of jackel-headed Anubis and falcon-headed Horus. "No, I don't know this game."

Khepri laughed. "Not this either? Well, sit and watch and try to learn."

Malina and Khepri played the game several times. It was simple. The sticks were tossed and counted according to the colors landing face up. The pawns were moved along the squares, trying to land on his opponent and move him back. The first set of pawns to clear the board won.

Khepri's moves weren't always logical and her counting frequently inaccurate. Malina followed with an unwise move, intentionally, so that her Mistress won every game.

"Enough. My stomach burns and I'm tired." Khepri's hand shook as she rubbed her temple. "Get me something, Malina."

Malina crossed her arms over her chest and looked at Eran.

Eran was the Healer, it was her duty. "Let's start with mint tea. Have you tried it before?"

"How do I know what all has been poured into me? Get me something!"

Eran stood and tried to keep herself from scolding the woman like a child. Her little Lilies had better behavior. "I'll return shortly."

Malina followed Eran out the door, for once, the one needing to move briskly to keep up. Eran made her way through the halls to the garden where she had started the day. Her assigned patient was a spoiled and irritable thing.

"Don't make her angry." Malina watched Eran rip leaves from their stems, hands on her hips.

"Seems she does that on her own."

"She can't help it. It's the sickness."

"Is that so? How would you know?" Eran words came out harshly but she didn't stop them. "Do you have it too, then? You're both inexcusably rude."

Crimson rose up Malina's cheeks and her hands fisted. "I know because-"

When she didn't finish, Eran stopped and faced her. "Because why?"

"That's what happened to her mother." Malina looked off into the distance.

"She died of irritability?"

"No. She wasn't like that. She was a kind woman. She became irritable as she got worse, like what's happening to Khepri." Malina wiped a finger under her eye, smearing the black makeup into a dark smudge on her cheek. "Khepri isn't really the beast who you saw. She wasn't like that until a few years ago."

There was sadness in Malina's explanation, a loss that touched her heart. "Tell me about her mother," Eran said gently. "Help me to understand. I can't find answers without your help."

Malina drew in quick breath. "It was the same. The fatigue and nausea. Headaches. Then mood swings and memory loss. It went on a few years until one day she didn't want to get out of bed, the pains were so great. And she never did. She died."

"She had physicians. What did they say? What did they do?"

Malina let out an exasperated sigh. "They tried everything they knew, prayed to every god and goddess. They didn't know how to stop the illness. They had no answers for Okpara and Khepri."

Eran gathered the mint leaves, and some hyssop for the tea concoction. Malina stopped her from leaving the herb bed when she finished. "Don't make her angry."

Something about the woman's tone made the hair prickle on Eran's neck. She looked up at her and waited for an explanation.

"Khepri's other physicians, before you. No one knows what happened to them. They've disappeared."

♥

The smoke was dark, thick with burning debris. Shem was desperate to quench the fire but could find nothing to drown the flames. Then his father was there, telling him again not to struggle, telling him he was responsible for the Promise.

Shem awakened from the dream, automatically reaching for

the reassurance of Eran's presence beside him. She wasn't there. He was alone in a tent in Abraham's camp. He rolled to his back and closed his eyes but already his mind was too busy for sleep, so he got up and dressed.

The fabric wrap of turban was still heaped where he left it, after showing his forehead to Abraham and explaining the danger to the camp. He didn't need to fear, he was told. Scouts knew well in advance of approaching danger, and there were plenty of places to tuck him away out of sight if need be. Kings from other lands had little influence among shepherds and the local tribes were on friendly terms with Abraham. They would protect his guests. With a little apprehension, Shem left the seal uncovered.

The camp was quiet in the early dawn. It would awaken soon and the routines of survival played out. Grain would be ground and bread put into ovens, goats would be milked and eggs gathered from squawking hens. Things that were dirty would be scrubbed and things that were clean would get dirty. Children, flocks, herds, and fields and gardens, tended. Life continuing.

Life continuing. Sarah carried a child of her own. Shem found a rocky point overlooking the green lands below, speckled with cattle. The serenity of the scene was a needed contrast to his jumble of thoughts and emotions. It was indeed a blessing, this baby. A life timed by God's design.

Like his own children, and those of Ham and Japheth. The first grandsons of Noah weren't meant to be conceived into the corrupt ways of the earth as it was before the Great Flood. The first generation was born on the new earth, a fresh start. Eran's inability to plant a child in her womb had been out of Shem's control.

God understood his frustration, the years of waiting for a firstborn, the ache of emptiness with each passing moon. He

176 - Rachel S. Neal

offered no explanation. He alone knew the plan and when the timing was complete, the babies came. Shem's prayers hadn't bounced from deaf ears and the answer hadn't been 'no.'

It was the same for Abraham and Sarah. In their younger years there were hopes and dreams, unmet as the decades passed. How they must have agonized, and questioned. Now her withered womb had no ability to sustain life. Yet it did.

Through their son, the name and ways of the Creator would live on, everlasting.

Everlasting, a term he could hardly comprehend. Shem's generations through Abraham would know God's presence. Forever.

Shem's heart ached for Noah at the thought. He would have so loved seeing his father's joy as the promises to Abraham were revealed. It's what they had prayed for, longed for, what seemed so impossible at times. He wished his father had lived to see this day.

Shem's heart ached for himself too. His own inability to raise a nation hadn't mattered. God chose another man, found another time to let his plans unfurl. He shook the stinger of rejection from his mind.

"Can't sleep?" Abraham sat down beside him. He smelled of wood smoke, and carried two mugs of strong tea.

"You've given me plenty to think about."

"I still can't believe it at times. Of course, one look at my wife and it's all confirmed."

Shem chuckled. "She glows like a newly wed bride." He saw Eran as he spoke, the thin girl dressed in flowing red linen, too shy to maintain his gaze.

"I have to confess, I laughed when God told me about the baby. I believed him of course. Who was I to doubt the one who formed the heavens by words alone and created man from the mud of the earth? But to think of my Sarah carrying a child at her age, her body filling out like that of a young woman, it was an image in my head that made me laugh out loud. I didn't tell her that. I'm not sure she would've allowed me back into our tent."

Shem nodded. "You wisely held your tongue."

"She gets younger by the day, it seems, more beautiful than ever. I still question it all. Why me? Why her? Why now? So many questions. So many I still can't answer."

"You've been faithful to honor God. He chose you for a reason. He knows you, Abraham, he knows your heart. Better than me, thankfully. I wasn't too sure about you and your reasons for leaving the camp. My faith wasn't at all exemplary."

"For good reason. Who would have guessed after all this time the promise of a nation was still alive? I don't blame your doubts. I may have doubted my own self if my wife didn't remind me once in awhile that I really had heard from God."

"Wives do that, don't they? Confirm truth. Confirm our actions when doubts spring up. One glance at Eran sometimes and I can tell if I'm doing right or messing up." Shem blew on the steam wisping from his mug and chuckled. There were far more wrongs than rights those early years of marriage. "I'm glad Sarah's part of the plan, and that your boy will have a Hebrew mother. She was hand-selected by God, too."

Abraham looked at him and grinned. "You were as well. Son of Noah, father of the Semites, the Hebrews, of myself and soon of Isaac and all the people who will call God their own. You've been chosen, Father Shem. Your name will be remembered with mine and that of my son. The seed, the people promised to Eve, will come from your offspring. And so will the Seed himself, the One who will conquer. He will come from your generations."

Shem set his mug on the ground, trembling. Linking the

prophesies together brought new realization that hit him with the force of a thunderbolt. First, the seed, the nation promised to Abraham, would rise from the boy Isaac. Then from it, the Seed promised to Eve would rise and defeat the evil of man's sin-filled blood. Redemption would come from Abraham's stars, from among his grains of sand on the seashore. The savior and blessing to all nations of the earth would carry Shem's blood.

And the course was already in motion.

Shem clasped his hand over his heart. Fulfillment of the Promise wasn't up to him.

He could stop struggling, stop trying in vain to preserve the ark, the way of salvation. It was God's responsibility to save mankind, God's responsibility to see that baby boys, and nations, were born, not Shem's. He could unleash the burden from his soul.

Maybe now the dreams would end.

Shem grappled with the feelings tumbling over one another like a pack of wolf pups in his mind. Elation. Relief. Awe. And one that stood separate from the rest, trying to remain hidden. Shem summoned it forward. Disappointment. His father's deathbed words weren't from God after all.

"Father Shem? You're far away. What are you thinking?"

He tried to put order to the chaos of thoughts. "First, how humbled I am, to be blessed in such a way. How grateful I am to be here with you and listen to your words and see for myself that you are a man of obedience. To know God's faithfulness, see his promises fulfilled…"

Abraham lifted his eyebrows. "But?"

"I have to admit an element of sadness. I thought I was responsible for the fulfillment of the Promise. Something my father said to me once. I'm responsible for your existence of course, but I thought there was more. I was ready for more. Am I making sense?

Do you understand?"

Abraham nodded. "You wanted to be used in a mighty way as your father was. You wanted to prove yourself to God, to Noah. To everyone."

"Prove myself?" Shem allowed the niggling of defensiveness to rise, then pushed it down again. Abraham pulled Shem's heart out and left it for them to examine together. It hurt, but the man was right. Shem did want another chance to show himself worthy, to prove that he was faithful as Priest of his God, that he was more than the sum of his faithful heirs. He took in a deep breath and expelled it loudly. "Yes, I suppose that's what it is."

Abraham smiled and shook his head. "You've walked obediently in the path of your fathers. That's what God has required of you. I worship him because of your faithfulness, and the truth you passed to your generations."

"I'll have to be content with that."

Abraham watched his face closely. "Do you resent me, Father Shem?"

Shem shook his head, willing the action to represent the truth. "No. No, my son. God chose you wisely. How could I resent the father of hope? Do I wish it was me he spoke to? Yes. I don't resent you Abraham, but I'm envious. He speaks with you, made covenant with you. You have been, and will be, blessed exceedingly."

"But not because you failed."

Shem turned his eyes to the drink in his hand, swirling the fragments of tea leaves in a circle around the perimeter of the cup.

Abraham continued when he didn't respond. "All men choose for themselves who they will serve. You taught your sons the truth of the Beginnings. You modeled righteousness. Just because the kingdoms of this earth aren't what you envisioned doesn't mean you failed."

Shem wiped a line of tears from his cheek, turning his face to the rising sun.

Abraham peeled the bark off a twig. Neither spoke for a while as he picked at the persistent covering. When it was smooth, he turned to Shem and pointed it at him. "Eran has the eyes of the Lord upon her."

Shem tossed the contents of his mug into the grass, grateful for a change in the course of the conversation. He felt uneasy as Abraham read his soul, exposed, and was eager to push the turmoil in his head aside until he could address it later, on his own. "I know. But I have to keep searching. I need her whether she needs me or not. I'll never rest as long as there is chance of finding her."

Abraham nodded. "I would do the same for my Sarah."

Shem's young relative was a man of wisdom, of strength not of his own making. How had he doubted God's call on his life? He wrapped his arm around Abraham's shoulder.

"Father Shem, I'm blessed in this land. There are many tents, many people who tend my herds and work my fields, but there is room for more. For the Hebrews, the rest of the camp. No one will take the children from among us. They can live in peace and worship the God of our fathers without fear. I'll send word to them at any time. You let me know, and I'll see to it."

"Thank you Abraham. That's generous. Let me think on it awhile?"

"Of course. It's the land of Canaan, I understand. It was hard for me to move here, even with God nudging me along."

"And yet he will fulfill his words to you in this place. Your sons will be as the stars in the heavens, the sand on the shore. Eber and his camp will be eager to be among them, I imagine."

The morning light shone from Abraham's eyes as he surveyed

his lands, blessed by the hand of the One he served. "You didn't fail, Father Shem," he said.

Shem allowed the truth to penetrate, loosening the shackles of guilt. "I would abandon everything to do what he asked of me. I would build him another ark."

Abraham smiled warmly. "He knows you're willing. He knows."

Chapter Twenty-five

The Lilies sat in the grass watching Eran diligently sew the skin of a peach back together with tiny crossed stitches. "See how I stay back from the edge a bit? The thread has to be in firm flesh or it will just tear out and make the wound bigger."

Malina stood with her back to a tree, arms crossed, trying not to reveal her interest in the procedure. Every one of her latest lessons was absorbed by three attentive pupils plus the one acting disinterested. Her posture was closed, her eyes and ears open. Today, Eran brought four extra needles along with thread and a basket of scrap cloth.

"You're all sticky," Hehet said. "You would be all bloody if this was real."

Eran smiled, enjoying the fear-free banter that accompanied the sessions now. "Yes, I would. Then I'd clean my clothing with hot water, or cold?"

"Cold!" the Lilies chimed.

"What would you add to the cold water?"

"Salt!"

"Correct. Lots of cold water to rinse then a salt and water paste gently rubbed into the stains. Well done, girls. Now you get to try sewing." She handed each two scraps of fabric and needle and thread. "First thread your needle."

Malina looked away as Eran glanced up at her and patted the ground. "I have another one. You may join us."

She stiffened as she decided, finally relaxing enough to sit with them. Mint rose from her skin, not completely concealing the lingering odor of the pots, but masking it sufficiently to be tolerable. Eran held her breath, praying the girls wouldn't choose this moment to speak freely. She didn't have to worry. They concentrated on their assignment without more than a glance at the new student.

Eran quizzed them on the last few weeks of training. They had sniffed, felt, tasted, chopped, and mixed every growing plant in the garden, save one. The bright poppies were plentiful, and she had harvested many already, but it was too soon to introduce them to the girls. The juice was beneficial when used correctly, deadly when not.

"We need to go gathering beyond this garden," she said. "There are wild trees and shrubs I want to show you, if they grow here. If not, we'll see what native plants are nearby and see if we can utilize them. It will be fun to explore."

All the students stopped working and stared at her. None of them smiled. "Where?" Keket asked.

"Anywhere plants grow freely. I've never been in Zoar so I don't know specifically. An open field, or along the road." She thought they'd be excited to leave the confines of Okpara's lands.

Keket shook her head. "We can't. It isn't safe. The city isn't safe."

"We'll take guards, if we're permitted, and go into the hills outside the city, away from people."

The children looked horrified. Even Malina's eyes were wide

184 – Rachel S. Neal

and her mouth drawn.

"Why does that frighten you?"

Maat glanced over her shoulder, as if someone was there. Her eyes watered as she leaned forward to whisper. "Be-, because *he's* out there."

"He? He who?"

Maat dropped her stitching and buried her face in Keket's shoulder.

Eran turned to Malina. "Who's out there? Who are they afraid of?"

"Amun. Amun lives in those hills. He's an evil god who-"

"He eats little girls!" Hehet interrupted, followed by a volley of input from the Lilies.

"He can touch fire and not be burned."

"He comes in the night to gobble up children then spits out their bones."

"He takes girls and they never come back."

"We can't go out there!"

"Don't make us go!"

Eran held up her hand to stem the flood of fear. She knew of the sins within the larger cities of the region, of Gomorrah and Sodom especially. Outside the caravansary, there was no promise of safety for the women or the men within the city walls. The residents preyed upon the innocent and the unprotected travelers for their pleasures, putting their lusts before their morality. She had no desire to see how Zoar compared.

Outside the cities, it was wild beasts and bandits to fear. Still, the hills called to her, the open space and wild flowers, the big sky and soft grasses. Could they not be safe with armed men in the daylight? It wasn't like they would have anything to steal and Okpara had guards in plentiful quantities.

"Have you seen this Amun? What does he look like?"

Malina shrugged when the girls had no descriptions to offer. "He's disguised as a man, mostly. He hides himself in his robes so no one sees his flesh shimmer. If you do, it's too late."

"So I could meet him on the street and not realize it was him?"

The four nodded.

"So any stranger could be Amun? Any man, anywhere?"

They nodded again.

Fear of everyone outside their protected walls. Frightening tales passed along until no one knew how they originated. The unseen terror of the god Amun was powerful.

"My God will protect us." Eran spoke softly. The Lilies snuggled into her side and waited to hear more.

Malina's eyes narrowed, then she looked away from Eran.

Khepri openly mocked the worship of one deity. Teaching the girls of Okpara's household that only one was real would not be taken favorably. Would Malina tell her Mistress?

Eran ran her hand over the girls' backs. How would they ever know truth if she held her tongue? She started at the beginning and told them about their Creator and his power and how he watched over them from his heavens.

The Lilies were full of questions. Malina said nothing. She continued creating a line of stitches between the pieces of linen. When she ran out of thread she knotted the ends and tossed the joined pieces back into the basket then got up and walked away.

Eran examined her work. Tiny, even, perfect stitches connected the halves.

♥

Khepri made them wait while her exquisite hair style was undone and redone, looking the same the second time as it had the first. The kohl was on and off again, the line thicker and reaching further from the corners each time. Then the henna was wrong on her nails. Then she was too fatigued for company and they were dismissed.

"It gives her a sense of control," Eran said as she followed Malina through the hallways. "One area of her life she can still manipulate."

"She likes her appearance. Always has. When we were-" Malina cut her words short and looked down.

Eran changed the subject. "You've sewn stitches before. Your hand is steady, precise."

Malina spun around and glared down her nose. "What of it? I'm not the Healer in this house."

The venom in her voice answered the question Eran was going to ask. Had she trained to sew garments or human flesh? Someone taught Malina how to close wounds already. "You aren't in my lessons to make sure I don't run off, are you? You were assigned to be there as a student. To continue training."

Malina scowled. "I didn't ask to be there. It was Okpara's order."

Eran connected pieces of the woman's puzzle. "Khepri always looks to you when she wants medicine. She expects them from you. You were training with someone to be her physician."

Malina crossed her arms over her chest, anger dissolving and a glimmer of tears emerging. She nodded.

"Someone who is gone."

Malina swiped at her eyes and sucked in a breath. "My father. He was the Healer for Khepri and her mother."

Eran handed her a cloth to blow her nose. "The woman died.

Is your father one that, that disappeared? Do you know what happened to him?"

Malina shrugged. "He was taken away after she stopped breathing. I was spared because Khepri and I were friends. She asked to keep me."

"Is that why you collect the pots every morning? That's your punishment? Because your father wasn't able to keep Okpara's wife alive?"

"Yes. Okpara would have preferred to make me disappear, but he didn't want to upset Khepri any more. When you came, he decided to put me back in the training lessons. So I can fail like my father and disappear, too, I guess."

"She has the same illness. And it's getting worse."

"Her moods especially. That's why I allow her to win at Senet. She could make me disappear over something so insignificant."

Eran tucked the warning into her mind.

She didn't want to just disappear.

♥

"I don't like it. It's too dangerous." Abraham shook his head. "Trade is favorable with the Ninevites right now, and loyalties to Amraphel are stronger than they've been in years. Kings intermarry and alliances shift all the time. One never knows. If anyone sees that seal on your head, it could be bad. You need back-up."

Japheth and Shem sat with their host at the fire-pit in the moonlight. "We don't want to risk your people. We don't know what we'll come across. Or who."

"Just the two of you, though? It's not safe."

Japheth ran his fingers through his hair. "It's easier to hide with only two. We had enough practice on the way here. It's simpler to stay out of sight without a large group. And it'll be a few weeks yet before any men in your camp feel like being on the back of a beast."

Abraham chuckled. "That's true. And walking would be slow. My men would be a pitiful army. But if you wait, we'll heal and I can send a dozen men with you, or a couple of hundred if you want."

"I can't wait that long," Shem said. "Every day puts me further away from her. I have to keep looking. And Japheth won't let me go alone."

Abraham sighed and looked between Shem and his brother. "I can't stop you, of course. I'll make a detailed map of the region, of the cities on the plain. There are only five and really only two where the caravans come and go frequently. Gomorrah and Sodom. But you must promise me this. You can't enter the city gates there. You can't step one foot inside."

Shem was surprised at the intensity of Abraham's voice. "How will we find Eran, then?"

"Lot, my nephew. Remember him? He sits at the gate of Sodom, a leader of the city. I'll send word that you're coming and he'll meet with you. Outside the gate. Let him ask around the twin cities. He'll want to redeem Eran if he can find her, and he has the means. Agreed?"

Shem caught Japheth's eye and both nodded. "Yes," Japheth said. "We'd appreciate his assistance. It will be good to see him again."

Abraham sighed. "Not like you'd think. He's a good man yet, knowing God in his heart, but he likes the city, the easy wealth he's obtained there. His daughters are betrothed to men who worship many gods. I tried to persuade him to find them suitable husbands, men from his own Hebrew kin, but he refuses. He has little to do with our ways anymore. Still, he's family and he will honor my request and treat you well."

"The wickedness in the cities is as we've heard?" Shem asked.

"It is. Day and night, it's unsafe there as a visitor. Only in the protected caravan corrals is there safety, and only then if you carry your own weapon. Men, women, children even. I don't allow my people to go anywhere near. Unless you have established ties within the walls, you won't leave unscathed. If you leave at all."

"We'll heed you advice. And pray that Lot has answers for us."

It was a place to start. If Lot couldn't find her in Gomorrah or Sodom, Shem intended to search Admah, Zeboyim and Zoar. These cities would be ruled out first, the most likely caravan stops. Then there were other cities to the south, and Egypt and... Shem fought against the flood of overwhelming possibilities. He put his head on his knees. They couldn't find Eran on their own.

Abraham read his thoughts. "Tomorrow we fast and sacrifice to the One God. It is he who will bring the answers."

Chapter Twenty-six

Permission to leave Okpara's land wasn't granted per se. There would be no wandering beyond the city in the verdant hills where native plants thrived in the rich soil of the plain. He understood the nature of Eran's request however, and today she would be escorted outside the walled perimeter of his land, to a safe zone near the dump. There were various indigenous trees and bushes there, if he remembered correctly.

Eran sat on her pallet and waited for Malina to come fetch her. Her heart was beating at a quick pace and though she welcomed new territory to explore, dread waited on the fringes. Not because of bandits or unseen gods of the hills. Because Okpara's home was flanked on one side by the river.

She spread her clammy hands on her lap to still the restless wringing. It was just water. Nothing to fear.

Nothing to fear. She wouldn't be swept away in its flow. She wouldn't even get in. The bank was safe and dry.

Breathe in. Breathe out.

The bubbling stream near the Hebrew camp wasn't a threat. She bathed in it. She washed linens, cleaned pots, cooled her feet on hot days without the blackness descending. A river was the same, only wider.

Deeper.

Swifter.

Capable of devouring all of humanity.

Since the Great Flood, water without a visible bottom had turned her into a rag doll. It was ridiculous, she knew. She could swim. She hadn't had the fear as a child. It was just water. Every river had banks, every lake had shores and none were truly bottomless. None would rise in judgment and sweep away all that she loved, not again.

Knowing this did little to stop the fears.

She had not moved to the Plain of Shinar with Denah and Naomi, to the first city-like settlement after the Flood. The waters drained away but a great river remained, the Euphrates, a turbulent path of terror. Choosing to live as far from it as she could had only made the problem worse. Instead of growing used to it, now the sight, even the thought of swift currents of unknown depths, set her heart to gallop.

Breathe in. Breathe out.

"You don't look well."

Eran looked up, startled by Malina's presence. "I'm fine." She made a point of smiling as she braced her arms on a small table to rise. Her knees grumbled as she did.

Malina scowled, then wiped it off her face. She had made efforts in the last few days to be more civil. If Eran failed to keep Khepri alive, Malina would be in danger again. They needed to help one another.

The woman did not help her stand from the floor, however. She waited, arms crossed, until she could lead her to the hall. Rez-Nahor followed, joining the Lilies and three other guards.

The long hall down the women's annex led to a heavy door.

The Lilies clung to her tunic as they walked, without the usual chittering like little sparrows. The space echoed with their footsteps. Eran shivered. The corridor was nothing like the ornate room where she waited to see Amraphel, yet the same dread surrounded her. The same fear and expectation and the desire to turn and run the other direction.

Malina showed no distress. Every morning she pulled her cart this direction, out to the pile of refuse. Every day she returned, not swallowed up by the river.

Eran patted the girls and whispered to them. "Don't be afraid," she said. To them. To herself.

Malina pushed the door open and walked out with Eran, the children and guards tailing. The men posted outside spoke to Rez-Nahor, and signaled to others on the wall. It was safe, they were told.

The door from the annex led to a short path, intersecting the walled perimeter of Okpara's land. Malina led them through the one gate in the high stone barrier. Straight ahead a packed path led to the dump where the river carried the waste downstream.

A little used dirt path ran parallel to the wall, flanked by trees and the riparian landscape. The river was hidden from view. Rez-Nahor turned to the left, upstream. Eran focused on the plants as she followed him. Willows and palms, grasses and rushes. She pointed to each new one and gave the name to the girls, keeping her voice as level as she could. Malina's eyebrows rose when she spoke, her eyes noticing the sweat trickling down Eran's temples.

The path took a sharp turn to the right and disappeared in the tree line. Eran followed the guard, the foliage becoming a mass of green on all sides. Behind her the Lilies followed, all in a row. Their fear of the outside was melting, the giggles returning. It could be a very beneficial training session. They would not be eaten by Amun.

And she would not be swallowed by the water.

Breathe in. Breathe out.

Clearing the tree line, the path led to a wide bank, soft and grassy and uninhabited. Gentle hills rose on the horizon beyond, touching the blue sky then dipping down to the earth again. It was peaceful, beautiful and should have been perfect. It wasn't because of the wide body of flowing water in front of her.

Eran tried to reason her fears away. Then little Hehet skipped toward the bank. Black spots formed. "No, stay close." She wasn't sure if her words were in her head or out loud.

A hand was on her shoulder and someone was talking. It didn't matter who it was. The sinking in her gut pulled Eran to the earth, the blanket of fear covering her mind.

♥

Eran opened her eyes, finding the faces of the Lilies and guards in the air above her. Malina held a cool damp cloth to her forehead.

They were back on the near side of the tree line, the river no where to be seen.

"I'm alright now," she said. "I'm alright." Malina lifted her to a sitting position.

The Lilies clambered around her, fear once again in their eyes. "Did you see him? Was it Amun?" Maat asked.

The name sparked the attention of the men. Even they locked onto her to await the response.

How to explain?

"It's the smell that got to her." Malina said. "I was watching. I didn't see Amun, unless he took another form…"

Eran raked the hair from her face. The smell by the river was unpleasant, the odor from the dump carried far from its site. But that isn't what made her senses whirl. Water, the Great Flood, the judgment of her God. There was so much to explain.

She could blame her condition on the odor and no would know the difference. They wouldn't go back there again and Eran's fears would be tucked away.

It wasn't right, though. The door was open to speak of the Flood.

She glanced at Malina, then the guards. Loyal servants of Okpara and his worship of many gods. Many ears to hear, many tongues to wag.

If Shem was here, he wouldn't hesitate despite the potential danger. "No," Eran said. "I didn't see anyone. And, it wasn't the odor. It's a silly fear. One that started long ago, when the earth was different than it is now. Back when there was no rain to fall from the skies. Back when I was a much younger woman."

She spoke of the sin among men, of Noah and his sons, of the ark. The Flood. The years afterward. No one spoke, listening to every word. Rez-Nahor stood beside Malina, eyes to the trail but ears to the words she spoke. With each description, Eran felt the chains of captivity lift. Her purpose was more than teaching healing to these girls. It was teaching truth to whomever would listen.

"That's why the water scares me. It beings back the memories of everyone drowning, my family, all gone. The constant, safe world I knew was changing and it was more than I could bear, I thought. I did of course. I had too, to survive. Later the fears returned. I know it's just water. But I can't stop the panic. Sometimes it overwhelms me."

Malina's eyes were wide open. She said nothing, turning away when she realized Eran was looking back at her.

The Lilies, as usual, had an array of questions, answered one by one until they were interrupted.

"We need to return." Rez-Nahor announced.

Eran couldn't miss the hostility in his voice. She slowly got to her feet, the episode draining her strength. "We haven't looked at all the plants yet. We'll talk on the way back."

Keket ran to a leafy shrub and broke off a branch. "What's this one?"

Before Eran could reply, Malina ripped it from the girl's hand. "Don't touch that one. Ever."

Eran caught her breath. There was more to fear outside Okpara's walls than the river. And a new fear inside the walls. On one side hemlock bushes grew among the ferns and on the other lived a woman who understood the power of its poison.

♥

A simple tincture of tea with hemlock leaves could ease pain and induce sleep if prepared correctly. Otherwise it could kill a man. The Hebrew pastures were systematically cleared of the plants so the herds and flocks wouldn't eat it, and the fields and stream banks, too, for the sake of the children. Eran kept a small patch, drying it and sealing it up in bottles. She used it sparingly, the nature of the poison too strong if mistakes were made.

For all the ailments Eran had run through her mind in search of a solution for Khepri, she had neglected to consider deliberate poisoning. Accidental, yes. Intentional, no. It never occurred among the Hebrews. This was frightening territory. Khepri's symptoms could easily stem from low doses of hemlock, dripped into a beverage, or stirred into a dish of food.

Eran chewed on a strand of hair and gazed out her window. Was Malina capable of poisoning her Mistress? Had her father poisoned Okpara's wife? Nothing was to be gained that she could see, except retaliation against the master of the home. Malina and her father were taken in a raid, forced from their homeland, and purchased as slaves. Neither chose to live in Zoar.

It was suicide for Malina if Khepri died. Their friendship was all that saved her from disappearing like her father. Would she avenge him with the poison anyhow? What else did she have to live for?

Eran eased onto her pallet. Any of the slaves had reason to hate Okpara, and many hands were involved with the preparation and delivery of food in the home. Yet only Malina and a handful of men had access to the land by the river where the hemlock grew. It was ground Eran needed to tread discreetly. Vengeance bore deep roots.

Chapter Twenty-seven

Lot's entourage was visible for a long distance. Shem and Japheth stood among the trees and watched them approach the meeting place, a grove of shady palms on a small rise. The three hour walk at first light of day had been uneventful, invigorating almost, and Shem felt his mood lighten. The twin cities of Gomorrah and Sodom utilized caravan merchants routinely and with Lot's influence, he felt certain there would be an answer of some sort today.

Shem examined each figure in the group approaching his location. None were Eran. It was too much to hope for, he knew, that somehow Lot had found her already and would bring her along. Disappointment pulled his heart down a notch.

He had prayed long into the night, falling asleep with Eran's name on his lips. He tried not to hope beyond reason. He knew his God listened, and watched. And he knew his prayers were not always answered as he expected. It was a struggle to keep his frustration pushed aside so his prayers could get through. He didn't want to be angry with God. It didn't help matters. This he learned over the years, over and over. When he was without an heir. When his children formed their own tribes and left, knowing he would never see most of them again. When the persecution ramped up, and he was forced to move his aged parents from their village to the camp of Eber. When the children were taken. When Eran was taken.

There was purpose to some of his trials, this he could see long after the events, though it didn't eradicate the pain when the next chaotic event occurred. Softened, yes. Even losing his heart-song, his wife, more precious to him than life, he knew the hand of his God controlled the outcomes. He had to pray, to ask, to seek favor all the same. He had to do something and lifting his heart to God was the one action he knew was most important. Trust. Belief. And more trust.

Abraham and Sarah were having a son. God still moved among the Hebrews. Shem had to rest his hope in that fact. The sinful nature of the cities had not chased the Almighty from the land of Canaan.

The city of Sodom rose from the land, a great walled fortress nestled in the verdant oasis, fed by streams on three sides. It was a beautiful place with ornate spires and multi-leveled rooflines pressed against the sky in an endless pattern, in gleaming colors of tile and paints and metals. It was whitewash, of course. The outward elegance covered a deplorable morality within. The main gate was open wide, its arched entrance eager to devour the unsuspecting and those who relished the nature of the city alike.

"How can he live there?" Japheth asked.

Shem shook his head. "He was like a son to Abraham and Sarah. I can't imagine their grief if it's as bad as its reputation."

"Lot has prospered and that's where his heart lies. In his wealth and power."

Shem brushed dust from his clothing and checked the position of his turban. "We can only hope ties to his family remain as strong as Abraham believes."

A dozen well-fed donkeys stopped at the tree line. Ten men dismounted, all armed, including Lot. He was draped in layers of brightly striped clothing. A gold band rested on his forehead, its gems reflecting the light, and gold hoops dangled from his ears and wrists. His skin was pink and pudgy as if he rarely saw sunlight. Most disturbing was his face, with lips stained crimson and a shimmer of gold paint above his eyes, like a woman would wear.

Shem's skin crawled, as if the evil of Sodom stood in his presence. He pushed it aside to greet his relative in a friendly manner. The man was his kin and lived in another culture. Shem knew better than to judge the man before he had the opportunity to understand his ways.

Lot wasted no effort on any formalities in front of the men protecting him. He hugged Shem and kissed his cheeks, then Japheth, exuberance in his demeanor. He smelled of spikenard, an expensive perfume.

"Welcome my relatives! I never dreamed I'd see you again. What a wonderful blessing. I wasn't sure I believed Uncle Abram's messenger at first. Shem and Japheth, in these lands of Canaan. I'm not sure I believe it now."

Lot turned to his men and gave instructions for the pack animals to be unloaded. Business would not begin right away. Their host would first set out a meal and talk of other matters, of his choosing as was custom. It was all Shem could do not to blurt out his questions.

A woven carpet was spread on the grass and covered dishes placed on top. The three men sat before the chunks of fish drenched in pomegranate sauce, breads stuffed with olives and goat cheese, grapes and apricots, and foods Shem didn't recognize. There was enough for all the men but only the three of them ate while Lot's men kept surveillance.

"Is it dangerous out here?" Japheth asked. "Are bandits common so close to Sodom?"

"One never knows. I like to be safe."

"And the city, you find it safe for your wife and children?"

Lot grinned as he slurped down an oily tidbit of lamb. "My Uncle has filled your head with exaggerated tales. Sodom celebrates the pleasures of living, that's all. You would be safe with me there, in my home. Old men aren't in demand."

"But your wife?"

"Happy, dressed as fine as anyone in Egypt. She has slaves for all her labors. What more could she ask?"

"A life pleasing the One God," Shem said. "Among your Hebrew relatives."

Lot laughed and waved his hand in the air as if sweeping the thought aside. "Abram thinks man must work his bones into the dust of the earth to please the God of Noah. Not so, not so. I've had my share of that and now I live off the works of the men I own. I treat them well, mind you. I never separate a man from his woman at the auction unless he is through using her."

Shem set his dish down, his appetite gone. "Your uncle goes by Abraham now. Did you know? He had a vision again, and Sarah is pregnant."

"She's going to have a baby? At her age? I was replaced by Ishmael and now he will be replaced by another. Well good for them. I'll send my congratulations when it happens. Now, tell me of your father, and the others."

Japheth and Shem filled in the details about the Hebrews, concluding with their own recent experiences. "I need to find Eran," Shem said.

Lot looked down at his city and sighed. "Yes. It's why you've come so far from your home. The messenger told me and I wish I could give you news. She isn't here, not in Sodom. I've checked the entire city and no one knows of her. I have men asking in Gomorrah, but I'm not optimistic. She's, well, old, like you, and I see no reason for her to be purchased. It would not be in the tastes of the men and women there."

Japheth reached over and squeezed Shem's arm. "What of the other three towns?"

"I can send men there too, if you wish. They're smaller, less caravan traffic, but one never knows. I can't rule out the possibility Eran was sold for some reason. Stay with me a while. I can have an answer within a week. In the mean time I'll fatten you up on the best the land has to offer. Whatever your pleasure, I can secure it, or them. We have visitors from the exotic regions of the world, if you want something new."

Shem shook his head, the man's intentions too clear, too repulsive. "We can't stay in the city. We promised Abraham. Thank you anyhow. We'll see what we can find out ourselves in the other cities."

Lot chuffed. "Of course, he made you promise. That isn't a surprise. You can borrow some of my men to escort you, then. You need the protection."

"Thank you for that offer, but we prefer to travel alone. It's easier to stay hidden among the trees." Japheth was quick to nod in agreement.

Lot wiped his lips on a delicate linen napkin, then gestured for his men to help him rise. "I'm sorry I couldn't bring you better news. I'll send word to Abram if I get a positive word from Gomorrah, but as I said, I can't imagine anyone there wanting to purchase her."

Three men tugged Lot to his feet. "It is so very good to see you both. If you reconsider, I'm usually near the gates with the other city leaders. Ask for me. Everyone knows who I am. You're welcome to stay with me anytime."

Lot's animals were packed and with a final kiss, he turned for his home.

Japheth shuddered. "I'm sorry Eran isn't in Sodom, yet, so grateful she isn't. There's an oppressive air hovering over that town. I'll be glad to move away from here."

Shem agreed. He and Japheth packed their belongings after plotting a path for Admah, the nearest city. He didn't have Eran in his arms, but he knew one place she wasn't, probably two. It was an answer, not a dead end. It was a turn in the path. There would more, he knew.

♥

By nightfall, Shem and Japheth were secure beneath a tent made of branches above and moss below. Still fully dressed, Shem covered himself with his cloak and leaned onto his elbow, then folded a makeshift pillow, the fabric wrap he used for his head. His hand felt beneath the fabric, finding the knife hilt in easy reach. The money bag was still strapped to his waist, beneath his clothing. Sandals were on, strapped tight, and the packs of food were stashed in the space between them.

They traveled light, no soft covers or pots to cook a stew. Not that either felt like chasing down game. The hike across the hilly terrain took longer than they anticipated and both were exhausted. Shem pulled provisions from his pack, fresh rations thanks to Lot. He uncapped a skin of wine and gave it to Japheth. "I don't have a plan for tomorrow," he admitted. "Except to enter Admah as travelers."

"I thought we could find the caravansary. Maybe the owners or guards will remember if-"

A twig snapped outside the tent.

Both fell silent. Both put hands to weapons.

Silence. The night was suddenly void of its usual rustle, as if the local creatures stopped mid-scurry and held their breath. It was still. Too still.

Shem was acutely aware of his own breathing, short and fast, and loud, it seemed. For a long moment they waited. They heard nothing to indicate a predator lurked nearby, beast or human. That meant nothing. Anyone or anything could keep a pose, waiting as he did, to determine whether or not to strike.

The hair on his neck stood at attention. Anticipating the unknown was torture.

He didn't have to wait long.

The tree boughs shook then flew away, exposing four men against the night sky. They grinned down at the two men they had uncovered.

Shem raised up onto his knees and lifted his dagger. A man kicked it from his hands. Another fell in behind Japheth, slipping a knife to his throat. He growled words in a tongue Shem couldn't understand. His meaning was clear. Back down. Stop fighting.

Shem held up his hands and eased back to a sitting position. Japheth kept still, the blade pressing his neck, his eyes wide and angry. "We won't fight," Shem said, to his brother more than the robbers.

Three burly men swept through their belongings while the fourth held Japheth. Shem could do nothing. The invaders were young and strong, determined in their search, and obviously unhappy with the meager selection.

The oldest of the four tossed Shem's cloak on the ground and mounded it with the food rations and extra clothing they pulled from the rucksacks. He pawed through each bit, searching for more. When he couldn't find anything of value, he slammed a hand on Japheth's shoulder and yelled at him.

Japheth flinched from the obvious cursing. "That's all we have," he growled back.

The man turned to Shem, sour breath and angry words pouring into his face.

Shem clenched his teeth, and shook his head, struggling to keep himself restrained.

In one shove, the thief pushed Shem to the ground, then pinned his shoulders to the earth while another patted him down, finding the bag of barter coins. With one meaty hand he grabbed Shem's tunic at the neck and ripped it, stripping it down to where the stash was secured at his waist. The knot was slashed with a knife, the contents taken.

His brother was pushed and held down in the same manner.

The men cursed them again in the foreign tongue as they counted the stash. Shem held his breath, fearing the worst, until the men stomped off, disappearing into the wooded terrain. He and his brother waited until the gentle night sounds resumed before moving. Neither had been harmed and he breathed a prayer of relief.

Then fear began a steady march up his spine.

In those brief moments, they lost all their provisions. All the food, all the money, the water skins and clothing that could have been traded, all gone.

Chapter Twenty-eight

"Name three remedies for a toothache." Eran tried to focus on the Lilies as they recited the lessons. Her mind was foggy, needing sleep. Khepri had called for her Healer during the day and night for the past three, complaining of abdominal pain. The standard remedies were barely keeping her placated. A stronger medicine was needed before she grew too uncomfortable, and too disagreeable. Eran needed the poppy juice.

Beyond the hedgerow of rue, poppies bloomed in the afternoon sun. She couldn't keep her eyes off the saturated scarlet hues, swaying in the breeze.

She was reluctant to gather and process it. There was no way to do so without Malina's awareness. Did she know about this potential poison too? Eran didn't want to teach her a new one. Especially one so easy to administer and impossible to detect.

"Is that correct? Mistress?"

The Lilies were speaking. She missed their answers. "Oh, yes. Well done."

Eran turned to Malina and took the terebinth tree branch she held. She had been gathering samples from the land near the river when she completed her morning chore. No one had suggested they venture out again as a class beyond the safety of the walls.

The explanation of terebinth to keep wounds from infection was explained simply, then Eran dismissed the girls, earlier than normal. After walking them back to their room, she turned back to the garden. The nap would have to wait.

Malina followed. "We aren't finished?" Her hostilities toward Eran had diminished considerably. Eran wanted to trust her, to have a friend. She didn't know if she could. She couldn't hide her activities either. She walked toward the red flowers and offered no explanation.

"Eran?"

"I need to make an extract for Khepri."

"For the belly pains?"

"Yes."

"From mint?"

"No."

"Why aren't the girls allowed to watch?"

Eran let an exasperated sigh escape. "I need to prepare this one alone."

Malina stopped on the path and put her hands on her hips. "What happened? How come you aren't nice to me any longer? I'm trying to like you, but you're making it impossible. You're more than grouchy from being tired."

Eran faced her. There was no subtle way to find the answers she sought. "How did your father treat Okpara's wife? What did he give her?"

"What does that have to do with you being mean?"

"Tell me."

"He did the best he could. There were many treatments. Dill, I remember, mixed in everything for a while. And rue, ointments with rue. I crushed it for him. And there were offerings to the gods. Bastet mostly. Myrrh was burned to her on a regular basis."

"Did he-" Eran stopped the words on her lips. She was about to ask if Malina's father killed the woman of the house.

"Did he what?" Malina's arms crossed, her spine stiffening so that she towered over Eran.

Eran made herself breathe in deeply, then phrased her question differently. "Did he use the hemlock bush, or the poppies for treatment?"

Malina's eyes narrowed. Her hand swung back and smacked Eran's cheek with enough force to knock her to the ground. "Not like you think."

Eran pulled her knees up to her chest, not sure if there was more coming. Her cheek stung. She rubbed it, swiping away tears that leaked out and ran down the hot surface.

Malina started to stalk off, then stopped with her back to Eran. After a minute she turned back around, her eyes red.

Eran took a breath and waited for another blow, but Malina dropped to the ground beside her. She glared openly. "Why would you ask me that?"

Eran swallowed the lump in her throat. "I'm sorry. I thought perhaps...I realized I don't know who I can trust."

No response.

"Khepri's symptoms, it may be poison." Malina's face showed no surprise. "Your father disappeared. I thought you might seek revenge. You know about the hemlock. It made me wonder."

"My father didn't kill anyone. And I'm not either. She's my friend."

There was an element of anguish in her voice. It was real. "I'm sorry." Eran said. "What I said, what I thought. That was unfair. I had to know, though. I need to trust you."

They sat in silence for a long while. Eran broke it, feeling she could speak freely in the moment of hurt. "I'm scared, Malina. If it is poison, who's responsible? If it isn't poison killing Khepri, I don't know what is. I don't know any more than your father or the others. I don't want to just disappear."

♥

"I can't think of any reason anyone would want her dead. Okpara treats his people well for the most part. And his wife was kind, as was Khepri. Demanding at times but not unreasonably so. Not before they were ill."

Eran showed Malina which immature poppy seed pods to harvest, adding them to a small basket. They had discussed Khepri's condition many times and were doing so again, hoping for a glimmer to lead them to the cure. "An allergy to something, then?"

"All the foods were systematically ruled out, and no one was permitted to burn incense of any sort for a time, but it made no difference. Even the goat's milk she bathes in sometimes was suspect. Nothing added or withheld from her routine affected the illness."

"Does she leave the home? Is there something outside these walls we don't know about?"

"She used to. The temples, the market, parties. Not any more. She has very few friends as you might imagine."

"Any who would poison her?"

Malina shrugged. "No one visits. Not anymore."

"The guards then? Or the poor girls stuck doing her hair over and over?"

The woman pinched her lips together for a moment. "No. There is loyalty in this house. I've never heard animosity of any real threat from the women. The guards are here by choice. They could leave if they wanted and the men in the fields have no access to Khepri."

"Not everyone who serves Okpara is here of their own will. No one resents being enslaved enough to retaliate?"

Malina looked over her shoulder at the wall and the hills beyond. "He mostly buys people in Egypt, where they are driven hard as slaves. Coming here is a better life. His people want to serve him. Very few even attempt escape."

Eran caught the wistfulness in the woman's voice. "And you? You aren't here by choice. Why do you stay?"

"Where would I go? My family was taken in battle years ago, before my father and I were purchased. I don't remember my old home anymore. I grew up here."

"But you're still a slave, and you could disappear, like your father. Do you think about leaving?"

Malina yanked off a pod and spun around. "We have enough, I'd think."

Eran caught her arm. "Every day you walk out of here with the cart, unhindered, past the guards."

The woman squared her shoulders. "I'm loyal to Master Okpara." She didn't look Eran in the eye.

"Your family may be gone but you could return to your people. There are many Hittite tribes in the lands of Canaan."

Malina looked back to the hills, not answering.

"You're scared to leave."

"The gods protect me here."

"You trust them within Okpara's walls, but not outside?"

Malina exhaled forcibly. "You're one to talk. You speak of a god all-powerful, watching you, yet fear of water drops you to the earth in oblivion."

Eran sucked in a breath, heat crawling up her neck at the blatant observation. "Yes. Point taken."

"You aren't here by choice, either. You could escape. Then what? Where would you go, Eran? No one in Zoar would take you in and protect you. No one defies Okpara. He controls too much of the commerce. You'd be out on your own, in the streets and the city would eat you. You'd be dead before you could crawl your way back here to beg for his protection." Malina pointed her finger in Eran's face. "Don't assume you have all the answers. You may not care about your life but I don't want to die like that."

Escape? The notion penetrated Eran's mind. Her prayers had been for Shem to rescue her. Other than riding the caravan with Tolo, she hadn't considered freeing herself. Would she do it if she could?

"Leave Zoar, then," Eran said. "Go to the hill country. I could live outside the cities, in a cave. I can hunt well enough and provide for myself. You could, too."

Malina's long fingers shot out and snared Eran's arm. "No. I can't go there. You can't either."

Eran looked into the woman's eyes, intensity shooting out like arrows.

"Amun." Malina said. "It's better to stay here than to fall into his hands."

♥

Eran scratched the poppy pods to allow the liquid to ooze out into a marble bowl. "It will dry out some, leaving a sticky residue. We'll spread it into a thin sheet and place it in the sun until it's nearly dried to a powder. It will store without going rancid that way."

Escape. The notion burrowed into her thoughts, finding itself neither accepted nor rejected. Could she? Would she?

Her husband wasn't alive for certain, and if he was, he didn't know where she was. Or if she still was. That was Amraphel's intention. Japheth and Denah would want to find her, and all the Hebrews for that matter, yet the reality of the situation was clear. They wouldn't know where to begin. They would have been here by now if they had known.

Shem wouldn't come. None of the Hebrews would rescue her. Her life would never be among them again. Eran brushed tears from her eyes. Not quickly enough.

"In time, it's better. Missing your mother, your family. Your husband." Malina said.

"I want to go home."

"It's still there at least. Mine is gone."

Was it true? The Hebrew camp might have disbanded since she was taken from there. But they would be somewhere in the land of the two rivers. Somewhere, she had people of her own blood.

Leave. Stay. Obey her master. Find her people. Teach the Lilies. Die in her husband's arms. She had never done anything risky on her own accord. Eran shivered. Escape? Was she strong enough to even consider it? The seed had been planted and like it or not, it was taking root.

Chapter Twenty-nine

Shem crawled to a clump of weeds and threw up what little was left in his belly. The burning sensation didn't diminish, the twisting of his gut warning of more to come. After the third round, the pains eased. The shiny red berries he found were definitely not meant for consumption. Thankfully he ate only a few.

It was unfortunate. The tiny fruits were plentiful. If they were inedible, it would be their fourth day without real food.

He sat back on his heels and wiped his mouth. Japheth scooped water from the stream and held it to his lips. Shem slurped it down, but it didn't stay down, landing beside him before he could move away. They could survive four, maybe five weeks without food as long as they stayed near water, but not if he was compromised. Not if every drop he put in came back. His strength would diminish rapidly.

Shem forced himself to crawl back to the shade where he could rest his back against the trunk of an olive tree. They stumbled across the untended grove a day ago and made camp there, beneath the developing fruit. There was little promise for a meal in the overgrown vegetation and the rabbits had been too swift to capture. Without a blade of some sort, they couldn't fashion effective traps and so far the primitive nets they wove had captured nothing but leaves.

"Admah isn't as large as Sodom, not as much activity. I'm sure I can get in if I follow another group of travelers though." Japheth climbed onto a rock and looked down into the valley below. His mane of graying curls traveled in every direction but down. There were bits of debris in his beard and if a sparrow suddenly emerged from its tangles, Shem wouldn't have been surprised. The ripped tunic was knotted over his shoulders, pulling it above his bony knees. He was dusty, and scratched, and overall appeared like a scraggly old beggar.

Shem couldn't help it, he chuckled, holding his belly from the agitation.

Japheth looked back at him, eyebrows arched above his blue sky eyes. Eyes he inherited from their mother. She would be appalled at their condition.

"You don't exactly look like a respectable citizen of the region, or any region. I wouldn't let you into my city. You're rather frightening."

Japheth ran a hand through his hair, only to have it get stuck in the mess. He pulled it out along with a twig, which he tossed at Shem. "Not in our prime, are we?" He flopped down in the weeds and picked tidbits from his beard.

"Remember when Ham convinced us to dress like beggars? We snuck out of the house and went into the city?"

"Ha! He hoped to get gambling coins. Then Naomi walked by and recognized him. That ended that adventure."

"Never seen him get so red faced and run so fast. Still, she married him."

"Remember what Grandfather Methuselah said when he

found out?"

Shem tented his fingers beneath his chin. "Don't practice being who you don't wish to be or the time will come when your practice pays off."

"Well, he was right. Here we are. Beggars." Japheth scooped water from the trickling stream and splashed his face, sending dirt rivulets into his beard. "I can do it, Shem. I'm not ready to meet up with our grandfathers yet. I can go beg. I'll get some food to settle that grumbling gut of yours."

Shem pressed his fingertips into his temples to stop the pounding. "I'll go with you. We're safer together."

"You can't walk that far. There may not be water, and I'm not sure I could carry you back here."

"You might get killed."

"I have to try. If I can at least get some bread…"

Japheth was already on his feet. He would go, putting himself at risk no matter how loudly Shem protested. That's what oldest brothers did. His at least.

"What a mess I've made," Shem said.

"No. Not you. God finds no fault in you, Shem. And either do I."

With that, Japheth walked away.

The tree was quaking behind him. Shem put his hands to the earth to steady himself, then realized it was because of him, he was shaking, head to toe, his head swimming in circles. He forced his eyes to keep open and track his brother, the blurring image getting smaller and smaller. Smaller.

Smaller.

Gone.

♥

An owl swooped near him, snatching a mouse from the brush and retreating to a limb above Shem's head. It paid no attention to the withering figure propped among the roots, a full, hearty meal in its clutches, the means for strength and fight to live another day.

Still no Japheth.

Shem focused his thoughts once again on his brother's safety, praying to his God between the bouts of dizziness and sweating and dry heaving.

The moon was a perfect crescent. He stared at it, for no reason other than because it was there, and bright and caught his attention at the moment. When it wavered back and forth in the sky, he lowered his gaze. And saw the outline of a man coming toward him.

"Japheth." He said it, but knew it wasn't. The walk was all wrong.

Running his hand along the ground, he found a stick. He gripped it with both hands.

The figure multiplied. Three? Five?

"Stop," he said, or whispered, or thought.

The images grew larger. Stretching towards the moon. Tall, broad men.

Amorites.

A pulse of nausea wracked his gut, forcing his face away from the giants and into the earth, his head hammering in his skull until it knocked consciousness from its tentative hold.

♥

Khepri tossed the sticks. Three colored side up, one facing down. A three. She moved her pawn to the end of the row, two more than she should have. The game piece rattled on the wooden board as she placed it. The tremor was worse.

Malina tossed a four but moved only two squares so she wouldn't land on Khepri's pawn and send it back. She dabbed a thin cloth across her forehead after handing her friend the sticks. The kohl smudged as trickles of sweat crossed her temple, leaving a trail of gray tracks. Eran watched them silently, her own anxiety rising as the afternoon wore on.

"We should burn incense for Bastet today." Khepri gathered the sticks in her pale hands, tossing them so that two of the four landed on the floor. Eran picked them up and handed them to her to toss again.

Fragrant resin already burned in the copper bowls scattered throughout her room. "I lit myrrh when I came in." Malina said. And she had re-lit the incense twice already at Khepri's request.

Khepri looked furtively around the room, her gaze finding the smoke as it rose toward an open window. She turned back to Malina. "I know," she snapped. "I want new incense. Put that out and start again. This batch isn't working."

"I'll see to it." Eran rose and partially snuffed the first bowl, allowing the smoke to fade before fanning it back to action. The burning aroma would do nothing to heal the woman. Eran lifted prayers to her own God as she tended the bowls. As she fanned the last one, she noticed Okpara observing his daughter from the doorway.

"How's my sweet girl?" He crossed the room and kissed her forehead, then ran his hand over her sleek hair, straight today, a black curtain resting just below her thin shoulders.

Khepri looked at Malina to respond. Malina looked to Eran.

Eran put the incense down and clasped her hands together. "She kept fruit in her system. And there have been no pains today."

Okpara kept his eyes on his daughter. "All of it. What else?"

Eran took a calming breath. "The shaking is worse, the tremors are increasing."

"She's pale as an apparition. What are you doing for her?"

Eran listed the remedies, knowing it wouldn't make a difference. He had heard them before, no doubt. And he could see the lack of results.

"I don't know what's making her ill. I'm treating her symptoms as best I can."

Okpara's lips twitched. His eyes flickered over Malina before resting on Eran again. "Like the rest, then. You're no better than the rest of the lot of Healers."

Eran stared at her feet, allowing her fingers to wring themselves together.

Khepri clapped her hands. "We should light incense for Bastet. That always makes me feel better. Malina, get the incense."

Okpara's eyes darted around the room. The fragrant, smoky haze had obviously been filling the room for some time already. His expression darkened. "Yes, Darling. You're right." He ran a jeweled finger along his daughter's cheek, forcing his voice to sound light. "Whatever you want."

The Master fixed a cold, narrow stare on Eran. "See to it, Healer." he said. "See that my daughter gets what she needs to get better. Understand?"

Eran nodded.

He kissed his daughter's hand then stalked from the room, slamming the door behind him. The jarring tone of his words vibrated through Eran's core.

♥

Eran stared at the sleeping pallet in her room. It was no longer on the floor. It was raised on four wooden legs, a proper bed with a real stuffed mattress.

Malina grinned. "For your old knees," she said.

"How did you arrange it?" Eran sat on the edge and ran her hand on the soft surface. Malina had connections within the household, then. With Rez-Nahor, of course, though they hid it well. Were there others? "Thank you."

Malina turned away, avoiding the question. She stared out the window to the hills beyond.

"What's on your mind?"

"We can help each other. Not just with Khepri. Teach me not to fear Amun. I'll help you face the river."

"The river?"

She turned and sat on the window ledge. "That which you fear. It controls you. It regulates where you go and what you do. Fear makes you weak. Don't you want to be free of its power?"

Eran gripped the edge of the bed. She could live her life away from the waters that drained her senses. If she stayed here, in Okpara's domain. If.

Malina watched her closely, reading her thoughts. "Your fear will determine how your life is lived out. Where your life is lived out. Walking out the front gates isn't an option."

The river was the way out. If she could get to it and swim across, she'd be free. The fear of Amun would stop anyone from chasing her too far. The irrational fear of an imagined threat could ensure her escape.

"I, I don't know."

"In the water is death. In the water there is life. It can harm. It can heal. If your God controls the waters, don't you think he can lead you through them? Won't he decide if you live or if you die? Is your fear stronger than the one you worship?"

Eran sank back on the cushions. Stunned. The woman's faith was stronger than her own.

God was in control. How many times had she said that to the little Hebrews? How many times did she console herself with the thought as the raiders tore through the camp? Did she not trust him to deliver her from the fear?

He could.

Would he?

Faith required taking the first step from the safe shore into the realm of fear. Only then, would miracles be seen. Only then would the hand of God be evident.

"Alright," Eran said. "I'm willing."

She was an old, old woman. Still, she had much to learn.

Chapter Thirty

Smoke swirled around his head. Shem blinked against the brightness of it, the intensity sending daggers into his skull. He tried to turn away, but couldn't. His head wouldn't move. A hand. There was a hand on his forehead. He forced his eyes open, the brightness gone, replaced by his father's face. "Take it easy, Shem. It's alright."

Noah. He was with his father. His father was dead. He was dead then.

No, not dead. It was the dream. Only different. He tried to move again but the hand stopped him.

Shem couldn't keep his eyes open, couldn't manage to say anything. He stopped resisting the touch of the man in his dream. Noah wouldn't hurt him.

♥

The Lilies remembered no other life than that in Zoar. Their parents lived in tents near the fields they tended for Okpara, a master they chose to follow from the land of Egypt. Like him, they worshipped a bevy of gods and goddesses. Some from the homelands, some from Canaan's lands, some picked up from travelers. Eran guessed the girls could name and describe at least thirty gods and goddesses.

She had introduced her God to them and prayed to him in their presence. They had prayed for his favor as well, but not as the only God yet. He was just another in their retinue.

Maat repeated her question. "What is your God's name?"

Teaching truth meant dispelling lies, contradicting all these girls had been taught regarding the beings of the sky and of the earth, those with power over the elements and man. Her approach was gentle, but not compromised. Bite-sized nuggets until they could see and understand and determine for themselves whom they would serve.

Malina's fear of the unknown would be defeated in the same manner. Eran would teach the healing of the body and the healing of the soul in the daily lessons. If she were another of the Healers to disappear, she would know the foundation of truth had been laid. If the time came for her to leave on her own, her time would not have been for nothing.

"My people call him the One God mostly. Or the Creator, The Almighty, or the God of Adam. We don't speak his formal name any longer. That right was taken when Adam and Eve were sent from Eden, their hearts blackened with sin."

"Does he ride the boat with Ra in the night?" Keket made a sweeping motion with her arm from horizon to horizon.

Eran looked to Malina for explanation.

"Ra is the sun god. He travels the sky at day and in a boat at night, under the world. He must defeat the Evil One each night before he can reappear."

Eran moved her students to the shaded gazebo, altering the lesson she had in mind. They needed to inspect a bunch of feet today. An irritating rash had developed between one guard's toes and had apparently spread to others. She'd seen it before and planned to demonstrate the preparation and use of an ointment, one made of lemon juice, basil and cinnamon. But itchy toes would have to wait.

"In the Beginning," Eran repeated the words she leaned in the recitations at Noah's home, before the flood, as a new bride, scared and isolated from all that was familiar. The words of the Beginnings brought comfort. There was stability in the recitation, a rock more solid than any she could stand on. One that stood before she was born and would continue far after her bones were sprinkled in myrrh and buried away. They weren't Noah's words, after all. They came from the Creator himself, a breath of knowledge whispered to Adam and all his generations.

It was time her pupils fully understood the nature of the God she worshipped, the only one with ears that heard and eyes that followed and a hand capable of sparing the righteous. And the only one with the power to wipe evil from his presence.

♥

Eran sat with her back to the river. Malina sat with her, Rez-Nahor and two other guards nearby, pretending not to be interested. It was the first time Malina led her to the far side of the tree line since the day she passed out. Her hands were clammy. Her heart thumping.

"Just listen," Malina said. "For a few moments, listen as it sings."

Eran prayed again under her breath. If she fell over backward, she wouldn't fall in. The ground around her was dry and firm.

She focused on the running water, the sound of it as it cascaded over the stones near the bank and the deeper rush further out, where the rocks fell away and the depth increased. Isolated splashes came and went at irregular intervals. Fish, she imagined, seeking flies skimming along the surface. It was one sound composed of many. And the sound couldn't hurt her.

Malina sat quietly. After only a few minutes she stood and reached out to Eran, clasping her arm and helping her to stand. "Time to leave," she said.

Eran's knees were quivering, her breathing quick and shallow. But she would walk away on her own power.

"Tell me why you don't fear Amun," Malina said as they left.

Rez-Nahor glanced at Malina and raised a quizzical eye. She gave him the hint of a smile. Both expressions were quickly wiped away, but not quickly enough. Eran saw the interaction. Fear was perhaps not the only chain preventing Malina from leaving.

Eran's mind played an image from long ago, of a giant, a Nephilim, being tortured and executed. It was the first of the evil tribe she had ever seen, and though he was tall and broad boned, he looked like any other man, formed in God's likeness. She expected them to be different, monstrous somehow. This one felt pain. Shed blood. Tried to cover the fear in his eyes as he faced death.

The thought made the hair tingle on her arms and she rubbed them as if to obliterate the gruesome memory. Centuries later, Nephilim blood still flowed to some extent, in the giants living in Canaan, owning their reputation as brutal warriors. But they weren't gods. They were men who chose evil or chose good. Tall and powerful, they were still only men.

"A god who touches fire and eats little girls? I don't believe this Amun exists, that's why I don't fear him. It sounds like an invention of Okpara's to keep his people from leaving Zoar. If you all fear him, you won't run to the hill country, you'll stay here

224 – Rachel S. Neal

where you believe you are protected."

"He's been seen."

"No one seems to have seen him directly. All I've heard are tales that have been repeated over and again."

"Girls have gone missing."

"Men are wicked. Men take what they want. How fortunate to blame an unseen god rather than admit to an evil deed."

Malina kept her eyes to the path. The walls of Okpara's home didn't shield anyone from knowing about the merciless ways of all the cities along the Salt Sea, the indulgent, sinful ways. Missing women and children were a consequence of the selfish lusts in the heart of man. It didn't require a god-like being to explain their empty beds.

♥

Emerald eyes smiled at him. Familiar eyes and soothing voice. "Try to drink," it said.

Someone lifted his head and gently put a cup to his lips. Shem allowed the liquid to trickle down his throat. He was in a room, a dark room.

"Your brother is so worried about you."

Japheth. Japheth was worried so Japheth was alive. Japheth was here. Where was here? "Sarah?" Was he back at Abraham's? "Sarah."

The voice spoke softly, growing farther away as tender hands tucked warm layers of skins over his shivering body and ran a hand over his forehead.

Safe, his mind said. Japheth was worried. His brother was here so here was safe.

♥

It wasn't a tent. The room was constructed of stacked stone, so he wasn't with Abraham. Nothing appeared familiar. He was on a raised bed, a soft one with several layers of skins to keep him warm. The only window was covered in a dark curtain. A table nearby held a pitcher and toweling. An oil lamp sent a soft glow into the room. Friendly, comforting. Shem didn't know where he was, just that he had been spared from death in peaceful surroundings.

The droning noise that woke him came from his brother, snoring, stretched out on a bench nearby. His long legs draped over the end, poking out of a tunic that Shem didn't recognize. There were no fetters around his ankles. Shem felt the relief immediately. Whatever their situation, they were in it together and didn't appear to be in imminent danger.

He lifted his head and allowed dizziness to pass before slowly rolling onto his side and sitting up. He needed his arms to hold himself, locked at the elbow and braced on the bed frame. Weakness tried to pull him back onto the soft bed. He resisted, needing to be aware, needing to understand.

He was dressed in a simple tunic, his hair cut short, above his shoulders and his beard to a tidy hand breadth in length. Scrapes on his arms and legs, open and festering the last he remembered, were nearly healed. How long had he been here? And where exactly was here?

"Japheth?" He wanted to keep his voice low and was surprised how dry and gravelly his words came out, too soft to wake his brother. He cleared his throat and tried again. No response from the sleeping man.

But the door opened.

And Noah walked in.

Chapter Thirty-one

Shem yelped, his mind spinning circles. He really was dead? This was, was, what? Where?

His father was beside him in a few long strides. He sat on the bed, his weight making a ravine that Shem fell into, collapsing against his shoulder despite efforts to pull away. The man wrapped his arm around Shem's waist and held him up effortlessly. "Shem, Shem," he said, emotion distorting the words.

He looked to his brother. Japheth was awake now and pulled himself up to sitting. He leaned forward with his hands on his knees, his eyes bright. And a grin on his face.

Shem leaned away from the man holding him. The man who smelled of wood shavings and pine oil. Something wasn't right. Japheth didn't look dead. And Shem had a headache. He didn't feel dead.

The man turned so they were face to face. Thinning gray curls shooting all directions, deep brown eyes in crinkled skin, a smile wider and truer than the great sea.

"It's me, Brother!"

Shem grasped the man's arms, confusion melting beneath the warmth of his gaze.

It wasn't Noah.
It was Ham.

Chapter Thirty-two

"Stop it, Shem. You're making me nervous."

Shem pulled his eyes from Ham's face again, trying not to stare. It was him, really him. His baby brother, gone forever, was alive. He couldn't get enough. The familiar eyes were nestled in crevices now, the easy smile revealed gaps in the line of teeth, the thick eyebrows that rose and fell as he talked contained wiry strands that stuck out like porcupine quills, matching the ones poking out of his ears. It was a beautiful sight.

Naomi put a bowl of watery broth on a table in front of him and stuffed more pillows behind his back so he could sit easily. Her green eyes were leaking again. Happy, joyful tears.

Shem glanced at his brother again and shook his head. "When did you turn into Father?"

Ham laughed. "I hadn't realized I did. Age does that I guess. Now eat."

Japheth sat next to him on the bed, attacking the dish of food Naomi placed in front of him. He stabbed a hunk of stew on a skewer and devoured it as if he hadn't eaten in years. The fullness around his jaw line indicated he had been eating well for more than a few days, in fact long enough to sprout a pudge roll around his belly.

"How did we end up here? How long have I been sick?" Shem was eager to fill up on the details.

Ham leaned back in the chair, crossing his arms and resting his feet on an overstuffed cushion. His right arm ended at the wrist in a rounded knob. Smooth, well-healed scars made a stitching line across the top. "You've been here ten days, flirting with the door of death. Whatever berries you tried didn't agree with you."

Shem lifted the bowl and slurped the brown liquid, trying to keep his shaking hands from sloshing too much over the sides. "Ten days? Japheth left to find food. I remember, he didn't come back. He found you in Admah?"

"No. Some local men saw him wandering along the stream bank, looking like a crazy man." Ham caught Japheth's eye and laughed. "They stopped him, scared the last wits out of his head, but managed to figure out he was harmless, and hungry. Japheth led them to you, and the men brought you both to me."

"Were they Amorites? There were men, I think. Really tall men that found me."

Ham nodded. "They are. Good men."

Shem paused mid-drink, then lowered his bowl. "Good men?"

"Good men. They brought you here, didn't they?"

"Why here, and for that matter, where is here?"

Naomi helped him lift the bowl for another drink. "This is our home, outside the cities, between Zeboyim and Zoar."

"They brought you to us because they didn't want to nurse you, but they knew we would. Naomi and I do that sort of thing, helping where we can. It's provided us a measure of protection. We rarely have theft anymore. We're left in peace up here. Like I said, the locals are good people for the most part."

Shem caught his breath for a moment. Was his brother aligned with the Canaanites in his heart? Had he abandoned the God of their fathers?

He leaned into the back rest, letting his head be supported. "You're alive. I can't believe you're both alive."

Naomi squeezed his hand. "We'll help you find Eran. With God, nothing is impossible."

Shem felt another wave of drowsiness descending. There was so much he wanted to know, so much time to fill in. But it would have to wait.

♥

It was obvious Malina and Rez-Nahor had more than a casual bond. Whispering outside her door in the morning, subtle glances, inside humor they tried to suppress when she glanced their direction. She was glad Malina found companionship and could be admired for the lovely young woman she was, despite the odor that lingered in her presence. Marriage was encouraged among Okpara's people. Babies left little room for running away. Malina could still have a fulfilling life. If she didn't disappear.

The guards weren't slaves. Devotion to their employer was by their own choosing. It was that loyalty that made her apprehensive. Rez-Nahor understood the unspoken reasoning behind Eran's attempts to be rid of her fear. Without fear of Amun, nothing but the rushing current stopped her from crossing the river and walking away from the self-titled King of Zoar. Was her guard's loyalty to Okpara stronger than his affection for Malina?

Eran let the thought slide for the moment. She stood on the bank facing the river and was about to put her bare feet in. One concern at a time.

Pounding steps on the trail broke her concentration and she turned toward the winded man, sweat dripping from his forehead. "The Healer. Okpara has summoned the Healer to come right away."

Malina snatched Eran's sandals from the ground and they ran to Khepri's room. Her screams reverberated down the hallway.

Inside, Okpara stood beside her bed, red faced, trying to keep hold of his daughter's flailing arms while avoiding her kicking feet.

"You have to make them go away. Look at me! Look what they're trying to do to me!"

Against the wall, three servants huddled together, faces pale. They were Khepri's personal servants, the ones who endlessly applied makeup and restyled hair.

Eran looked at the woman's face. Kohl circled one eye, ending in a wavy line across her cheek.

"She wouldn't keep still. I couldn't help it," one of the girls squeaked. "I didn't mean to."

"You did! You don't want me to be pretty! Evil little rat!"

Okpara dropped his daughter's wrists and backed away. "Do something!" His finger shook in Eran's face.

She turned to Malina. "The juice. Get the poppy juice."

Malina spun on her heels and left the room to retrieve the medicine. Okpara followed her out the door despite Khepri's demand for his attention. After he was gone, Eran nodded to the girls. "Go to your room and stay there for now, and try not to worry."

Eran was alone with Khepri. The young woman continued screaming curses after the girls but was fatiguing rapidly, making it difficult to keep thrashing. There was a wild look to her eyes, an element of incomprehension and fear along with the irrational paranoia. Her nails raked Eran's arm a few times before her arms finally dropped to the bed and the ranting diminished. She lay on her back sucking in air.

Eran grabbed supplies from the table and sat beside her on the bed. "I'll fix it. I see how the line is messed up, but I can fix it." The screaming would rise up again, Eran was certain, once she had enough air in her lungs. In the lull, she would seek to calm Khepri's anxiety.

She dipped the tip of a soft cloth in almond oil and wiped the line gently, then again with more pressure, continuing the strokes until it was finally removed. "You will always be beautiful. No one can take that from you and no one means you harm." Eran kept her tone low and even, cooing like a mother over her newborn.

Khepri closed and opened her eyes repeatedly, remembering to shut them so Eran could work, then forgetting and opening them, startled until Eran explained what she was doing. Fear and inner turmoil alternated, with only brief periods of full awareness.

Malina tiptoed into the room and hovered beside them. Eran took the small pot of poppy extraction from her and dribbled a tiny amount onto Khepri's tongue. It would quiet her mind, calm her limbs, and put her into a restful state.

Pulling a simple song from her mind, Eran hummed it softly, soothing the girl until the tension in her limbs released and she lay quietly on the bed. She systematically wiped all face paint from Khepri's skin, surprised at the true color. She had the bluish tint of someone who had lost too much blood. Not pronounced, but a symptom a Healer would recognize.

And dread. Somewhere inside, Khepri was oozing the fluid of life from her veins and there was no remedy to stop it.

Chapter Thirty-three

The scruffy canine chomped onto Ham's right forearm, determined to keep it locked tight in his jaws no matter how hard its owner wrestled it back and forth.

Shem laughed, a rich satisfying laugh at the two at play. His brother had devised a hollow wooden tube to fit over his arm. The closed end was a simple hook where his hand should have been. It was a tool of necessity to him, a wonderful toy for his dog.

"What made you decide to remove it?" When Ham left the Hebrew camp, his right hand was still there. It was useless, frozen in a claw, but still had life blood flowing through it.

"Too many projects that I couldn't do. And without feeling, I nearly chopped off a few fingers. More than once. This made more sense." He raised his arm in the air, lifting the dog off the ground.

"How did you ever convince Naomi to make the incision?"

Ham gave the dog a final jerk and it went flying into the grass. He inspected the new teeth imprints. "Oh, I couldn't. She refused. I had to let the dog take care of it."

Shem's stomach churned. He had been lifting a rock up and down, strengthening his arms, but suddenly had to let it fall to the earth. "Oh," was all he could say, the image in his mind unthinkable.

Ham's laugh was good and deep, from his belly. "Don't go all passing out on me again. I wasn't serious. It doesn't know how to chew a straight line."

Same old brother Ham. He should have known.

"I used an axe."

Shem looked up to see his brother's expression so he didn't get fooled again. Ham waited for a response, his eyes wide beneath arching eyebrows.

"This time you're serious?" Shem asked. "You cut your own hand off?" That was no better image in his mind than that of the dog chewing on it.

"I knew it wouldn't hurt too much and had some men here to tend it afterward. They wouldn't do it for me, either. It's much better this way. I have hands in the shape of all manner of tools."

"You built all this yourself, didn't you?" The room he woke up in was only a tiny portion of the stone dwelling. It resembled the home they grew up in, a center courtyard surrounded by four long sides of rooms. To his surprise, there were quite a number of people living there. As he had been told, the local Amorite and Hittite tribes often brought their sick and dying to Ham and Naomi. Some recovered, and left again. Some stayed and worked the fields, or helped with the flocks. As distant kin, they were left alone when it came to mischief. No one raided the camp or threatened their safety.

They were in the courtyard now, beneath the shade of fruit trees, overlooking the nearby hills that were dotted with burial stone mounds.

"Mostly. The house grew over time. We stayed in a cave before that. It's a good place to be, this country. A good place for me, among the children of Canaan. I'm needed here."

"You were needed in the old camp."

"It's different. These are my people, my blood."

Shem nodded. He understood the desire to be among those who called him Father. Like Abraham.

"Remember Abram?" Shem asked. "Came up from Ur with his father?"

Ham shook his head. "Not really. Vaguely recall the name."

"Married to Sarai-"

"Sarai!" Ham plopped onto the ground beside him. "Of course, I remember her." He jabbed his elbow into Shem's side and grinned. "Who could forget? Abram won the prize snagging her from her father's tents. What of them?"

Shem told him of the call to leave the Hebrews and go to Canaan, of the visits from God, the promise of descendants like the stars of the heavens. Of the baby on his way and the covenant seal.

"They did what? All of the men? And I thought I was brave to chop off a hand."

Shem picked up the stone again and lifted it over his head, slowly repeating until his left arm was fatigued, then switching to his right. He waited while Ham got past the dreadful surgery in his mind and absorbed the significance of Abraham's interactions with God.

"God spoke to him, man to man like he did with Father, then? Huh."

Shem forced his arm to lift and straighten without responding.

Ham turned his way and watched him thoughtfully. "You did well, Brother."

Shem didn't know what to say. He dropped the weight and rubbed his arm.

"You don't believe it, do you? That you've done well. You

hold yourself to an impossible measure. Your blood will flow into a nation chosen by the Creator, claimed as his own. Isn't that enough? He chose you, Shem. God chose your tents in which to dwell."

"There is no better blessing. I know this in my head. In my heart, I wish all of my generations were faithful. I hoped all would stay true and we would be strong."

Ham scratched his head with the point of the hook. Shem flinched, waiting for blood to flow but his brother used the tool with precision. "As did I. And Japheth. We all made mistakes, me more than the two of you. And our children all made the choice for themselves. Now there's hope. Your Abraham, sealed into a covenant with the God of Adam, and of Noah. Don't make little of it, Shem. It's your blood in him, and in that baby of his. You've done well, Brother."

Shem allowed Ham's words to soak into his heart, needing to know that his life had not been years and years without purpose.

"Speaking of being sealed." Ham's eyes locked onto Shem's forehead. "My grandson did that to you. I'm so sorry. I miss Nimrod, believe it or not. I miss those earlier days of teaching him to string a bow and swim against a current and hunt game and tan hides. I had so many hopes for him."

Ham dropped his eyes to stare at his right arm, maimed intentionally by Nimrod. "Little boys grow into men and men choose the right or the left. I wish I had pushed him harder to stay on the way that led to truth. When Japheth told me what he did to Eran, and Mother…"

Shem draped his arm over his brother's shoulder. "You've stayed true all these years, though, haven't you? You cling to the One God and his ways."

"I do. I can't repair the damage I did, can't help what my sons have become, but I can make a difference here. Only our God is worshipped in my home and anyone who comes for care leaves with knowledge of truth."

Japheth was the brave, smart brother, full of logic and reason. Shem was the compassionate and spiritual one. He tried to look beyond the surface of a man's actions and understand his heart. And Ham, always the laughter of the family, walking the line of rebellion and seeking pleasure. As his brother spoke, Shem realized Ham had turned from the line, choosing what he knew to be right and true. He saw how wise, how compassionate, how brave, and how spiritual this little brother of his actually was.

♥

"We missed you, teacher!"

"What's wrong? Why were you gone?"

"Are you sick? Are we having lessons again?"

The Lilies clung to Eran, patting her arms and spitting out questions and concerns.

"I'm not sick, and yes, we will continue our lessons. Malina and I have been with Khepri. She's the one who is sick."

Hehet brightened. "You'll heal her then. We'll help you."

Eran caught Malina's eye. They had spent most of the previous three days and nights in Khepri's room, sleeping in shifts, monitoring her breathing and how fast her heart was beating. They gave her liquids for nourishment and a drop of poppy juice when she was agitated, keeping her calm and asleep as much as possible. Today she would hold the pain relievers and sleep aids to see what condition the woman was in.

Both she and Malina prayed to their gods for healing beyond their abilities. One to the God of Adam, the other to Bastet. Only one was truly alive and able to hear the words of supplication. As Malina burned her incense and said her prayers, Eran felt the pain of separation between them, united in purpose but not bound by cords of truth. It was a great gulf, one that most of her own children had leapt across at one time, their feet landing in flowery meadows. They remained rooted there, not seeing the weeds, or the withering of the reasoning they had chosen. They saw what they wanted to see, held to the gods that promised the most, adding others if one or another didn't live up to expectations.

As a young bride, God had opened her heart to his words of truth. He could do so for these pupils in her charge. She would speak what she knew until they knew it, too, and hopefully chose to believe.

Malina stopped before the statue of Bastet to offer prayers. Eran stood with the girls to one side and waited until she was finished, then led them to an ornately carved pedestal positioned in a ring of soft pink roses. It stood empty, anticipating the arrival of another god once Okpara discovered its existence. He would add it to the others.

She pointed to the empty stand. "How many gods are there?"

The girls silently counted the ones they knew in their minds, believing there was an ultimate answer.

"There are very many, aren't there?" Eran interrupted the calculations. "Some you pray to when you are at war, some when you are sick, some for your fields and some for the blessing of many sons."

Eran sat down and indicated they should as well. "I pray only to one."

"The One God, of Adam and Noah," Maat said.

"That's correct. And I believe there is but one. One with power over all. It is he who I seek when I pray."

"You've prayed to him about Khepri, then?"

"Yes."

"Will he listen? Will she be better?"

"He hears. I don't know if she will be made well. It is the decision he must make."

"If she dies, will you choose another god?"

If she died, Eran in all likelihood would as well. How would they understand? "No. I will go to my grave standing for the One who saved me from the flood. Him, and no other."

Like Shem. Willing to risk his life, and hers, to be faithful. Could she be so brave? She wanted to be, wanted to be strong like that on the outside and in. She wanted to stand unwavering, despite any threat that challenged her footing.

Her husband had not bowed to Amraphel, surrounded by sharpened weapons, he held fast. Could she? It wasn't a test she wanted to take. If a knife was held to her throat, she didn't know if she could follow his example.

♥

Khepri was sleeping soundly after eating a small bit of bread. Eran finished cleaning her skin, noting the pink tones in her cheeks and lips. Not blue.

Malina gathered soiled linens from the rim of a washtub and started a heap on the floor. "She'll be demanding a sound hair washing and brushing soon."

Eran dumped ashes from the incense bowls into a lined basket. They were supposed to be spread at the feet of Bastet in the garden. She had never done this, instead alternating where they went. Sometimes to the roses, sometimes to the herb beds, or to whatever plants needed to be nourished. Some she had given to the

Lilies for making kohl before realizing the soot was sacred.

Malina stared at the ashes, then looked up and frowning.

"Master Okpara assumes you pray to the gods of healing, to Bastet especially, since she is Khepri's chosen. If she gets worse again and he finds out, he'll blame you based on that alone. He won't see that you've done your best to save her. He'll see that you were negligent. He won't understand why you don't add other gods."

"I know."

"You'll disappear."

Eran stopped her task and looked Malina in the eye. "I know."

"You want to die, then? You miss your home so much, you'd rather die than pretend to worship his deities? What of the girls? Have you no feelings for them?"

Of course she loved her Lilies, and Malina, too. "I don't wish to die, or to harm anyone. But I can't be untruthful. It's wrong. Lies only lead to more lies."

Malina watched her for a moment before returning to the soiled linens. She jerked sheets from the bed and wadded them into tight balls before pitching them to the pile. "You realize, it isn't just about you. We might all disappear."

Chapter Thirty-four

Denah spilled from the donkey and into her husband's arms, puffs of dust from her clothes enveloping them in a cloud. She clung to Japheth's neck just long enough to adequately express joy in seeing him after so many weeks then pulled free to embrace Naomi. It was a heart-rending reunion. They cried. The men cried. Even the donkeys seemed to bray in a spirit of thanksgiving.

The household of Ham feasted, entertaining the young men from Abraham's camp who escorted Denah back to her husband. Everyone was full of questions, full of stories, full of awe. Shem finally managed to catch Denah's ear to ask about Sarah. "Is she carrying a baby? Is there really a little Isaac getting knit together in her womb?"

"You can tell now if you're looking." Denah patted her own belly. "And believe me, everyone is looking. Poor Sarah. She doesn't seem to mind though. She and Abraham walk as if there was nothing but clouds beneath their feet, and she's healthy."

"And the men?"

Ham groaned dramatically.

"They healed just fine." Her expression turned serious. "And, if we want men for any reason, to help us find Eran, Abraham says he will send as many as you want and they will be willing to come. They are eager to be of service."

An army. It was good to have the support. Good to know they had back-up in strong, fighting numbers. But where would he send them? He didn't know where his wife was.

Japheth stared up into the night sky, his arm holding Denah securely against his side. "Abraham. Our future." He dropped his head and smiled. "On the ark, I remember the first time I stood outside, in the darkness, alone. The rain had stopped and there was nothing. Just water below and stars above. The flood happened and it was all like Father said. And still, still I stood there and tried to figure it all out. Tried to make a plan. As if it was up to me. God did his thing, now I was supposed to take over."

Shem had to smile. Japheth made the first chore list. What beasts to feed when and how much, who cleaned which messes, who fed the humans. His forty-day plan had to be repeated many times over as it became evident they wouldn't be leaving the ark as soon as they thought. There was far more water beneath them than any had ever imagined.

Japheth chuckled at his own memories. "Then as I stood there, I thought about that door, how I worried we wouldn't be able to close it."

All five of them laughed.

"God shut us in the ark. He would let us out when he was ready. It was all his timing. For the first time, I really understood that he was making the decisions. It's his timing now too. He promised to live in Shem's tents, and has chosen a man of Shem's generations to bless with that promise."

Naomi put her head on Ham's shoulder. "A baby, and one day a nation in covenant with the Creator. For all the sin and rebellion, the hope remains."

Hope gave strength. The future was secured in the hands of the divine. But there was also the now, the present, and the emptiness of his arms. Life had pain. Children were taken, men were killed, crops destroyed. Families split. And wives were stolen, never to return home.

Shem needed hope for today.

There were only five of them huddled around the warming fire. Not six. Shem quietly stood and walked into the night, leaving his brothers with wives held firmly against their hearts. His ached for Eran.

♥

The cool flow on her ankles was unnerving. Eran shifted from foot to foot, fighting black spots. Malina and the girls splashed around her, enjoying the water as she was trying so very hard to do herself. She focused on the hills beyond the river. The peaceful landscape, the freedom it appeared to offer. Cross the river and be there, she told herself. Walk away from captivity.

And do what? Fight for survival. She had done it before, when they left the protection of the ark. She wasn't alone then. No one relied on her to provide all the food and shelter. She could do it, though, or at least try. If the Lilies were in danger, she'd take them with her. And Malina, if she wanted to go.

Khepri had been getter stronger for over a week. She was genuinely pleasant at times, and seemed to be past the illness. Then she would ask Malina the same question two or three times and the irritability would start its rise, as if she knew her mind wasn't functioning as it should. It hadn't escalated to tantrums of screaming. Not yet.

244 – Rachel S. Neal

She turned to find Malina studying her face. When their eyes met, the woman turned her gaze to the hills where Eran's had been.

"Can you do it? Are you going to leave?"

Eran stepped out of the water and tried not to appear flustered. "What?" She glanced at the girls. They were pinching their noses and ducking under the water, paying no attention to the conversation. Rez-Nahor's gaze was fixed on the river and he didn't flinch at the suggestion. He heard though, and Eran bit down on her lip.

Malina turned to search the bank, picking up a stick which she sent flying across the water. It fell into the churning flow, bobbing past them on its way down river. "No," she said. "You can't leave. You'll take your chances here. You can't find your freedom if you can't swim."

Eran snapped her head around. Malina put her hands on her hips and pointed at the river with her chin.

"Do again, Eran," she said. "Get back in."

Eran filled her lungs with air and unclenched her fingers, stepping back into the river, less aware of the sinking in her gut this time. More aware of the necessity in overcoming her fear. Malina's intentions were obvious. She was training Eran to make an escape.

♥

"Keep away Denah." Ham tossed the last biscuit in the air above Shem's head and a little beyond so that he had to run. He managed to snatch it before it fell, just before Denah's hands grabbed his arm and pulled it down. With quick maneuvering, he dodged and slid from her grasp, tossing the prize to Japheth, who jumped up behind his wife to catch it.

Denah was all over Japheth like a bear after honey, growl included, clawing and nearly climbing up his trunk. Japheth squirmed into every conceivable formation, the biscuit held high above his head until she jabbed his side with her elbow. Shem darted behind his brother, ready for a backward over-the-shoulder toss. He didn't see Ham's dog. He fell, grunting as he hit the earth.

The biscuit sailed over his head and bounced just once before the dog clamped on and turned it to crumbly wet bits.

Ham laughed, his wonderful deep-from-the-gut laugh. "That was pathetic! When did my brothers get so old?"

Shem bent over at the waist, hands on his knees, winded. How many years since they played that game? It was their great-grandfather Methuselah's favorite. He was always offered the last of the food, usually a piece of bread baked a little too long. If he didn't want it, he offered it to the three young sons of Noah with a toss and a "keep away" from one of them. It would be an all out battle, despite the fact the item of desire wasn't even remotely edible by the time they were spent. Of course, that took a long while and by then, the meal was cleaned up and the adults winding down for the night. Years later it occurred to him that it was an intentional ploy for the three to run off excess energy before bed. And that his mother seemed to over-bake a roll or two every so often. On purpose.

They played a similar game with the little ones of the Hebrew camp, just not with food. It was too valuable to destroy intentionally. A ball of cloth was adequate, just never the same.

"That. Was harder. Than it. Should've been." Shem laughed as he sucked down air and forced the words out.

"It's good for you," Ham said, rewarding the dog with a scratch behind the ears for spitting the treat remains at his feet. "Now you should check the road again."

His little brother took it upon himself to see that he and Japheth were getting stronger. And it was paying off. He could feel the tone in his limbs again and was walking more each day. He nodded and started up the short rise from where they were to a point where he could see the road below.

A caravan was expected sometime today, and they were watching to see whether it turned for Zeboyim or kept on the road toward Zoar. Daily for the past three weeks they had monitored the arrivals. Once they knew where a caravan was headed, Ham's men took silver coins and fast horses to intercept and ask about Eran.

Shem looked down at the forked road. The caravan itself was a dust cloud still, another hour perhaps until it reached the point below Ham's land. He sighed and stood for a minute. For all the silver paid out, they had garnished mostly great humor from the caravan guides. No one traded in old women.

The caravans came and went at fairly regular intervals, according to Ham, and could be tracked. Some were six months coming and going, others a month or two, depending on the distance. For the most part, the large caravans kept to the same paths, knowing water sources, dangerous areas, and merchants along the way. Smaller groups joined the larger ones, but there were always identifying features of each long line of camels, carts and donkeys. They were taking note of each one. They would know in time when all the regular caravans had been questioned.

Then what? He didn't know. He didn't want to think about it, praying his answers were in the next stream of travel weary merchants.

He was about to go back down when he saw a movement in the hills to his right. Automatically he reached for a weapon before remembering he didn't have one on. Keep Away was dangerous with sharp objects tied to one's waist. He stooped behind a rock.

A young girl stumbled from the brush, falling to her hands and knees.

Shem called down to his brothers then ran to the girl.

She tried to push him away, then gave up and fell to her side. Her eyes were full of pain, her arms cradling a very round abdomen on her thin frame. Shem helped her lie in the grass and spoke reassuring words over her, gently brushing the tangles of hair from her face.

The others dropped to the earth beside them. "She's too young to have a baby." Denah took her hand and tried to communicate. The girl spoke a different tongue, her words laced with fear as she looked from face to face. Denah rubbed the young mother's arm as they watched anxiously for Ham, who had gone for more help.

It was a short wait. He came with a litter and four young men to lift it. Two other men were sent to the ridge. "They'll keep watch," Ham said. "And go to the caravan when it is close enough. Come pray with us."

Shem had been strong enough only the last few days to ride to the caravans. He hesitated, not wanting to leave the questioning to others any longer. What if they missed something, or gave up too easily. What if-"

"It's alright, Brother." Japheth interrupted his thoughts. "They'll ask the right questions."

Shem turned away and followed the litter to the house, taking focus from Eran and directing it toward the agonized cries of this new presence among them. She was someone's daughter. A stranger, dependent upon the kindness of others in her time of great need. Her face reflected the intense fear alongside the pains, not knowing what would come next.

Had Eran found a refuge like the home of his brother? Had God led her to a place of safety?

At once he knew it was imperative that he pray for this young woman and that they did all they could for her. He prayed someone was doing the same for his wife.

♥

The girl had a wreath around her neck, beneath her outer cloak. She had been unwilling for it to be removed, clinging to it desperately through the pains. When she finally birthed the tiny boy and had fallen asleep, Naomi had removed it to bathe her properly. It was on top of the heap of clothing outside her room, where Shem paced and prayed.

It was simple, woven with an unpracticed hand. Cloves of garlic and wild onion were tied on with pieces of vine. The girl probably made it herself as a talisman of sorts.

Shem's hand shook as he examined it. Anyone could form a wreath. Even here, in the land of Canaan, the craft was practiced. It wasn't a skill inherent to the Hebrews. It wasn't a skill belonging to Eran alone. He found a wreath on a grave and clung to it as proof of her presence.

He pursued his wife based on nothing.

Eran was still in Nineveh. Or Haran or Damascus. She might at that moment be asleep in their tent, his tent, among the Hebrews.

Or she might be dead.

He dropped the wreath and went outside, to the dark stillness. Finding a stone requiring both hands to lift, he hoisted it overhead, holding it as long as his arms could before the muscles burned and quivered. He rested briefly then lifted it again.

And again.

And again.

Chapter Thirty-five

"The weave of her clothing makes me think she's from Zoar." Naomi held the tiny infant while his mother slept. "And not a prostitute. She doesn't have the scars of abuse and was clean except the grit under her toenails. I suspect she's a farm hand's daughter."

They had all awakened early to the meek wail of the newborn. Mother and child still lived, but neither thrived.

"Why was she out here alone?" Denah set a tray of grapes, goat cheese and flat bread in front of them, then collapsed back on a pillow. It had been a grueling night, fighting off death for both newcomers.

"I imagine she knew the birth wasn't going to be easy," Ham said. "She's so young. Or her mother did, or the father, or a master perhaps. She was sent to Naomi on purpose."

"Alone, though?"

Ham caught Naomi's eye and smiled. "They're a mighty superstitious lot down in Zoar. No one leaves the safety of home without good reason, even to accompany a pregnant girl to a midwife. But the fact that she was sent is a good sign. It means someone actually cares about her and the child. Odd as that sounds, she probably has family. If we don't have to bury them, we'll bring her and the babe back to her people in a few weeks."

"The wreath." Shem tried to form a logical question. Two words were all that came from his efforts.

Naomi ran the tip of her thumb on the baby's tiny nose. "More superstition. A ward against evil. The smell is supposed to keep death away and it's been prayed over, blessed by the girl's gods. Of course, if her boy lives, she'll believe it was because of the gods and goddesses asked to bless it, and her. We'll tell her otherwise of course. She'll hear truth from one of our shepherds who speaks her language."

Her gaze re-directed to Shem, understanding the turmoil in his mind. "They are common in this region, made for idols and as talismans for the living. I've never seen one placed on a grave."

Shem nodded, his whole body fatigued. He would not relinquish hope. That much he decided in the night as he pushed his body to build its strength and pushed his spirit to stand strong on a rock of faith. He had a home with his brother or with Abraham, and could be useful, finding purpose as they did until God allowed him to find Eran.

God knew the timing and he could bring Shem and his wife together. It wasn't a matter of "if" he could. Would he choose to?

♥

A light rapping on the door startled Eran from the verge of sleep. She folded the covers back and sat up as the door opened and Malina slipped in, quietly shutting the door behind her.

"Malina, what's wrong? Is it Khepri?"

"No. Here." She pulled a cloth bound bundle from beneath her arm and handed it to Eran then pulled the drapes apart enough to let in the moonlight.

Carefully unwrapping the package, Eran found a pair of sandals. They were like her own, leather strapping attached to a sole. The only difference was the wooden base fastened beneath the sole. It was a very simply carved base, and as tall as her fist.

"Practice wearing those," Malina said.

"Why?"

Malina sighed, briefly irritated at her lack of comprehension. "I'm taller than you. It'll be obvious when you take the cart down the hall that you aren't me."

She clutched the shoes into her chest, the pieces of Malina's escape plan connecting.

Eran would disguise herself and take the cart of pots down the hall, outside, to the river, where she could swim to freedom. The guards turned their heads, she remembered, avoiding the woman and her insulting duty. Only Rez-Nahor would notice.

Would it work? Could she do it? A weight sunk in her gut.

Malina was staring intently at her face, her eyebrows raised.

"I understand. I'd have to swim. I, I can't. You know that."

"You can."

"And you? Will you come with me? And the girls, can we get them out?"

Malina's mouth fell open. "You expect a lot."

"You could find your people, start a new life. Or you could come with me. I have relatives in Hebron. We could find them. All of us."

Malina shook her head. "The girls won't disappear. No one will blame them for what happens to Khepri. They are safer here than anywhere you take them."

"And you? If we time it right, we can both get out. One morning, together. With Rez-Nahor, if you want, if he is willing."

Malina snapped her eyes to the door, then back at Eran. "Why would you say that? Why would I want him to go?"

"I can see the bond you have with him. I know he's loyal to Okpara, but if you mean enough to him-"

"Don't think about taking anyone, Eran. When you're ready you'll go. Alone."

"I don't want anything to happen to you."

Malina eased the door open and looked out. Rez-Nahor checked the hall in both directions, ignoring her except for a quick nod. Malina looked back at Eran. "I have to go. The guards switch for the night soon. And don't worry so much. I don't intend for anything to happen to me."

She didn't elaborate. "Why? Why are you doing this for me?"

Malina absently ran her hands over her arms. "My father didn't deserve whatever happened to him. And you, you don't deserve to disappear either."

♥

Denah's hand on his shoulder was gentle but persistent. "Wake up. Open your eyes, Shem."

Shem roused from the dream to wakefulness, finding himself lying under a mound of soft covers in the room where they had been praying for the mother and child. It was dark, and the others were gone. He sat up and ran his hand over his face, cranking his neck back and forth to loosen the knots.

"The baby?"

"He's weak, but alive. His mother is sleeping. I was just checking on them. You were dreaming, thrashing about. I thought I should wake you."

"Dreaming. Yes." The dream again, the words of his father

repeating over and over this time. He swallowed the bile it left in his throat, the unfulfilled expectancy. Why had it returned?

Denah paused a moment, allowing him to continue if he wanted. He didn't. He pushed it away. It had no meaning for him any longer. Abraham was the object of God's favor, and the fulfillment was through him.

She sat beside him, gathering her long hair behind her head and pulling it into a knot. "On the ark, I found a basket tucked into a corner. It held my essential clothing and a comb that once belonged to my mother, and perfume, and other bits and pieces that mattered to me for personal reasons. I thought Japheth put it there."

Shem didn't respond. It had been a time of chaos, loading the ark, facing the reality of judgment. They hadn't known what would become of Denah then.

"He didn't. Eran did. Eran gathered what I needed and put them on board, days before I came back to Noah's land. Hope, she told me later. She held onto the hope that God would restore me, lead me back into his plan for salvation."

"She prayed constantly for you."

"She understands hope. And faith. She acted in my behalf without any guarantees I would choose to return. There is strength in hope, Shem. Where ever she is, she has the strength to persevere. I know she relied on you, on Noah and Jael, on me even. But it's in her, a sound trust in her God, ears to hear his voice, and the strength to follow his leading."

"She's stronger than she realizes." Shem smacked his hands on his knees. "And I'm weaker than I thought. I say I trust God, but I'm fighting anger. I feel he's let me down."

"It's hard to understand why he allowed her to be taken."

Shem stared into his tented hands so Denah wouldn't read the extent of shame in his confession, sure it was visible in his eyes like the ugly mark on his forehead. "There may never be an end to it. It may not end all nice for me like it did for Japheth, when you came back and healed the rips in his heart."

Denah was quiet. Too quiet. Shem looked at her, ready to apologize for the uncensored words he allowed to spill from his mind. Her eyes were closed so he took her hand and squeezed it, finding no words.

"No." Her tone was smooth and forgiving. "You may never find her. And still you will trust in the One who saves. It's alright to be angry when life hurts, when you think God has turned a deaf ear to your heart. It doesn't mean there's no purpose in the pain, even when it seems senseless. Hope rests in God's ultimate goodness, Shem. Your hope, and Eran's."

♥

Three caravans snaked their way down the valley, the links separated by short lengths of the road between them. Each was a block of similar colored tarps and painted wagons. Shem and Ham monitored their positions. Three groups of scouts and three bags of silver were needed for the unusual confluence.

"There must have been a hold up along the way for them to be that close together. Bad for them. Good for us. Prices will be low in town," Ham said. "I'll send extra men for supplies."

"How long has it been, since you went yourself?" His little brother once loved the busy chaos of city life. He frequented the markets and bartered like no one else, stealing deals before the merchants realized they were taking a loss from the slick tongued young man.

Ham scratched his clean shaven chin. "Several years. Maybe

eight or ten even. It didn't go well the last time. The people of Zoar are frightened of most everything and anyone they don't know. It's not so bad in the markets and the caravansary, but beyond that, they don't welcome strangers. It isn't somewhere to be at night, for sure. Being outside the safety of your home in the darkness is asking for a trouble."

"Your men are safe there?"

"They are. Most come from this region and speak the local languages, so aren't so suspect." Ham raised his right arm. "Plus, they have all their parts. Even missing a hand makes the locals tremble, as if it's contagious."

Shem nodded. He'd seen the looks his brother got after the hand was maimed. "You miss it though, don't you? You want to be in the midst haggling over the goods yourself?"

Ham smiled. "I was good at it, huh? It's just better that I don't go now. Nimrod has spies everywhere. You think he'd forget about hating his Grandfather after all this time, but I can't rely on it. If he knew where I was, there would be trouble." He glanced at Shem's scar. "He doesn't forget his grudges. To protect Naomi and the others here, I have to stay out of sight."

"That's why we didn't hear from you after you left, isn't it? You were protecting us."

Ham shrugged. "It was safer for you, safer for me. The less anyone knew, the better for us all."

Shem turned his focus to the road below. "Abraham warned us about the sin in the cities of the plain, in Gomorrah and Sodom mostly. Is it as bad as he says?"

"It is. Immorality is the lifestyle they've chosen. The rich own the land, leaving the poor to fend for themselves, intentionally creating an endless supply of prostitutes to meet an endless supply of lust. Parents give their children up for a night in exchange for a meal. Women are traded like cheap trinkets. Travelers have to stay with their guides, it's so bad. There's no guarantee of safety and no law to protect them. It's appalling. When anyone comes to us for care, we offer them a home away from that life. Some stay. Some don't."

"Such a lush valley. It's unfortunate."

"Food and water come readily to the land owners. They're left with plenty of time for pursuits of an ungodly nature."

Shem pushed the image of Eran from his mind. He didn't want to see her there.

Ham read his thoughts. "She's an old woman, Brother. Not likely one to be bothered."

"If she isn't in Admah, Zoar, or Zeboyim, I don't know what I will do, where I will go next...."

"Stay here. I don't think Japheth will be able to pull Denah away from Naomi. Let's all be together again."

"Thank you. Your purpose is certainly in this land. I don't know where mine is yet."

Ham kicked at small stones, sending them over the hill top one by one. "Don't know where to build your ark?"

Shem collected a handful of stones and tossed them at the ones his brother sent over the edge, trying to careen them off course. "Care to explain?"

Ham gave him a one-sided smile. "Son of Noah. Hard to escape the shadow."

Shem missed his target by several cubits.

Ham laughed. "I see my observations are correct. Priest of the One God, you believe you're supposed to have a great destiny, a memorable one like Father's."

Shem stared at his brother, amazed at his insight. "It's been a struggle, I admit. A confusing one. Father told me the future was

258 – Rachel S. Neal

my responsibility. I've held that belief for a century, not knowing what I'm supposed to do. But, it isn't up to me any longer. Abraham has the covenant. Not me. Somehow I've done my part. I guess by fathering the lineage of Sarah and Abraham, I fulfilled Father's prophesy. If it was prophesy."

"Great and mighty things will happen through Abraham. Not an exciting end for you. Is your pride feeling stomped on, Brother? Is there a bit of jealousy in your heart?"

Shem bristled, choosing to launch a rock from his arm, watch it soar into the sky, then plummet into the stream far below before responding. In that length of time, his defenses crumbled beneath the weight of his conscience. The ugly spot had festered since they left Abraham's camp. He tried to heal it but it persisted, poking him like a thorn caught in his sandal. "Jealous? Maybe. Maybe more than a bit."

Ham raised one eyebrow. "It's pouring out of you like a wine bag stuck with a knife."

All his life he tried to serve his father's God. He questioned the whole flood thing, of course. Not out loud, and not for long. He chose to believe and act in faith. He chose to trust in the God of Adam.

He chose to believe after the ark was fixed on the new earth, and after God splintered the generations of Noah into seventy-some tribes. He chose the path of faithfulness every step away from his home to the land near Haran, where he taught the Hebrews how to stay true. He didn't get it right every moment, but there was never a time in all his many years that he stepped away from the truth of his beginnings, the Truth of his God.

But God had not chosen to speak to him.

And he asked nothing of Shem beyond the ordinary duties of all men.

Shame tightened a noose around his pride. Shem inhaled and dropped the rocks from his hand. "I'm behaving like a spoiled child. How can I hold it against Abraham, son of my own blood? God has chosen me, my lineage to bear his name. I need to see it as the blessing that it is."

Ham said nothing as he gazed over the countryside.

"I'm an old man now Ham. I'm tired of turmoil. Really, it's good that Abraham has the weight to carry now. I don't know if I could anymore."

Ham dropped his arm on Shem's shoulder. "Oh, you could. We aren't that old. And you do realize that Abraham wasn't asked to build an ark either, right? He has it easy compared to Father. He had to move around some and spend time with his wife, is all. Well, that and the whole circumcision thing."

Shem exhaled and allowed his heart to lighten.

"Think about it, Shem. We're the ones who are really blessed in all this. We see the future, secure. And we don't have to start cutting down trees, or cutting any body parts either."

Footsteps interrupted their laughter. Japheth ran up the hill and stopped beside them, pointing at the road. The first caravan had made the turn toward the city, its black banded awnings moving steadily toward its destination. Ham's men were already in pursuit.

"Shall we go after the second one?" Japheth asked. He had a pack of supplies already strapped to his waist, the eager glint in his eyes, anxious to do something. "They can't move too fast and I imagine they'll be eager to earn any extra profit available." He jiggled the stash of coins.

Shem looked down at the line of beasts and burdens in their monotonous plod toward water, food and rest. The faded pinkish colored coverings of the second caravan were followed by the third group, a chain of brighter colored ones, yellow and white striped, glaring beneath the sun's rays.

In a moment, he was back home, sitting among the rocks on a ledge, praying for Eran as the caravans passed. His head, searing with pain, was wrapped in fresh bandages. His heart was shredded. The yellow striped awnings had rumbled below him in a hazy flow. It spoke in its rhythm, to his soul, beseeching him to leave his post, leave his home, and start life again away from all that brought him sorrow. He thought he heard his name out loud once too, shouted into the dusty wind and melding with the sounds of life moving on.

He didn't imagine then that the voice might have been real.

His heart pounded.

"No. Not that one. We'll chase the last caravan," he said. "I've seen it before. It called me once. It calls again."

Chapter Thirty-six

The sharp pinch on her upper arm drove the darkness away. Eran recoiled from Malina's hand, her foot automatically stepping further into the water. The sudden cool, wet surge on her thigh made her gasp. She steadied herself in the current, planting her feet between slippery rocks and allowing the water to churn around her on its journey. Breathing in and out with concentration, she talked out loud. "I'm alright. It's just water."

One goal had already been achieved for the day. Eran walked the corridor in the tall shoes without stumbling. She was certain it was Rez-Nahor who helped with shoe construction. He didn't comment on her growth spurt but she saw him suppress a smile when she opened her door and took the first few clunky steps. He didn't trail as far behind her either and his hands were weapon free, ready to put her upright if she tipped.

The second goal was to stand in water up to her waist.

The guard watched her from the bank, ready to dive in and catch her if she fainted. He was responsible for her safety, and her imprisonment. Eran knew the man understood the purpose in the shoes and the lessons in the river. He was choosing to ignore the obvious. At least, for now.

Malina stepped further into the river. "You have to get to your waist at least. Try again."

Eran shivered, unable to move. It made no difference if the shoes were successful, if she could fool the guards at the door and in the hall, and make her way outside. The river imprisoned her. At her speed of progress, it would be a year before she could actually swim across. If then. Perhaps Rez-Nahor understood that too. He wouldn't lose her anytime soon.

"I can't. I-"

Her words were cut short. A guard pushed past foliage and found her with his eyes.

Eran immediately clasped her hands over her heart. They only came running after her for one reason.

He turned to Rez-Nahor. "She's needed inside. Quickly. Khepri's room."

Malina grabbed Eran's arm and pulled her out of the river. Two days ago, Khepri had been out of bed and dressed when they checked her, immaculate in appearance though thin and obviously lacking stamina. Eran believed the episode was over and prayed she could conquer her fear of the river before the next bout of illness arrived. The bouts were getting worse according to Malina. Just like the ones ending the life of Khepri's mother.

Eran stooped to retrieve her shoes from the bank, then hid them in the foliage. She couldn't wear them now. She had no choice but to run barefooted.

Okpara paced the room in front of the wall of windows, stopping when Eran and Malina entered. His eyes traveled up and down her body, over her clinging wet tunic and her muddy feet. His displeasure was evident.

Eran shifted her eyes from his scowl to Khepri. She sat in a high back chair sipping wine from a goblet with a steady hand. Her eyes were bright, her skin tone pale but not gray. She was relaxed, a hint of a smile on her lips, as if watching a good performance.

Against the wall behind Khepri stood six girls, three older ones clutching the hands of the three little ones.

Eran's heart jumped. Her Lilies stood with Khepri's servants. Their eyes were wide and laced with fear.

Okpara pointed his chin at Eran, his eyes tracking the footprints on the otherwise spotless floor. "Took a day from your duties to go swimming?"

"We-"

Malina interrupted. "We were looking for river weeds, for ointments."

Okpara nodded. "That's why the lessons ended early? Shouldn't your little pupils be assisting? Isn't that why you are their teacher?" He addressed Eran.

She swallowed hard and tried to sound calm. "I didn't ask them to go to the river today. I asked them to pray for your daughter rather than go with me this time."

Okpara licked his lips and clasped his hands behind his back, resuming the pacing. "Yes. So I understand." He stopped moving and stood before Bastet, a golden one with emerald eyes. She was adorned in a lavender wreath and a shroud of incense. "Pray to whom?"

Eran breathed in, praying at the same time. "To my God."

He nodded, no surprise written across his face. He knew the answers already. "And who else?"

"No other."

"No. Other. Not Bastet, or Horus, or Ra?"

"No."

"The girls have been forbidden to seek the gods of my household? Of their homeland?"

"No. It is for them to choose, ultimately. I asked them to pray today to the One God because I know it is he who hears. It is he who can take the sickness from your daughter."

Khepri smacked her goblet down on a tiled table, sloshing wine over the rim. "No wonder I've been sick. You've angered Bastet."

Eran watched her pick up a bite of fig and nibble at it. Last week Eran had to hold food to her lips, she tired so readily. She fed herself today, was clear minded, and sat unsupported. Khepri was clearly improving. For now, at least.

Okpara turned to the girls. They stiffened under his gaze. "Your pupils were heard praying to your god. Out loud, in the children's quarters."

"I didn't ask them to seek his favor in secret."

"It was suggested they take incense and prayers to the garden, since they were so intent on seeking blessings. They were asked to appeal to all the esteemed ones whose divine assistance I require. They didn't want to."

Eran swallowed hard.

"The Healer asked them to pray to her god and that's what they intended to do. One unknown god. No more."

Okpara ran a hand over Bastet's feline features. "You've poisoned their minds. Now what good are they to me?"

Eran's heart hammered uncontrollably. "It's my fault. They're following my instructions."

"Then you'll stop this nonsense? Teach them the prayers of Bastet? Give her the homage she deserves?" His face was the color of beets, his hand clenching and unclenching.

It was a meaningless ritual. It would save her, and the Lilies.

Eran felt the quaking in her limbs, standing on the precipice of decision.

She was Shem before Amraphel.

And there was only one truth.

"I serve only one God. I can worship no other."

♥

All sound evaporated from the room.

Eran looked each child in the eye and tried to give reassurance. Had she given them a sentence of death?

Malina was trembling. Eran found her hand and gripped it tightly for a moment then let go, not wanting Okpara to connect them, and condemn them together. Malina had the chance to separate herself from Eran's stand, to spare herself if she chose. It was a decision only she could make. And her Master knew it.

Okpara lifted a bowl of fresh myrrh resin from the table and inhaled the fragrance, then offered it to Malina. His dark eyes were narrowed, offering her a choice that needed no words to define.

The woman hesitated, her chest heaving up and down. Without looking at Eran, she stepped forward and took it from his hands. "Shall I light it and say the prayers now?"

Rez-Nahor released a breath. Khepri clapped her hands. Malina dropped her head.

Okpara didn't respond, his focus on Eran alone. His finger was in her face. "Why did I buy you? I should have known nothing but ignorance came from the land of the two rivers. You backward stubborn lot. Don't understand anything. Primitive. I treat you well and you repay me by spreading lies among my people. You're trying to ruin me! You anger my gods and threaten my good fortunes."

Eran folded her arms over her chest, holding herself from collapsing under the tirade.

"You risk the life of my daughter." The accusation was spit at her, venomous and searing, the one insult he could not forgive.

She was aware of Rez-Nahor's breath on her neck, standing ready to follow his Master's commands. His breathing was fast, anticipating what? She stiffened her spine, preparing herself.

The Lilies were crying in the arms of Khepri's maids. Okpara's voice raised over their sobs as the insults continued. On and on it went. Finally he was spent of his fury.

"What should I do with you, Healer?" Okpara turned from her and walked to his daughter's side. He stroked her silky hair and smiled down at her.

Khepri took his hand and kissed it. "Are you finished, Father? I want my hair braided."

Okpara stared past Malina, frozen with the bowl in her hands, to Bastet's gleaming image. "Put her in the storehouse."

Rez-Nahor grabbed her arm.

Eran looked to Malina, desperate for an indication of compassion.

Malina closed her eyes and turned away.

♥

The cell had light only from the perimeter around the door. Eran sat on the floor on the opposite side, her back to the stone wall. It was a storage room, lined with shelves and smelling of cinnamon and cumin. The wooden planks were mostly empty, the crates of spices on their way to some city or another. Traded and sold as she had been.

And would again?

Okpara imprisoned her in the vacant room hours ago. For how long? She had no way to know. She hadn't been killed. Or taken away. Or put in a proper prison cell. This confinement was temporary, and she figured Khepri's health would determine when it ended. And how it ended.

Eran rubbed her hands over her ears, the terrified cries of the children still ringing there. They had listened to her teaching and followed her example, and she was proud of them but they hadn't realized the cost. Not that she would have taught them differently. Warned them, perhaps. Prepared them somehow. Now she could do nothing to protect them. They were in God's hands.

Malina made her choice, too.

"I serve only the One God," Eran said, out loud. Her words reverberated in the closed space, bouncing from the walls and covering her with a blanket of assurance. It was truer now than ever. Although fear crawled along her skin as she waited, deep inside Eran found bedrock, a firm, unmoving foundation. Her faith rested there, in the God who saves.

♥

The strip of light widened. Eran blinked her eyes against the brightness.

"Eran?" Malina found her in the darkness, quickly stepping away from the cracked open door. "Are you hurt?" There was concern in her voice.

Eran let go of her knees and straightened her spine, stiff after the long hours in prayer. "No. I wasn't beaten."

The woman crouched down and set a chamber pot nearby. "I brought this."

Malina wasn't sent to release her or take her to Okpara. Eran reached for her hand, the contact comforting. "Thank you. Am I here for the night?"

"I don't know."

"What happened after I left? The Lilies...?"

"Khepri told her girls to fix her face and hair, like nothing happened. Like that's all that mattered. Okpara dismissed the little ones. They won't be held responsible for, for what you taught them."

Relief broke through her stress. "And you?"

"I'm to continue their lessons for now."

"While he searches for a new Healer."

Malina squeezed her hand firmly. "I don't know if he's made that decision yet. I think he'll see how Khepri does before..."

"Before I disappear."

Eran leaned back onto the wall. Malina and the girls were safe. She was not. "When your father and the others disappeared, do you know what happened to them?"

Malina shook her head. "Not for certain. My father was pulled from Bastet in the garden where we were praying. Guards pried his arms from her and dragged him away. I never saw him again. Supposedly there's a valley nearby where men are tossed, gifts to appease Amun. No one dares look for it, to know if it exists."

"Bastet didn't save him, or Khepri's mother."

"No."

"She has no power."

Malina dropped her head. "I know. I wanted, I couldn't-"

Eran cupped the woman's face in her hands, her words of comfort interrupted by a sharp rapping on the door, and the flash of Rez-Nahor's face as he peered in.

Malina pulled back and stood. "I have to go. What I came to tell you is that the caravan is expected in the next few days."

Routine would continue as it always had in the household of Okpara. People and goods bought and sold. Her room of confinement would be needed for storage so a decision would be made-

"Do you understand, Eran? *Tolo's* caravan."

The door creaked open a few more inches. "I have to go. I'll do what I can." Malina slipped out the door and was gone.

Tolo's caravan. The one that traveled north, then east to Nineveh. The one that passed the Hebrew camp.

Eran smiled in the darkness. If she made her way to the caravan, she could hide in the wagons until they left again. It was risky. Tolo would find her, but he wouldn't turn the vast array of beasts and men and carts and goods around to take her back. Not likely. He might toss her out alone on the road. He might not. She had given him the gift of her skills when his men were injured. He might have a grateful heart.

He might take her home.

Eran stretched out her knees, the grinding making her wince. Another thought made her laugh out loud. She could ride the cart over the river. She wouldn't have to swim to escape the hand of death.

Chapter Thirty-seven

The caravan didn't turn to Zeboyim. It kept to the road heading for the small city of Zoar. Without the congestion to slow its pace, it moved ahead of Shem and Japheth in no time and they didn't catch up to it until it stopped in a vacant field. The men were unleashing donkeys and unloading merchandise, transferring it to smaller carts. They were directed to a tall man in the midst of the buzzing swarm.

"Are you Tolo?" Japheth asked.

The man turned from a stack of crates and frowned down at them. "Not here. No purchases. In the market, tomorrow." He whipped out a knife and sliced the cords binding a stack of wooden boxes together.

Japheth jingled the coins tied to his belt, subtly, but enough to gain the attention of the man again. "We aren't interested in buying anything yet. We're looking for someone. Wondered if you'd be kind enough to speak with us a moment."

Tolo ran his eyes up and down both of them with an irritated expression. "I'm busy."

"Please," Shem said, pulling out his own knife and separating crates as the caravan leader was doing. "We're looking for an old woman. She may have come this way four or five months ago. Perhaps she traveled with you."

Tolo's eyes stayed fixed on his work but Shem noticed that he blinked, and paused, just a hair's breadth in time, but it was there. His heart quickened. The man said nothing.

"She was alone, coming out of Nineveh originally but maybe you saw her in Haran or Damascus?"

Tolo sliced a box open, the scent of frankincense escaping the confines. "I don't trade in old women." He turned his back to them.

"It's important that I find her and of course your name will be forgotten. I don't mean to stir trouble for you, but if you can tell me-"

Tolo turned and put his hands on his hips, then spit on the ground between them. "I said I don't trade in old women. Now get out of here. I'm busy." He looked over Shem's head as he spoke.

Shem reached for the man's arm as he walked away from them. Japheth pulled him back.

He shook off his brother's grasp and strode in front of Tolo, between the man's knife and the boxes. He knew something. Shem couldn't walk away. He found Tolo's eyes, forcing contact.

"She's my wife. Please tell me where she is. Tell me something. Anything."

Tolo's knife was pointed at Shem's heart. The man glared and sucked in a deep breath, exhaling foul air into Shem's face.

Shem didn't flinch, holding Tolo's gaze until the sharp squint softened.

He lowered the weapon and gave one curt nod of his head. "King Okpara bought an old woman. She was here, in Zoar, last I knew."

The man turned and strode away, leaving the coins in

Japheth's hand, and jubilance in Shem's heart.

♥

The young man eagerly took the silver Ham offered. He came in and sat among them, also accepting a mug of beer and a dish of lentils. Naomi helped his wife deliver twins a few years back, boys that were tangled together and didn't want to come out on their own. Now they were rowdy and independent as any two year olds. The young father was eager to help. He had donned the clothing and kohl of his ancestors and paid a visit to Okpara.

"She's there, in Okpara's home, but I didn't see her. He says he bought an old woman Healer and paid too much for her. He didn't want to talk about it. I bribed one of the men standing guard on the way out but he was tight lipped too. All I know is she lost favor somehow and was locked up recently. She's alive though. He seemed sure of it. Surprised, but sure."

"Why surprised?" Naomi asked.

"Okpara's people are fortunate. He treats them well, slaves included. But when he's dissatisfied, they go away rather suddenly and are never seen again. Killed, of course, though you'd never get one of his men to admit it. The unknown gives the man power, and he likes power. He uses fear to his advantage. The guard I spoke with was surprised the old woman was alive. Apparently the entire house could hear him screaming at her and it wasn't pleasant."

Eran was alive, and in danger. Shem excused himself, seeking the vineyard to pray and think. He needed a plan to get her back, and soon.

♥

"Wake up, Brother." Ham shook him vigorously.

Shem groaned. He'd fallen asleep not more than a couple of hours ago. Without a sound plan to rescue Eran. An army of men from Abraham's camp stood ready if asked, he knew, but his heart couldn't settle on it. He didn't want bloodshed. And Okpara was far too wealthy for them to offer anything of value in trade.

Ham slid his arm under Shem's shoulders and hoisted him up. "Come on. We're wasting time." His brother pulled him to his feet, threw a cloak over his shoulders and put a mug of hot tea in his hand.

It was barely morning, the sun just spilling over the eastern hills and into the windows. Shem yawned, shifting the hot beverage from hand to hand so he wouldn't get burned. Ham held a second cup with his right hand, with a makeshift hook that clamped onto a sturdy handle.

He followed Ham to the room where Japheth's snores rose and fell in regular intervals and waited, propped against the wall, while his brother crept in. In a moment both of his brothers emerged. One disheveled and juggling his own hot cup, the other wide eyed and urging them down the hall.

Ham led them across the courtyard and opened the door to a large room attached to the end of his home. His workshop, filled with the familiar array of tables and tools and shelves and bits of this, fragments of that.

Shem located a tall stool and plopped down. "You have an idea itching to get out, Ham?"

His brother nodded vigorously as he started digging around the room, searching under piles of wooden parts and through bins of tools and scraps of leather, bone, and whatever else the earth gave up.

"It may not be to your liking. But-, oh here it is." Ham pulled out a tube made of hammered copper. Charred leather bits crumbled from a series of straps, flittering into the air as he inspected it.

Japheth caught Shem's eye. He grinned. "It was a wild idea we had last night. I guess our brother intends to act on it." His hair was flying all directions and bags under his eyes spoke of little sleep. "It was our only solution that seemed to have merit."

Shem ran his eyes over the odd contraption. "I'm listening. We're going to sell that, that, whatever that is, to barter for Eran?"

Ham laughed. "No. It's a much better idea." He removed the hook from his right hand and tossed it onto a table with the other adapted contraptions for the arm. Holding the old copper one between his thighs, he yanked off the remaining bits of strapping. "We'll simply ask for her."

Shem felt the plummet of disappointment in his gut. He'd thought of that already. The last time he tried it, the meeting hadn't gone so well and he was forever reminded of it by the seal on his forehead. "Do you have connections with Okpara? Favors he can return?"

"No. Never met him. Just know about him and his household. They worship both local and Egyptian gods. There's a deity for everything that happens. One makes sure the crops come up, another sends the locusts that destroy it. Gods send rain, gods send floods, gods give sons and take sons. For everything good, there's a god to thank. Every bad fortune comes from the displeasure of another. Okpara is superstitious and religious and full of his own self importance. We can use that to our advantage."

Ham pulled the tube over his arm so it covered his forearm from stump to elbow. He fished around some more and pulled out another shorter piece. This one he put over the open end so the stump was enclosed. Five thick hooks projected from the metal base. "One of the earliest models," he said. "Until I realized how hot and heavy it was. Wood and leather are better."

Japheth found a wad of fabric and tossed it in the air near his brother. Ham stretched out his arm and allowed the metal claw to snag it as it fell.

"Uh, I still don't get it," Shem said. "How are we using that contraption to get Eran?"

"I need to fix it up." Ham slid the parts off, turned his back to them and was already absorbed in the project.

"Ham?"

"Oh, I need to put straps on again so it stays in place. It fits nice and snug on my arm but it will slip off if I add weight to the end. It needs straps to attach it to my shoulder. And I can make this finger part better."

Shem turned to Japheth who was watching his face and still grinning. "Explain it to me, Japheth. What's he doing? What are we doing?"

"Okpara fears a god of these hills. One that devours women and children. Ham wants to allow that god to ask for Eran."

"Utilize the man's fear. What does the arm have to do with it?"

Ham laughed and shook his head, his attention back on his brothers. "I wore it to the city once and it caused quite a stir. Especially when I showed some boys how I could reach into a fire pit and pick up a burning stick. I thought they'd be entertained. Instead I scared the heartbeat out of them. Never seen boys turn so white and run so fast."

"He's achieved god status himself, it seems." Japheth could hardly talk, he was laughing so hard. He set his tea down before it ended up all over his lap. "Our brother is a local deity."

Ham drew himself up tall and puffed out his chest. He spoke

in a deep resonating voice. "Hear me King Okpara. I am the god of the hills. I am Amun!"

Chapter Thirty-eight

Denah sewed furiously on the linen robe she was creating. It was composed of long colorful strips, dyed the same day Shem had agreed to Ham's insane plan. The reds, purples and blues ran vertically and would be lined and hemmed in a bright gold. Two of the young mothers in Naomi's care stitched on new ones for Japheth and Shem too, since the brothers refused to allow Ham to go alone.

"What if he won't see you?" Denah asked.

Shem turned toward his brother only to have his head thumped.

"Stop moving," Naomi said. "Or your ear will come off next."

Shem forced his head to be still while Naomi wielded her cutting blade. Locks of hair littered the floor around him.

Ham fiddled with the leather straps securing the metal arm to his shoulder. Internal strapping connected to the new riveted finger joints and by moving his shoulder and elbow the right way, the tension made the fingers open and close a bit. His arm appeared to be alive without human flesh and bone.

"He will," Ham said. "He'll be more scared to refuse than to appear before me. I can appease him with blessings of favor."

Shem caught his breath.

"Or not," Ham interjected quickly. "I won't Shem, I won't make false promises."

They had agreed not to lie outright. No saying he was Amun, no divine incantations. Okpara could make connections in his own mind and even with that, Shem felt a twinge of reluctance. He fought against deceit, allowing none in his home and punishing it severely when it did. Lies were not to be tolerated. Lies led to more lies. But he had no other plan.

Japheth handed his wife a long length of thread. "Still alright with this, Shem?"

He shrugged. "I can't believe we found her and I can't take the chance of losing her when we've come this far."

"If we had more time…"

"I know. We'd find alternative solutions. But we don't. This is the plan for now and God can choose to bless it or not. We'll come home with Eran or…"

"You'll come home with Eran," Denah said. "Don't even think otherwise."

It was a dangerous endeavor. They could predict the movement of the stars in the heavens, knowing by the alignment when to till the earth and plant their crops. They understood the clouds and the winds, predicting thunderstorms or endless sun-filled days. Even the migration paths of the great dragon packs could be determined with a little logic and careful study of their habits. But King Okpara? The plan was based on their assumptions of him, the pattern of beliefs and behaviors they thought he would follow. There were no guarantees. Despite centuries of learning, they couldn't accurately predict the actions of any single man.

They all knew the risks involved and all agreed to proceed anyway. Shem said a silent pray for each of his brothers and their wives. The cord that bound them had never been tighter.

♥

Six days and Eran was still confined in the storage room. Now she wasn't alone. The shelves were packed with packages of spice and rolls of silk and stacks of intricately woven tapestries. She stood against the far wall with her guard as the last of the merchandise was tucked away. Tolo's caravan was in Zoar. It was unloaded. It would leave again soon.

"Did Okpara forget that he put me in here?" Eran asked Rez-Nahor a question that would go unanswered, like all the others she had asked him as the men traveled in and out of the room, certainly curious as to why a woman was living in there. None of them spoke to her either, taking their cue from Rez-Nahor's rigid position. The only time he made eye contact was when she asked after Malina, and it was accompanied with a scowl.

She hadn't seen Malina, though she came every day. The guard allowed her to deliver food and water through him only. At first the two argued outside the door, under their breath and in the tongue of the Hittites. As the days passed, Malina came and went and as far as Eran could tell, she made no efforts to see her any longer.

She was alone.

Rez-Nahor left the room behind the last man and closed the door.

Eran slumped against a crate and did what she had been doing for nearly a week. Waiting. Praying. Waiting some more.

♥

Shem re-wound the silky turban on his head, increasing the tightness. The indigo swath matched his new inner tunic. The outer robe and sash were sewn from fabric dyed in same bath, but left in the vinegar fixative longer, so the shade was deeper and richer, like the plump grapes from his father's vineyards. The new sandals revealed trim, clean toenails that he scarcely recognized as his own. Hair trimmed short, clean shaven and flesh scrubbed and oiled, he felt like misplaced royalty.

Japheth was dressed similarly in tones of crimson, while Ham wore the colorfully striped garments and an impressive headpiece made of a golden band around his forehead, complete with linens cascading down his back. Naomi outlined his eyes with kohl to add an aura of mystery and familiarity to Okpara. The copper arm was secured, straps hidden beneath his tunic. The hand gleamed, smooth and polished.

They were an impressive trio, Shem had to admit. In all their years, even in the bountiful times, they had never dressed in such finery. He and his brothers were born with tools in their hands and soil beneath their feet and nothing in life had turned them from the delight of labor beneath the sun to the delicacies of luxurious living.

They stood in a grove of trees on the rim of a narrow valley. The land below was a cemetery, small stone stacks dotting the terrain in irregular intervals with wild flowers growing freely among them.

"When we find remains dumped here, we bury them," Ham said. "Men mostly, throats slashed. They're wrapped in white linen and left for the scavengers."

The feel of the place was peaceful in some respects, yet the aura of death made Shem eager to move on. Murdered men, dumped and abandoned. He couldn't help but make a connection to Okpara, who made men disappear. Women too? He turned away and pushed those thoughts aside.

Zoar was a short distance away, flanked by a wide river. The buildings were of simple construction, without the fussy tiled mosaics and ornate façades of Sodom, and the city wall was more like a fence. It was guarded, yet the main corridor into the town was freely accepting travelers and allowing them to leave without inspections or interrogations. Entering would not be a problem.

They needed to be aware of the time of day to be sure they could get out though. Ham warned them of this again, in case they were separated. Within Zoar, large estates were surrounded by high walls and defended. Common homes were sealed against evil, doors locked and protected. The debauchery and superstitions known to the cities of the plain rose with the moon so they needed to be out before nightfall, or be under the protection of someone with enough influence to see that they weren't harmed.

"I'd rather we ask him to meet us outside." Shem said. "It seems safer overall. More escape options that way."

"We can't risk a big crowd though." Japheth fiddled with a golden earring that was pinching his newly pierced ear. "And look at us. We will certainly be attracting attention."

Ham's grin covered his face. He was enjoying this far too much. "Ham," Shem said. "Try not to be too obnoxious. Don't intentionally terrify the residents."

"Understood. I'll mind myself. Unless Okpara needs a demonstration. I can dip my hand in fire again."

Shem shook his head at his brother. "I hope it won't come to that. Let's pray the man's fears take over and he can't see that we're just men in costumes. We know enough about him to make him nervous. I hope he wants to hand over Eran then be rid of us as quickly as possible."

282 – Rachel S. Neal

Ham sent men with jars of expensive Nabatean wine to the city for several days in a row. They used it wisely, gleaning information from the locals - gossip and slander and bits of inside knowledge about the self-proclaimed King. The loyalties within the city were less pronounced outside the walls of his land. It was a stab at being omniscient. Shem hoped the information was correct and not the exaggerations of a head filled with too much wine.

Ham looked at Shem's head gear, reached over and tugged it down a bit more over his forehead. "Feelings around here aren't generally favorable toward Amraphel, but there are some loyal supporters, and spies, and men eager to make a profit by returning run-away slaves. From what I understand, Okpara trades regularly in Nineveh and profits handsomely so his loyalties may not be solely with the local kings. Keep that thing on, Brother."

Shem checked the position of the wrap again, then turned his eyes to the heavens. There was anxiousness in his spirit, a heaviness, like fear yet more than a need to fight or flee. Before the clouds unfurled over the ark, he'd felt it, and running down the tower in Shinar. It was unease that came from outside his own reasoning, a sharp awareness of God, of the need for protection, for deliverance.

It was the unease of impending judgment.

The trouble in his spirit made him pause. He had discussed the feeling already with his brothers and they understood. It had not been present for any of them until that morning.

"I still feel it, Shem," Japheth said. "We have to go on though. It's Eran."

Shem nodded. The urgency to find her was pressing. It had grown steadily within him and the others. Denah and Naomi were both flustered as the men left, scooting them out the door as if they were eager to have them gone. And back again. The five of them were united and despite the crazy plan, they were going to see it through. The need to fall on his face before his God was stayed by a higher demand. He had to save Eran.

He nodded. It was time. He collected his horse, brushing dust from the cushion on its back. "I don't like what I'm feeling. But I see no other direction. Ready?"

They mounted and rode side by side down the road, Ham in the middle. "Quit smiling, Ham," Japheth reminded him. "You're supposed to induce fear and awe."

Ham intentionally tightened his lips as they rode past gawking guards over the bridge and into the city of Zoar. If they hadn't already made it this far, Shem would've made him practice a solemn, emotionless expression instead of the one he wore. It was worse than the smile, oozing with theatrical exaggeration.

It didn't seem to matter. They drew eyes from every direction. The fancy clothing and horses first garnered attention to the men of means not from among them. Then the flash of copper. Shem looked discreetly at the faces going pale and knees going weak. No one thought they were acting. The chitter-chatter stopped abruptly, filtering in every direction until hooves on cobblestone made the loudest noise on the street. Shem exhaled through his lips and made himself relax his shoulders.

Okpara's estate was massive in comparison to what they had seen in the city so far. It had a high wall, protected by a line of men. They drew their horses in close to the guards frozen at the front entrance.

"We are here to see King Okpara," Shem said.

A dozen men stood still, visually inspecting them for a sign of goodwill or that of potential danger. All were tensed, ready to use the weapons in their grasp and equally ready to faint dead away. One finally stepped forward.

284 – Rachel S. Neal

"We are here to see King Okpara," Shem repeated, this time directing it to the one in command. "It's urgent."

"Whom shall I say desires his audience?"

Ham flicked his garment just enough for a flash of metal to catch the man's eye again. "He'll know."

Shem watched the man's jaw slip, trepidation registering in his countenance. "We are here to see King Okpara." He smiled at the man and handed him the reins.

The guard waved his hand, sending another through the door. The others backed a short distance away, fully focused on the trio of visitors and not daring to speak a word.

Shem glanced at Ham, noticing the trickle of perspiration on his temple. His false arm was hot and heavy and multiple layers of clothing added to the discomfort. It was not a god-like image for one who touched fire.

The man returned from within the home and dropped to his knee, bowing his head and motioning to the others to do the same. Shem felt the sting of guilt. "Rise," he said. "Take us to your Master."

Guards jumped up and helped them dismount without eye contact. They were led into a large open room and left with other guards, young men rigid in their stance, veins of apprehension bulging on muscled chests.

Japheth crossed his arm over his chest, his eyes surveying the niches carved into the walls and filled with odd looking gods. His brother's displeasure was easy to read. Shem felt it, too, the unseeing eyes mocking the real God, the futility of worshipping carvings of stone. It was not a home he would ever find peace in.

Okpara made a hasty entrance a moment later. The man was flushed and didn't know what to do, bowing at first then looking at Ham, then lowering his eyes. His hands were clamped together at his bare chest and he licked his lips repeatedly.

Shem suppressed a smile. The man was nervous and that was good.

Ham let the arm be seen briefly, long enough for Okpara to gasp under his breath.

"King Okpara," Ham said, his voice deep and resonant. "Do you know who I am?"

He cleared his throat, then simply nodded.

"Good. And congratulations. Two fine sons were added to your community. Allow the Ethiopian musician a day from his duties in your home, to celebrate the blessing with his family."

An intoxicated neighbor, disturbed by the commotion of the midnight deliveries, had given them that bit of news. Shem hoped Okpara hadn't yet been informed.

The King's eyebrows lifted. "Of course. Of course," he said.

"How is that rash? It needs to be kept dry if you want it to heal."

Okpara's eyes could grow no wider. He automatically rubbed one foot over the other, where the scaly skin condition lived beneath padded slippers. That news came from an herb peddler for a few coins and a few mugs of wine.

The King lowered his eyes again, and bobbed his head up and down.

Ham's face glistened with perspiration. The precise black line under his eyes had a smudged look and the fake forearm had rotated slightly, spinning downward so the hand was now in an awkward position.

Shem caught his brother's eye and lifted an eyebrow. His brother was enjoying his torturous presence and could go on for a while, watching the man squirm. Shem wanted to push on, the man clearly submissive already.

Ham winked at Shem and allowed his voice to boom. "You purchased a woman from the lands to the east."

Okpara glanced up and spoke softly. "I have many people in my possession."

"This one is old, a Healer called Eran."

The man's head shot up and he stared at Ham then shifted his gaze to Japheth, then to Shem. His voice was less confident. "Yes."

"I need her to come with me."

Shem watched the man closely. His fear would be tremendous if Eran was already dead. And he would wonder why the god Amun didn't know that already.

Okpara shifted from foot to foot and rubbed his chin. Nervous, not in a state of panic. "Yes, of course. I'll get her." Relief seemed to help him breathe easier. The god asked for something he was able to fulfill.

Shem controlled the hope wanting to break out as a smile on his face.

Okpara turned to speak to a servant. He was interrupted.

Men outside the front door yelled, then it crashed open and a man pushed his way inside, stumbling into the room. His richly ornamented clothing was coated in dust, his hands weapon-free, flailed in the air to keep the guards at bay, while desperate eyes searched. When he found Okpara, the man slumped to his knees, clinging to the King's ankles. "Help me! I beg you King Okpara! Help me!"

Three women followed the man and dropped behind him in a bow, heads to the floor, arms outstretched. Guards reached to pull them up but Okpara raised his hand and stopped them. He jerked his legs from the man's clutches and stepped back. "What's going on? Who are you?" he demanded.

The guard commander sheathed his sword. "More visitors, my

lord. This one says he's a city leader, from Sodom."

Shem couldn't suppress the shudder rippling up his spine. He heard Japheth groan. It wasn't just the untimely interruption. It was the man, desperate before Okpara.

It was Abraham's nephew.

Chapter Thirty-nine

Fran pulled herself to standing, forcing her stiff knees to comply. She walked in place, lifting her legs up and down for a full five hundred counts. Then she raised herself up on tiptoe, then down and up one hundred times. Growls arose from her belly, protesting the lack of food. She figured it must be morning, but had seen no one.

How long would she remain? Would Okpara forget about her completely? Eventually someone would come for the spices so at least her body would be discovered, if it came to that.

She wasn't afraid to die. After many long hours in the dark room alone, she had thought about it repeatedly. Her life had been long already and it was the nature of all things, to give up the life breath and return to the earth. Shem believed they would join their ancestors when they did, their souls within finding refuge with God. She hoped it was so, and looked forward to existing without the nagging aches of the current vessel she was housed in. Somehow, it would be alright to die.

But she didn't want to.

She wanted to feel Shem's lips on hers again and hear the early morning breeze rustling through the grass and smell curried goat as it simmered over a fire. She wanted to taste the summer rains that ended the droughts and see the bow of vivid colors afterward, arcing against the sky, a promise of long ago to the children of Noah. It wasn't time to die yet.

Was Tolo's caravan packed and gone already?

Eran sat on a crate and put her head on her knees. She woke with an unease tingling her spine, not knowing why. It was different than the prior days of uncertainty. It was heavy, a burden given to her that she couldn't carry on her own. Was this it? Was it her day to face death? Was God preparing her somehow? She would have preferred a blanket of his peace but it wouldn't come.

She turned her prayers to Shem, and the Lilies and everyone she could think of, spending her minutes, if they were her last, with the faces of those she loved in her mind and on her heart.

It didn't matter if Tolo was still in Zoar, or even standing at the front door of Okpara's home asking for her. She had no way to get out of the storage room.

♥

The sliver of light grew as the door opened. Rez-Nahor stepped inside with an oil lamp, closing the door behind him. "Get up. Hurry," he said. He set the lamp on a shelf and pulled a bundle of fabric from under his arm and tossed it at her. It clunked to the floor.

Eran put her hand on the white fabric but didn't lift it, watching the guard instead. He reached inside his tunic and withdrew a small vial. Eran pulled her hand back and clutched it over her heart. It was the bottle of poppy juice.

Rez-Nahor set it beside the lamp then pulled his dagger from its sheath.

Eran stayed on the floor, her heart thumping in her chest. She wouldn't fight the man but couldn't simply walk into his arms for her execution, either.

"Do you want to do it yourself?" He held out the knife.

Eran gasped. "No. I couldn't. I-" She stopped herself. If she had the knife, could she get past him?

"Stand up then." His voice left no room for argument.

Eran braced her arms on a stack of rolled carpets and pulled herself to her feet. "The juice, it will make it painless. May I take it first, before you…"

Rez-Nahor put a hand on her shoulder and spun her around so her back was to him. "It won't hurt. Hold still."

Eran pulled herself into a rigid line, chin up so the blade wouldn't miss. If this was it, she wanted his aim to be quick and sure.

The guard took her hair in his hand, pulling it away from her head. Eran fought against the backward tug. She squeezed her eyes closed, drawing the familiar words of history into her mind. "In the beginning-"

Thwack! The tension released and her head sprang forward.

There was no pain. Eran opened her eyes as the guard spun her back to face him, her long hair in his fist.

"Put those on and hurry." His voice was laced with agitation. He pointed at the bundle.

Eran put her hands to her head. He'd cut her hair off at the shoulders. "I don't understand. What….?"

Rez-Nahor pinched her chin between his thumb and finger and bent down to peer at her a hands-breadth away. "If you want out of here, put those things on. Now!"

Eran dropped to the floor and unwrapped the heeled sandals from the white linen tunic. A pot of kohl, small mirror, and an application stick was there too. She started with her eyes, drawing a line as she had seen Khepri's girls do many times. Her hand shook as the mark was made, the outlining emphasizing the trepidation in her features. It had to do. She didn't have the luxury of time to repeat the process to make it neater.

The clean tunic was like her own, but longer. It would hide the shoes as she walked.

As she walked! The realization washed over her. Rez-Nahor was giving her freedom. Hope seeped out of Eran's pores. "The caravan? I can still get to the caravan?"

He shook his head, then averted his gaze as she lifted her garment to exchange it for the longer one. "I don't know about the caravan."

"Why are you doing this? Okpara will kill you for helping me."

The man's jaw clenched for a moment. "My sister's wishes."

"Sister?" Only one other person knew about the shoes. Eran clapped her hands over her mouth. "Oh, of course. I thought-"

"I know what you thought. Malina is my sister."

Eran strapped the shoes on, putting the details together. "She's a slave. You aren't. You came here by choice. You followed her here, took a position intentionally?"

His back stiffened. "Yes," he said.

"Malina has family. I thought-"

"No one knows."

Eran smiled. "You'll help her escape. You came to take her home."

Rez-Nahor didn't respond. He turned away and put his ear to the door.

Eran stood and wobbled on the shoes before getting the rhythm smoothed out. Tall, with cropped hair like Malina, with eye make-up like Malina. If no one looked too closely...

"But Okpara. How will you explain?"

He picked up the poppy juice. "I'll be asleep. You tricked me into the room, then Malina. You used your God's powers to render us unconscious."

"But-"

"If your God is stronger than Amun, my sister and I will live when we leave this place. She tells me she is ready to run to the hills, and she'll do so with prayers to your God on her lips. She endangers us by saving you, but she wouldn't let me take her out before, too frightened. Now she is ready. We can all be free."

The clatter of wheels echoed at the end of the hall. Rez-Nahor sat against the wall and poured the drops into his palm then licked them up. He handed her the vial and leaned back, waiting for the drowsiness to take over. "Get out quickly or we'll all disappear."

"May you find my God strong, Rez-Nahor, and find peace in your own home."

He nodded then closed his eyes.

"Thank you," she said quietly.

"It's time for you to go."

Eran took in a breath and said a prayer, opening the door as Malina approached.

Malina pressed the cart handle into Eran's hand then wrapped her arms around her shoulders, kissing each cheek. "Khepri is worse."

Eran nodded, the lump in her throat making it difficult to speak all the words she wanted to say.

Malina put a finger against Eran's lips. "Don't cry. Your eyes will smear."

Eran handed her the poppy juice. Malina carefully dosed herself then dropped the vial in the pot of refuse with the kohl.

"May your God protect you, Eran," she said, then closed the door between them.

"And you," Eran whispered.

The hall was empty. Eran gripped the cart handle and walked to the end, mindful of the pace so nothing spilled. As she turned the corner, she held her breath. A guard caught the first glimpse of her, wrinkling his nose. And turning away.

The gut churning aroma seething from the full pots enveloped the air around her.

Eran suppressed a wide smile, grateful for the wonderfully offensive aroma.

♥

There was nowhere for them to hide, no way to slip from the room unnoticed. Shem could only hope the distraught Lot would be too preoccupied to notice who stood in the room with him.

"They were men of God, two of them. Told us we had to leave and struck everyone but us with blindness so we could get past them in the street. They led us out and, and they intend to destroy my city!" Lot's voice quivered. He was on his knees, rocking back and forth. "They're going to destroy Sodom. They wouldn't let me take anything from my home. My home, my fortune, my city. What will I do? Help me. Protect me!"

Shem felt the sinking fear that comes with understanding, with knowing the truth of a situation, no matter how implausible. Sodom had reached her endpoint, her sin too great to go unpunished. God was ready to show his hand of judgment.

He pressed his hands to his temples. Only Sodom? There were five cities on this plain.

"Why are you coming to me? Why are you bringing wrath to

my home? If you offended your gods, make your restitution. Pay homage and make your sacrifices elsewhere. Don't involve me!" Okpara's face was strained. His eyes shifted between Lot and Ham.

Lot inhaled a ragged breath, quelling his demanding tone and adding flowery words. "Great King Okpara, as an influential man such as yourself, I seek your favor and will repay your generosity. You're the only one who can help me. You must provide me shelter and protection. I was forced to leave quickly and I have nothing except my wife and daughters. Nothing. Protect me, as I would do for you."

Shem's heart pounded. He felt eyes on him and turned to his brothers. Ham didn't recognize Lot, didn't understand the danger they were in if the man recognized them. His brother seemed to sense the same urgency to act as Shem was feeling though, the same weight in the air that made them both shift from foot to foot. Japheth was nervously running his hands over his garments as if repeatedly searching for a weapon that wasn't there.

Okpara glanced at Ham and nodded as if he understood an unspoken message. "The gods test me." He grabbed the neck of Lot's tunic and pulled him to his feet. "Who am I to interfere with the anger of your gods? You'll bring disaster on my household if I show you favor. Pray to Amun and save your city, save yourself!" He spun Lot around and pushed him toward Ham.

Lot stumbled toward Ham, staring at him without comprehending. Then his gaze shifted to Shem. Recognition filled his face. He fell to his knees again, the composure lost. "You! Father Shem, pray for us! Pray to your father's God for Sodom!"

Shem backed away from Lot, refusing to have his legs in the man's desperate clutches.

Okpara pulled a dagger from its sheath and placed the tip on Japheth's throat. "What is this? Who are you?!"

"No! Don't hurt them! Make them pray!" Lot grabbed the hem of Okpara's tunic, and leaned back, yanking the King off balance.

Japheth snatched the dagger from the King's hand and tossed it into the air. "Keep away!" His brother called out the game as the King of Zoar recovered his stance. He slammed a fist into Japheth's chest, sending him crashing to the floor.

Shem caught the handle with his right hand, guards rushing toward him as he did. One clamped a fierce hand onto his shoulder. He shifted the weapon to his left hand and tossed it to Ham before his legs were kicked out from under him and he too was on the floor. As soon as he let go of the weapon, he knew he messed up.

Ham automatically reached out with his dominant arm. His right arm. The metal tube continued its rotation on his brother's sweaty skin as he reached out, sliding around until the palm faced down. He couldn't catch the falling dagger. The weapon hit the back of the metal hand and bounced onto the floor.

♥

The chaos was swiftly controlled by the armed men. Shem, Lot and Japheth were on the floor. Lot's wife and daughters stood in a corner, arms wrapped around one another. Ham stood in the center of the room, face grim, left arm holding the right one against his chest. It was silent except for heavy breathing and the sobbing from the women.

Okpara stared at Ham, eyes narrowed and piercing. He retrieved his dagger from the floor and sauntered up to him until they stood face to face. With the tip of the weapon he flung the colorfully striped robe back, exposing the metal contraption, then pointed it at Ham's heart. His eyes explored the metal arm, fully comprehending the ruse. With a few fierce moves, he sliced through the leather strapping. The arm clanged on the floor.

The raw stump of his brother's arm was exposed. Okpara stepped back, hands on his hips. He looked at Ham with evident disdain, then surveyed the sorry group of men and women in his presence. "Get up," he commanded.

Shem and Japheth rose and stood beside Ham.

Lot remained on the floor, bowing to Okpara. "Please. Help me. Please." His voice was low and urgent.

Okpara had had enough of him. He summoned his men. "Take him and his women out of here," he said. "Let them beg for safety in the streets. Don't allow them to return."

Lot wailed as he was dragged through the door, the mournful sound accompanied by his daughters. His wife held herself straight and openly scowled at Okpara as she followed. There was no fear that Shem could see, no remorse or resignation, just coldness, unforgiving coldness.

Shem shivered as the door slammed shut. He forced himself to breathe in a regular rhythm. Judgment on Sodom. When? How? Zoar too? His mind tried to find a direction, his feet needed to flee. But not without Eran.

"We owe you an explanation," Shem started. "An apology."

Okpara stared at him with an intensity that rattled his gut. He dropped his head and licked his lips.

That's when he saw it. His turban came off in the scuffle.

Shem slowly raised his head.

Okpara's eyes burned into the scar.

Shem's hand flew to cover it. It was too late of course. The burned seal of Amraphel was visible. He dropped his hand.

"What's this?" For a man unnerved by the gods in his midst,

he was not flustered by mere men. Okpara was no longer intimidated. He walked up to Shem and squinted at the mark.

"I belong to the One God." Shem said. "The seal means nothing."

"Yet you hide it. You mock me with your charade." He frowned and stepped away, hands behind his back. "Tell me the truth. Who are you and why are you here insulting me?"

"We're brothers, the sons of Noah, originally from the region of Shinar. We're peaceful men, not intending to cause turmoil. We're here to see your Healer. Eran is my wife. She was taken from me and, and I want her back."

"So you dressed up to deceive me? You almost had me fooled. Why the pretense? Why didn't you ask like men of honor?" He kicked the arm with his jeweled slipper, watching it slide along the tiles.

Shem squeezed his eyes closed for a moment. "We..."

Ham exhaled forcibly. "It was my idea. I thought you would honor Amun. We only wanted the old woman. If I can do anything, or..."

Okpara held up a hand to stop Ham's apology. He stood near a tapestry depicting a wide river, flanked with palms and women in white garments. He sighed then turned back to Shem.

"You are the property of King Amraphel. His slave in my house, under my swords." Okpara examined Shem's mark again. "I understand why you're afraid to expose that. He has men everywhere. Treating you well is disobedient to the mighty king. Did you know that?" He kicked the arm again, allowing it fly into the wall.

The sound startled Shem. He automatically placed his hand over his heart. "Yes."

"He's powerful. Not so much as he thinks though. Not

everyone plays his game." Okpara chuckled under his breath. "I'm not his pawn. Zoar is not his domain."

Shem jerked his head around to see the man's expression.

Okpara lifted an eyebrow. "The kings of the east are not my allies. Zoar strives to live a profitable and peaceful existence and they continually wage war." He watched Shem for a moment. "Tell me, what did you do to anger him? That scar is new and you are an old man. Why do you wear his seal?"

"He took Eran from me, from her people in the Hebrew camp. I asked him to return her. He was willing, for a price. For my worship. I could not. He marked me in his anger, and sold my wife to you. I've been searching for her."

"Hebrew? You are another of those Hebrews then. You pray to only one god?"

"Yes."

"An archaic belief. One that confounds me, I admit. Abram, the Hebrew of the hills worships but one. Is he your relative? Is this the same god for you both, and of your wife?"

Shem couldn't keep the surprise from his voice. "He is my relation, many generations descended. And yes, we pray to the same God Almighty. You know Abram?"

Okpara rubbed his chin. "Of him. His army fought for Zoar at one time. He is respected among us."

Both Ham and Japheth nodded vigorously. "He fought for these cities, against Amraphel," Ham said.

The knotted muscles in Shem's spine eased a bit. That battle was some fifteen years back and alliances changed overnight yet Okpara remembered the foreigner defending the cities of the plain, and also perhaps that Abram had an army. A small one, yes. One that was victorious against significant odds. One that recovered the treasures taken from Zoar.

Okpara walked the perimeter of the room, hands linked behind his back. He stopped beside a guard and ran a finger over the shaft of the spear he held. "What shall I do with the three Hebrews who ruined my day? I should punish them for humiliating me."

Shem pressed his lips together and folded his hands over his chest, memories of Amraphel, the hot iron, Eran's screams mixing in his mind. He tightened his legs to keep them from trembling.

Okpara soaked in the fear from each of their faces, looking them in the eye, stopping at Shem. "However," he left the guard's side and retuned to the tapestry, running a finger over the length of a woman standing in the shade. "I understand the desperate attempts to keep one's wife. I might be tempted to do as you have done. The gods are with you today. I am done with that Healer woman, and to give her to you is a strike against my enemy."

With a flick of his wrist the guards moved back and lowered their weapons. "Fetch Eran," he told one of them.

♥

The cart rumbled too loudly, the pots clacking together as if to draw attention to the woman it trailed. Eran forced herself to slow the pace, no hurry, no pressure, as if all was as it should be. As if she was Malina performing a required task. As if she was supposed to take the cart to the front of the house instead of out the back to the river. So far no one paid any attention to her and she prayed the guards at the door would turn away and ignore her too.

The caravans loaded and unloaded on the edge of town. Eran could find her way there from the entrance where she had come initially. It was a fairly straight path between Okpara's front gate to the market and beyond to the loading fields, where she'd search for Tolo. If he was gone, she would climb onto another one and pray for mercy. If she could get past the guards.

Commotion at the end of the hall slowed her steps. She stopped behind the statue of Ra, in the darkness of his shadow. There were people between her and the door. Several well dressed men stood together, surrounded by guards. Another one cried pitifully as he was hauled off the floor, and women cried in a corner. Okpara was in the midst and he was angry.

The way was blocked.

There were other doors out of the house. All protected. Eran pulled back to conceal herself further, her heart beating a strong rhythm. Most she had never been through. Would Malina have access?

There were too many uncertainties. The pressure to get away from the house was nearly overwhelming and she had to act. Eran moved away from the statue and went back the way she had come, heart pounding faster than she allowed her feet to travel with the jostling load.

There was only one choice.

The river.

Chapter Forty

"The Healer's gone. Malina and Rez-Nahor are dead." The servant was pale, reporting to Okpara on bended knee.

Japheth grabbed Shem's arm, keeping him steady.

"What!" Okpara's face flushed crimson. "How did she get away? She overpowered her guard? She killed him?"

Another servant entered the room with a limp woman draped over his arms. "She's not dead. She's breathing but I can't wake her up. Rez-Nahor is the same."

Okpara started to place his hand on the woman's skin then jerked it back and examined her face without touching her. "Alive. Under a spell, a curse. Struck by the Healer's god?"

Shem pushed panic from his voice. "No-"

Fury lit Okpara's face. "You helped her escape! You and your one god and your trickery! Get. Out." His finger pointed to the door. His men pointed their weapons.

"I have to find Eran, I-"

Okpara exploded. Cursing and ranting, he drew his own weapon.

Japheth and Ham took Shem's arms and pulled him away

302 – Rachel S. Neal

from Okpara and out the door. It slammed closed. There was no going back.

The burn of sulfur hit his senses. Again, the feeling of a heavy weight on his chest, of the need to fall to his knees, to pray. He grasped his brothers' arms to keep from collapsing.

"Judgment," Ham said. "We have to get out of this city."

"Not without Eran. How could she be gone? Where would she go?"

Japheth pointed to the walled gate leading from Okpara's estate. It was open, armed men waiting for them to pass through. "Those men wouldn't let her out. She has to be here, in the house or on the grounds."

Japheth spun to his left and ran from the gate, heading around the house. Ham smacked Shem's arm as he pulled up his garments and followed. "Come on!"

Shem lifted two handfuls of clothing to free his legs and join his brothers. What were they doing? They would be trapped inside the King's walls.

Guards yelled. Footsteps followed in pursuit.

Shem scanned the grounds as they dashed in and out of the trees and shrubs. "Eran!" He called out, joining the calls of his brothers, praying she'd appear from hiding.

They rounded the back of the house and abruptly fell short, heaving. A dozen guards stood in front of them. Shem braced himself. They were pinned between the two sets of men.

The men paid no attention to them. They stared over the far wall, to the landscape north of the city.

Shem looked up and shivered at the ominous darkness, at the thick gray fury swirling from the earth, joining golden flames from the heavens. It was as if a wall had dropped between them and the nearest city. Zeboyim was being consumed in a rain that burned while the sky above his head was blue. But if that city burned, and Sodom before it...

"Oh, God of the Heavens! Help us!"

The rear guards fell in behind them. Eyes to the hand of judgment, they fell to the earth and began calling out names of deities.

Japheth grabbed Shem's arm again and pulled. "This way," he said, and led them along a path toward a gate in the wall. They slipped through and ran, none of the men in Okpara's service lifting a hand to stop them.

The sulfurous burn and the putrid odor of a dump combined in his nose and mouth. Shem gagged, and coughed, trying to breathe and not breathe at the same time.

Japheth stopped at the river and ripped off his outer tunic.

"No!" Shem said. "She's not here. She won't swim. She's not here."

The gate squealed on its hinges. Someone was still in pursuit.

Ham glanced at the wall of fire, stripped off his garments and splashed into the water. "We have no choice, Shem. Hurry."

He hesitated. He couldn't leave her.

Japheth cupped his face in his hands. "Trust your God. He saved her once and he can do so again."

Shem prayed for it to be so as he dove into the rushing current.

♥

Eran abandoned the cart and her shoes, running the last length of the hall. Her soul was under pressure, as if the anxieties of the entire world were heaped on top of her, and she couldn't stand under them. She wanted to fall to her knees, to weep, to pray.

But she didn't. She couldn't. She had to get out of the house.

The door opened under her hand. The familiar stench was covered by another one, a heavy sulfurous one. The light of day was dimmed, the sky outside the city wearing an ominous gray veil. Fiery balls hurled from the heavens toward earth.

Judgment.

From the pit of her being, she recognized the pressure. She'd felt it before, on the last day of the old earth. Before the flood waters came. She gasped and stepped back into the house.

"Go." The sensation was strong, coming from nowhere and everywhere at the same time. She didn't question, bolting outside.

Several dozen men were gathered on the grass. They talked rapidly in other tongues. Some were face first in the soil, names of gods tossed from their lips into the furious skies.

Fire from heaven. Judgment from the Almighty. Didn't they know? It was moving toward Zoar.

"Get to the river."

Malina and her brother? Eran hesitated, then remembered the poppy juice. They were asleep and she couldn't carry either one on her own.

The Lilies? Could she get to them?

"The river."

Men and women of Okpara's estate poured out the door and turned their focus to the sky. There were screams of terror and some tried to turn around and go back in but were blocked by those trying to get out. The door was a solid mass of fighting bodies.

She couldn't go back in. She couldn't get to her Lilies. "God of all power, save them," she prayed. "Save me."

She ran, knees grinding in retaliation but not holding her back. The gate squealed in protest as she flung it aside. At the bank, she stopped.

The black spots hovered in the periphery.

"No!" She shook her head and took three long strides into the water.

Her gut gurgled. "God, help me. God help me."

Water splashed against her calves, then her thighs. Burning in her eyes and nose made her squint and cough. Another step.

Her waist was surrounded by river water, tugging at her feet, wrapping around her legs. It wanted to pull her off balance, drag her under. Blackness waited.

A low rumble from above tore through her fear, shattering the dark shroud.

Eran sucked down a breath and dove into the current. It yanked her down, forcing her limbs to flail against the pressure.

"Swim."

The command drew her attention. She focused, kicking her legs and pulling with her arms like she used to do as child. Right arm. Left arm. Right arm.

In little time she was exhausted, burning from the effort. She sucked in water then spit it out, frantically extending her legs for the river bed but there was nothing solid below.

Swim, she told herself this time.

One arm overhead, then the other. Kick. Keep kicking.

Muscles and lungs screamed for relief.

When her feet scraped on the bottom, Eran crawled onto the bank, gasping. The air was thick, getting thicker with the swirling smoke, burning her eyes. She squinted trying to find cover. On hands and knees she made her way to the brush-line, intending to collapse in the tall grasses. Then her hand landed on something that gave way under her weight.

Something that gasped and pulled away.

♥

The sky itself seemed to be sucking the breath from his lungs. Shem lay on his stomach beside his brothers, trying to capture air. They weren't far enough away from the city. It was bound for the fires from heaven, bound for destruction. They had to keep moving. But he couldn't. He couldn't get enough breath. He couldn't leave Eran.

The grasses rustled.

He rolled to his back and felt for the small dagger he usually kept in his belt.

No belt. No dagger. Both were at Ham's place. He had no weapon, no means to fight off the guards except with his bare hands.

A weight landed on his ribs. He gasped and jerked himself from it, opening his eyes a slit to see his opponent.

It wasn't a man. It was an Egyptian woman, black paint streaking down her cheeks. He grabbed her wrist.

♥

A hand caught her wrist. Eran jerked back and lost her balance, falling onto the man's chest. It heaved beneath her weight. She pulled her head up. An ugly scar dominated the man's forehead and his eyes were struggling to see who he had ensnared.

Eyes encircled by the deep wrinkles of a long life.

Familiar eyes.

It was Shem.

♥

The woman struggled to be released, falling hard against his chest. He grunted and looked into the fear written in her eyes, wanting to reassure her.

The fear vanished.

It was Eran.

Shem grabbed his wife's shoulders and pulled her close, tucking her into the safety of his arms. It was Eran. God gave him Eran. If it was their time to die in the fires of heaven, so be it. They would die as one.

Chapter Forty-one

Fran clung to her husband, her nose taking in rich perfumes from his skin. It was fitting, his body sweetly anointed for death, her soul held firmly near his heart.

But death didn't come.

The fury of the skies ended. The smoke thinned and blue reappeared. They rose from the grasses and held each other, their gaze to Zoar. It stood. Covered in ash of the burning sky, it was otherwise unscathed.

"God spared the city," she whispered.

"And us." Shem ran his finger over her chin and kissed the soot from her lips.

"Uh-hmm." A voice cleared behind them. "Don't forget you aren't alone."

Japheth's grin covered his face. He helped another man rise from the ground beside him. This one smiled just as broadly, black flakes peppering their teeth and coating their skin. Both were dressed like her husband in colorful, soggy garments.

The third man put his hands on his hips. Or hand. His right one was missing. "Well, my plan worked. Got what we came for. Hello Eran." He held out his arms.

Eran looked at the stump then clamped a hand over her mouth.

Shem nodded, tears collecting in his eyes. "God is good, Eran. So good."

The stranger stepped forward, his easy laughter rising above the frightened cries from beyond Okpara's walls.

Ham.

Eran fell into her brother-in-law's arms, then pulled away to search his face. Was it really him? Another blessing of her God piled onto the ones she had already received?

"It's me, really," he said, ruffling her cropped hair. "Wasn't sure it was you for a minute."

It was overwhelming. How could so much goodness be heaped upon her in so little time? God saved her again from judgment. She survived the river. She found Shem. The Lilies, Malina, and Rez-Nahor were spared from the burning sky. Now Ham.

The tears welled up. "Denah, and Naomi? Are they..."

"Eager to see you. Both of them."

♥

The little town of Zoar sat in a shallow nest of green, surrounded by devastation. The once fertile plain was scorched, smoldering, without so much as a thistle left to acknowledge the land once ripe with life. Black plumes rose from the land to the north, and it was as Lot had said. Sodom had been destroyed, and not alone. Gomorrah, Admah, and Zeboyim were gone. Only Zoar was spared. If there were survivors from the destroyed cities, none traveled the road to Zoar. Shem wasn't surprised. He doubted anyone was able to flee the wrath of God.

Except Lot. The divine messengers gave him a chance to live, his wife and unwed daughters at his side.

Where Abraham's nephew was now, they didn't know. His wife fled Zoar, that they knew. They found her standing alone on the hill on which they now sat. Her eyes looked toward her beloved city, to Sodom, unable to see the vacant gash in the landscape. She couldn't see. She was as dead as the idols of Okpara's garden, carved of salt by the hand of God.

Finding her took the last of their strength. They collapsed in each other's arms, releasing tears and expressing gratitude to the One who saves. If they'd had the means, Shem would have offered a sacrifice right there. Instead he urged them on, climbing the hills to Ham's land. Around them, birds twittered, rodents scurried, and antelope bounded from their path. Life remained in the hill country. Life remained for the sons of Noah.

♥

The night sky was clear, the stars more numerous than Eran could remember. Like Abraham's descendants would become. Her generations, the people God would call his own. It was the blessing of all blessings. She closed her eyes and relaxed against a cushion.

Naomi massaged Eran's feet in the moonlight while Denah brushed her hair. The six of them had talked for hours, after she and the men had stumbled back, black and sooty, barely clothed, filled with both the horror and joy of what had occurred.

Jael was dead, with Noah at last. Abram was Abraham, an expectant father. Ham and Naomi, alive and faithful. There was so much to think about, so much yet to ask. Eran kept the questions to herself. For the moment she enjoyed the peaceful silence beneath the stars.

Shem draped a warm cloak over her shoulders. The air was cooling without the warmth of a fire. There had been enough smoke and they welcomed the cool breeze to cleanse their lungs. Tomorrow they would work together to build a new altar and hold a proper sacrifice. Tonight she wanted-

Ham stood abruptly. Eran followed his gaze to the edge of the vineyard, to the silhouette of a man.

"I mean no harm," he said, hands held up revealing an absence of weapons. "I have women and children. They need food and protection for the night."

Eran rose to her feet. She knew the voice.

Shem took her arm and held her back. "Wait until we see if he's speaking the truth."

Eran patted his hand and smiled, finding energy she thought long gone for the day. "God has already seen."

Rez-Nahor gasped when she drew close enough for him to recognize her. "You?"

Eran squeezed his arm. "I swam the river."

The man smiled. "I knew you could."

"Malina? Is she with you?"

He nodded and led them to the cluster of people huddled together in fear beneath the trees. Malina lay on the ground among them, mumbling. "She's still sleeping off the medication. I had to carry her."

"Teacher!" Three flashes of grungy white emerged from the group. The Lilies.

Eran pulled them into her arms.

"I woke up and found the household in hysterics." Rez-Nahor kneeled beside his sister and lifted her into his arms. "I decided it was time to leave. My sister would have gone back for those girls so I took them too, and their parents. I don't know how we found you."

"My God led you, Rez-Nahor."

He looked down at Malina's face and nodded. "Your God saves."

Chapter Forty-two

Eran scrubbed the linens again, the ash blowing in from the plain managing to stain everything. A week since the destruction, Malina helped her for the last time. She and her brother would begin the journey to their homeland today, the hope of only one God in their prayers.

"Khepri will have an endless supply of ash for her kohl now," Eran said. "If no one else is content, maybe she will be."

Malina shook her head as her hands vigorously rubbed linens together in a hot bath. "She would never use ordinary ingredients. Only the finest Egyptian blend for her."

Eran froze. "Her mother too?"

The answer she searched for was so simple. Khepri's eyes never smudged in the heat, never dripped and smeared. Eran had to wipe it off with oil soaked rags.

Malina's eyes grew wide. "The kohl. The endless applications of Egyptian kohl. Yes. Her mother used it. The rest of us use plain old soot."

♥

314 – Rachel S. Neal

Shem knocked again, harder. A man opened Okpara's door a crack and peered out. The heady scent of incense poured through the opening.

"Please, I need to see your Master. It's about his daughter," Shem said. "About her illness."

The door opened as wide as the man's face. "He sees no one. No one."

Eran looked into the man's tired eyes. "Khepri then. If you allow me to see her, I can help her."

"No."

"Will you give Okpara a message, then? Tell him the kohl makes Khepri sick, the supply from Egypt has something in it that's poisoning her."

The man waited, as if the information was trivial and not worth his bother. "Is that all?"

"You must tell him, it's-" The door slammed shut in her face.

Shem knocked again but the door remained closed.

Eran mounted the horse behind Shem, holding him tightly and resting her head on his shoulder as they rode from town. She tried, and would do so again when the fears had settled among the residents of Zoar.

Silently they rode back to the valley where Okpara disposed of his enemies. Malina and Rez-Nahor would already be gone from there, after placing wreaths on all the burial mounds. Their father was under one of them. They would honor him then leave the land with a hearty supply of provisions.

She would miss Malina, her oldest pupil. Not the Lilies. She would see them every day, continuing the lessons while their parents helped Ham work his land. One day they would return to their homeland. Until then, they were hers to teach and train and love because she wasn't going anywhere. God brought them into

Canaan's land and in his land they would remain. Shem, Ham, and Japheth already drew up the plans for the additional rooms they would construct so the sons of Noah could be together again.

Chapter Forty-three

Eran dove into the river, into a deep pool where the currents swirled in and about the stones, polishing rough edges and leaving smooth glossy mounds. She touched the bottom of the bed then pushed herself to the surface, into the sunshine. Turning upstream, she swam until her muscles ached, then floated back toward shore.

There was no pain in her knees when she was in the water. And no longer any fear.

"Eran!" Denah waved from the bank. "It's time! The pains have started!"

Eran splashed from the water, yanked dry clothes over her head and ran behind her sister-in-law to the birthing tent on the edge of Abraham's camp. Hagar and Naomi prepared it over a week ago, anxiously awaiting the latest addition to the Hebrew tribe. The time had arrived at last. Time for new life, for promises fulfilled. Little Isaac was on his way.

♥

"How much longer will it be?" Abraham asked Shem, as if

this time he would have an answer. Time was stretching out into an endless length, unrolling from an infinite ball. It couldn't pass quickly enough for the hundred year old man awaiting his son. He paced and fretted and paced some more. That hadn't changed over the centuries. Babies never came quickly enough, and fathers never waited patiently.

Shem didn't dare go near the tent again. The women shooed him out when he poked his head in to ask about Sarah and Isaac, and the last time he wandered close, the sounds from within made him light-headed. He was grateful women had the duty of bringing infants into the world. It was rumored that Eve delivered her first few sons on her own. There was no one to assist but Adam. He took one look and hit the earth, passed out cold.

Shem clapped a hand on Abraham's shoulder. "I don't know. Let's recite together to pass the time."

Abraham nodded. "In the beginning, God created-"

An infant's indignant wail pierced the camp. Whether he wanted to leave the cozy womb or not, Isaac had arrived.

Abraham's eyes grew wide and he froze, staring at the birthing tent.

"Go!" Shem pushed the man's shoulders to get his feet moving.

The new father shook off decades of age and ran like a young man to see his newborn son.

Shem, Ham and Japheth fell into each other's arms. They cheered and cried, then fell to their knees in utter awe and gratitude. And a bit of apprehension. In eight days they would be circumcised along with Isaac, choosing to seal themselves alongside Abraham's boy, making covenant with the God of Noah, the God of the Hebrews, the God of mankind's hope.

Abraham emerged from the tent with the tiny swaddled

bundle. His red rimmed eyes overflowed. He gingerly gave the linen bound baby to Shem, honoring him as father of the tribe.

Shem's arms quivered as he raised the boy up to the heavens. "Blessed be the name of the Lord. His ways will not be thwarted. His promises not forgotten." Lowering the baby, he tucked him against his heart and rocked him, unable to keep his gaze from the miracle in his hands.

Isaac's red face scrunched up and a pitiful newborn cry emerged.

"Within your grasp, the Pledge cries out. The Promise is awakened!"

The words echoed through his ears. Shem jerked his head up. He was surrounded by family and the men and women of Abraham's camp. None of them had spoken. The words of his father's blessing didn't come from mere man.

It was the voice of God reverberating through his soul, through his own ears.

Shem stared at the babe as it cried for the reassurance of Sarah's arms.

A smile pulled at his lips, then chuckles spilled out, then laughter so deep Abraham took Isaac so he wouldn't be dropped.

Noah's words finally made sense.

Isaac was a Pledge, a miraculous guarantee that God had not forgotten his Promise. The Seed was still to come. Hope was awakened with the birth of this most blessed child.

Hope, confident assurance. It gave strength, sweeping away his fears and replacing them with fathomless peace. The future of God's name wasn't Shem's responsibility. It never had been. No one, not himself or any of the kings of the earth, could prevent the plan of God from unfurling.

He hadn't failed. The longstanding burden dissolved for good. His God was in control, as he always had been.

Eran slipped up beside him, wrapping her arm around his waist and laying her head against his shoulder. Her hair, still damp from the river, smelled of the healing herbs she prepared for Sarah. She sighed, relaxing into him. "God is good," she whispered.

Shem pulled her in close, his bride, taken, then returned with the steadfast faith of Noah steering her heart. She was stronger than before the raiders took her away, stronger of mind and soul and spirit than even she realized. And she was back in his arms. He kissed her forehead. His God was good indeed.

It's not

The End...

Isaac grew up, married and fathered sons of his own. One of them was Jacob, also called Israel. Jacob's twelve sons had numerous descendants, establishing twelve strong tribes.

After many generations, Jacob's son Judah became the ancestor of two young Hebrews named Mary and Joseph. God had not forgotten the Promise. The Holy Spirit impregnated Mary and unto her was born The Seed, The Savior of the world promised to Adam and Eve, promised to me, promised to you.

Thoughts from the Author

What made Khepri ill?

She had lead poisoning. Kohl, the black eyeliner used by both men and women in Egypt, was often made from a lead ore called galena. The toxic substance absorbed into the skin and could accumulate for years before the symptoms became evident. The delay in illness onset, the diversity of symptoms, and individual levels of susceptibility masked the source of the toxicity.

The dark outline seen on nearly every image of early Egyptians was not only cosmetic. It reduced glare from the desert sun, repelled Nile flies, inhibited eye infections, and was believed to ward off the Evil Eye. Kohl is still used as eyeliner in some cultures as a talisman against evil, especially on babies. Although lead is prohibited in U.S. cosmetics, it is used in other counties, putting children especially at risk for long term medical complications resulting from the lead based components.

What really happened to Nimrod?

He seized power and made himself a king. He was of Hamitic lineage but his followers were of Shem's descent, Semitic tribes living in Mesopotamia. The last reference we have to Ham's grandson is found in Genesis 10:10-11, where it lists the 'first centers of Nimrod's kingdom' then the other great cities he built, including Nineveh. Genesis 14:1 refers to King Amraphel as the King of Shinar, where many of Nimrod's cities are located. It has been postulated that he and Nimrod were the same man. Name changes were not uncommon in those days and one man may have been known by several names. An internet search gives various theories on his life and demise but none are confirmed Biblically.

Did Shem know Abraham?

Pinpointing Abraham's year of birth was impossible. There are many varied opinions on the matter, ranging between 1812 B.C. – 2050 B.C. Most seemed to center around 1948 to 2000 so I chose that time frame as well. With this range, and if you do the math yourself, you'll see that it was plausible these men knew one another. They were relatives, both alive at the same time for at least 150 years. They may have lived near one another in Ur or Haran, or possibly Canaan. Shem may have traveled to visit his descendants or young Abram may have been taken to meet the son of Noah.

Shem lived to be 600 years old and was still living as Isaac was growing into manhood. It is likely Abraham and Isaac heard *first hand* accounts of the flood and the building of the ark.

Giants, dragons and dinosaurs

I need a lot of pages to really cover these fun topics. I'll give you a brief summary and you can read more of my thoughts at gracebythegallon.com or look them up at answersingenesis.com.

Dinosaurs: As a believer in a young earth, created by God in the six literal days described in the Bible, dinosaurs were created in the beginning with the other creatures of land, sea, and air. They were taken on the ark, probably as youngsters, multiplied and migrated about the new earth. Most were hunted or died in unfavorable climates resulting from the ice age (a climatic upheaval after the flood).

Dragons: The original name for dinosaurs. Dragon images and descriptions are found around the globe, not as fairy tale material, but as real threats to communities and beasts for the brave to conquer.

Giants: The Bible refers to giants in Canaan, the most notable being Goliath. They were conquered by the Israelites. Were they descendants of the Nephilim described in Genesis Six? I gave them that heritage in Book II, but that was my own conjuring of ideas to make Naomi's little secret an issue that continued in Book III.

Noah's grave

There are four traditional sites claiming Noah's burial tomb, located in Armenia, Turkey, Iraq, and Lebanon. We don't know which one(s), if any, actually contain his bones.

Senet

This is a real game from Egypt that I discovered on the internet while doing research. It reminds me of the games 'Trouble' and 'Aggravation', where players try to be the first to move their game pieces around a board, relying on luck and strategy to pass their opponent. King Tut had an elaborate game board in his tomb, and there is a painting of one in a tomb dated back to 2686 B.C.

The Promise

From the beginning, mankind knew that a Redeemer would come and sin would be defeated (Genesis 3:15). As time passes, the rather vague Promise is narrowed down, more details given. God would be the God of Shem, then the God of Abraham's great nation, from whom all nations would be blessed. King David had further confirmation that the Seed would come through his lineage. Throughout the Old Testament we find prophesies that further define the Messiah. He was to be born of a virgin, born in Bethlehem, pierced for our sins, and many others, all which were fulfilled in Jesus. His death on the cross as punishment for our sin was planned from the beginning of history.

Those who believed in the Promise yet to come were counted as righteous. They didn't know the name of Jesus, or understand how all the prophesies would be fulfilled, but they found justification in the eyes of God by faith. Just as we who look back at the cross and believe Jesus took our punishment are seen as righteous in God's eyes, those who looked forward and believed were too.

Favor with God had never been about the quantity of our good deeds weighed against our bad ones. It isn't about the number of lambs sacrificed or the amount of money we give to the poor. It has always been a matter of belief and acceptance of grace that is offered freely to all.

Final Thoughts on Themes

Blood of Adam

Denah and Japheth contend with the blood of Adam, the sinful nature inherent to mankind. Theirs is a story of FAITH and personal decisions to believe in the God of creation and his words of destruction and salvation. It includes frankincense as a recurring thread and has an element of Romance.

Bones of Rebellion

LOVE for God and his commands versus love for ourselves is seen in Ham and Naomi's story. Once compromise was tolerated, it compounded, affecting their family and community in successive generations. Gold is key to this story, as is the Mystery component.

Breath of Knowledge

Eran and Shem rely on HOPE for strength and purpose in the midst of trials, striving to stand firm on Truth both at home and on foreign soil. Their story includes myrrh and a hint of the Action/Adventure genre.

♥

Thank you for sticking with me to the end of this final book, and may you find the God of all Creation a firm foundation for your life.

Made in the USA
Lexington, KY
25 October 2015